THE BLITHEDALE ROMANCE

DOVER THRIFT EDITIONS

Nathaniel Hawthorne

DOVER PUBLICATIONS, INC.
MINEOLA, NEW YORK

DOVER THRIFT EDITIONS

GENERAL EDITOR: PAUL NEGRI

EDITOR OF THIS VOLUME: JANET BAINE KOPITO

Copyright

Note copyright © 2003 by Dover Publications, Inc.
All rights reserved.

Bibliographical Note

This Dover edition, first published in 2003, is an unabridged republication, including author's preface, of a standard edition of Nathaniel Hawthorne's *The Blithedale Romance*, originally published in 1852. A new introductory Note has been specially prepared for this edition.

Library of Congress Cataloging-in-Publication Data

Hawthorne, Nathaniel, 1804–1864.
    The Blithedale romance / Nathaniel Hawthorne
        p. cm. — (Dover thrift editions)
    ISBN-13: 978-0-486-42684-6
    ISBN-10: 0-486-42684-X
    1. Collective farms—Fiction. 2. Communal living—Fiction. 3. Massachusetts—Fiction. 4. Farm life—Fiction. I. Title. II. Series.

PS1855.A1 2003
813'.3—dc21   2003040966

Manufactured in the United States by LSC Communications
42684X04   2017
www.doverpublications.com

Note

NATHANIEL Hawthorne (1804–1864) was born in Salem, Massachusetts. He was descended from several generations of Hathornes (he changed the spelling of the name when he became a writer), one of whom, John Hathorne, was a judge at the Salem witch trials. Hawthorne's father, a sea captain, died of yellow fever when the boy was four. His mother steered him toward a love of literature, and, when sidelined by a sports injury for an extended period, he discovered that he had an interest in writing as well. He considered his self-published first novel, *Fanshawe* (1828), a failure and attempted to destroy the copies. However, he went on to produce highly regarded tales such as "My Kinsman, Major Molineux" (1832) and "Young Goodman Brown" (1835). He finally achieved success in 1837 with the publication of *Twice-Told Tales*.

In 1842 Hawthorne married Sophia Peabody. They had three children, Una, Julian, and Rose. Hawthorne took a job at the Salem Custom House in 1846, all the while attempting to further his literary career. It was a time of great achievement in American letters: Thoreau, Emerson, Melville, and Bronson Alcott, among others, brought about the "American Renaissance," a flowering of prose and poetry that Hawthorne enriched with his works. In 1850 Hawthorne published *The Scarlet Letter*, a tale of intolerance that examines human behavior through the prism of harsh Puritanical judgment (an echo of the harsh judgment handed out by his ancestor at the witch trials). *The House of the Seven Gables* appeared in 1851, another of Hawthorne's novels to draw upon his family's historic connection with the witch trials. That same year he also published A *Wonder-Book for Girls and Boys*, a re-working of classical myths for young readers. In 1852 he brought out a biography of Franklin Pierce, whom he had known since his days at Bowdoin College. Pierce had entered politics and was elected president in 1853. He appointed his friend Hawthorne to the post of American consul to England. Hawthorne toured Europe and was inspired by his travels in Italy to produce *The Marble Faun* (1860), his last completed work of fiction.

The Blithedale Romance appeared in 1852. It reflected, to some extent, Hawthorne's experiences living at Brook Farm, a utopian community founded by George Ripley in West Roxbury, Massachusetts, in 1841. Brook Farm was developed with the support of the New England Transcendentalists, an intellectual movement whose beliefs were shaped by both Western and Eastern religion and philosophy. The community was designed to benefit both the individual and the group by developing each person's potential in an agricultural setting with socialist underpinnings. Residents were required to perform physical labor—supposedly a means of creating a classless society. In 1841 Hawthorne spent spring through fall at Brook Farm, partaking in the social experiment; he left the community in disappointment.

Blithedale Farm is the setting for the author's examination of the damage done to utopian dreams by the realities of human nature. Through the eyes of the novel's narrator, Miles Coverdale (whose character is based somewhat on the author), the complicated relationships between Coverdale and another male resident of the farm, Hollingsworth, and Zenobia and Priscilla, two female characters, are analyzed and mercilessly dissected. Hawthorne's opinion of the futility of the willful betterment of mankind is revealed in Coverdale's rejoinder to a fellow farmer who has offered him a meal from some fat pigs: "All the rest of us, men, women, and live-stock, save only these four porkers, are bedevilled with one grief or another; they alone are happy,—and you mean to cut their throats and eat them! It would be more for the general comfort to let them eat us; and bitter and sour morsels we should be!"

Contents

Preface by the Author

IN the "Blithedale" of this volume many readers will, probably, suspect a faint and not very faithful shadowing of Brook Farm, in Roxbury, which (now a little more than ten years ago) was occupied and cultivated by a company of socialists. The author does not wish to deny that he had this community in his mind, and that (having had the good fortune, for a time, to be personally connected with it) he has occasionally availed himself of his actual reminiscences, in the hope of giving a more lifelike tint to the fancy-sketch in the following pages. He begs it to be understood, however, that he has considered the institution itself as not less fairly the subject of fictitious handling than the imaginary personages whom he has introduced there. His whole treatment of the affair is altogether incidental to the main purpose of the romance; nor does he put forward the slightest pretensions to illustrate a theory, or elicit a conclusion, favorable or otherwise, in respect to socialism.

In short, his present concern with the socialist community is merely to establish a theatre, a little removed from the highway of ordinary travel, where the creatures of his brain may play their phantasmagorical antics, without exposing them to too close a comparison with the actual events of real lives. In the old countries, with which fiction has long been conversant, a certain conventional privilege seems to be awarded to the romancer; his work is not put exactly side by side with nature; and he is allowed a license with regard to every-day probability, in view of the improved effects which he is bound to produce thereby. Among ourselves, on the contrary, there is as yet no such Faery Land, so like the real world, that, in a suitable remoteness, one cannot well tell the difference, but with an atmosphere of strange enchantment, beheld through which the inhabitants have a propriety of their own. This atmosphere is what the American romancer needs. In its absence, the beings of imagination are compelled to show themselves in the same category as actually living mortals; a necessity that generally renders the paint and pasteboard of their composition but too painfully discernible. With the idea of partially obviating this difficulty (the sense of which has always pressed very heavily upon him), the author has ventured to make free with his old and affectionately remembered home at Brook Farm, as being certainly the most romantic episode of his own life,—essentially a daydream, and yet a fact,—and thus offering an available foothold between fiction and reality. Furthermore, the scene was in good keeping with the personages whom he desired to introduce.

These characters, he feels it right to say, are entirely fictitious. It would, indeed (considering how few amiable qualities he distributes among his imaginary progeny), be a most grievous wrong to his former excellent associates, were the author to allow it to be supposed that he has been sketching any of their likenesses. Had he attempted it, they would at least have recognized the touches of a friendly pencil. But he has done nothing of the kind. The self-concentrated Philanthropist; the high-spirited Woman, bruising herself against the narrow limitations of her sex; the weakly Maiden, whose tremulous nerves endow her with sibylline attributes; the Minor Poet, beginning life with strenuous aspirations, which die out with his youthful fervor;—all these might have been looked for at Brook Farm, but, by some accident, never made their appearance there.

The author cannot close his reference to this subject, without expressing a most earnest wish that some one of the many cultivated and philosophic minds, which took an interest in that enterprise, might now give the world its history. Ripley, with whom rests the honorable paternity of the institution, Dana, Dwight, Channing, Burton, Parker, for instance,—with others, whom he dares not name, because they veil themselves from the public eye,—among these is the ability to convey both the outward narrative and the inner truth and spirit of the whole affair, together with the lessons which those years of thought and toil must have elaborated, for the behoof of future experimentalists. Even the brilliant Howadji might find as rich a theme in his youthful reminiscenses of Brook Farm, and a more novel one,—close at hand as it lies,—than those which he has since made so distant a pilgrimage to seek, in Syria, and along the current of the Nile.

CONCORD (Mass.), May, 1852.

THE BLITHEDALE
ROMANCE

I.

OLD MOODIE

THE evening before my departure for Blithedale, I was returning to my bachelor apartments, after attending the wonderful exhibition of the Veiled Lady, when an elderly man, of rather shabby appearance, met me in an obscure part of the street.

"Mr. Coverdale," said he, softly, "can I speak with you a moment?"

As I have casually alluded to the Veiled Lady, it may not be amiss to mention, for the benefit of such of my readers as are unacquainted with her now forgotten celebrity, that she was a phenomenon in the mesmeric line; one of the earliest that had indicated the birth of a new science, or the revival of an old humbug. Since those times, her sisterhood have grown too numerous to attract much individual notice; nor, in fact, has any one of them come before the public under such skilfully contrived circumstances of stage-effect as those which at once mystified and illuminated the remarkable performances of the lady in question. Now-a-days, in the management of his "subject," "clairvoyant," or "medium," the exhibitor affects the simplicity and openness of scientific experiment; and even if he profess to tread a step or two across the boundaries of the spiritual world, yet carries with him the laws of our actual life, and extends them over his preternatural conquests. Twelve or fifteen years ago, on the contrary, all the arts of mysterious arrangement, of picturesque disposition, and artistically contrasted light and shade, were made available, in order to set the apparent miracle in the strongest attitude of opposition to ordinary facts. In the case of the Veiled Lady, moreover, the interest of the spectator was further wrought up by the enigma of her identity, and an absurd rumor (probably set afloat by the exhibitor, and at one time very prevalent), that a beautiful young lady, of family and

1

fortune, was enshrouded within the misty drapery of the veil. It was white, with somewhat of a subdued silver sheen, like the sunnyside of a cloud; and, falling over the wearer from head to foot, was supposed to insulate her from the material world, from time and space, and to endow her with many of the privileges of a disembodied spirit.

Her pretensions, however, whether miraculous or otherwise, have little to do with the present narrative; except, indeed, that I had propounded, for the Veiled Lady's prophetic solution, a query as to the success of our Blithedale enterprise. The response, by the by, was of the true Sibylline stamp,—nonsensical in its first aspect, yet, on closer study, unfolding a variety of interpretations, one of which has certainly accorded with the event. I was turning over this riddle in my mind, and trying to catch its slippery purport by the tail, when the old man above mentioned interrupted me.

"Mr. Coverdale!—Mr. Coverdale!" said he; repeating my name twice, in order to make up for the hesitating and ineffectual way in which he uttered it. "I ask your pardon, sir, but I hear you are going to Blithedale to-morrow."

I knew the pale, elderly face, with the red-tipt nose, and the patch over one eye; and likewise saw something characteristic in the old fellow's way of standing under the arch of a gate, only revealing enough of himself to make me recognize him as an acquaintance. He was a very shy personage, this Mr. Moodie; and the trait was the more singular, as his mode of getting his bread necessarily brought him into the stir and hubbub of the world more than the generality of men.

"Yes, Mr. Moodie," I answered, wondering what interest he could take in the fact, "it is my intention to go to Blithedale to-morrow. Can I be of any service to you before my departure?"

"If you pleased, Mr. Coverdale," said he, "you might do me a very great favor."

"A very great one?" repeated I, in a tone that must have expressed but little alacrity of beneficence, although I was ready to do the old man any amount of kindness involving no special trouble to myself. "A very great favor, do you say? My time is brief, Mr. Moodie, and I have a good many preparations to make. But be good enough to tell me what you wish."

"Ah, sir," replied Old Moodie, "I don't quite like to do that; and, on further thoughts, Mr. Coverdale, perhaps I had better apply to some older gentleman, or to some lady, if you would have the kindness to make me known to one, who may happen to be going to Blithedale. You are a young man, sir!"

"Does that fact lessen my availability for your purpose?" asked I. "However, if an older man will suit you better, there is Mr. Hollingsworth, who has three or four years the advantage of me in age, and is a much more solid character, and a philanthropist to boot. I am only a poet, and, so the critics tell me, no great affair at that! But what can this business be, Mr. Moodie? It begins to interest me; especially since your hint that a lady's influence might be found desirable. Come, I am really anxious to be of service to you."

But the old fellow, in his civil and demure manner, was both freakish and obstinate; and he had now taken some notion or other into his head that made him hesitate in his former design.

"I wonder, sir," said he, "whether you know a lady whom they call Zenobia?"

"Not personally," I answered, "although I expect that pleasure tomorrow, as she has got the start of the rest of us, and is already a resident at Blithedale. But have you a literary turn, Mr. Moodie? or have you taken up the advocacy of women's rights? or what else can have interested you in this lady? Zenobia, by the by, as I suppose you know, is merely her public name; a sort of mask in which she comes before the world, retaining all the privileges of privacy,—a contrivance, in short, like the white drapery of the Veiled Lady, only a little more transparent. But it is late. Will you tell me what I can do for you?"

"Please to excuse me to-night, Mr. Coverdale," said Moodie. "You are very kind; but I am afraid I have troubled you, when, after all, there may be no need. Perhaps, with your good leave, I will come to your lodgings to-morrow morning, before you set out for Blithedale. I wish you a good-night, sir, and beg pardon for stopping you."

And so he slipt away; and, as he did not show himself the next morning, it was only through subsequent events that I ever arrived at a plausible conjecture as to what his business could have been. Arriving at my room, I threw a lump of cannel coal upon the grate, lighted a cigar, and spent an hour in musings of every hue, from the brightest to the most sombre; being, in truth, not so very confident as at some former periods that this final step, which would mix me up irrevocably with the Blithedale affair, was the wisest that could possibly be taken. It was nothing short of midnight when I went to bed, after drinking a glass of particularly fine sherry, on which I used to pride myself, in those days. It was the very last bottle; and I finished it, with a friend, the next forenoon, before setting out for Blithedale.

II.

BLITHEDALE

THERE can hardly remain for me (who am really getting to be a frosty bachelor, with another white hair, every week or so, in my moustache), there can hardly flicker up again so cheery a blaze upon the hearth, as that which I remember, the next day, at Blithedale. It was a wood-fire, in the parlor of an old farm-house, on an April afternoon, but with the fitful gusts of a wintry snow-storm roaring in the chimney. Vividly does that fireside re-create itself, as I rake away the ashes from the embers in my memory, and blow them up with a sigh, for lack of more inspiring breath. Vividly, for an instant, but, anon, with the dimmest gleam, and with just as little fervency for my heart as for my finger-ends! The stanch oaken logs were long ago burnt out. Their genial glow must be represented, if at all, by the merest phosphoric glimmer, like that which exudes, rather than shines, from damp fragments of decayed trees, deluding the benighted wanderer through a forest. Around such chill mockery of a fire some few of us might sit on the withered leaves, spreading out each a palm towards the imaginary warmth, and talk over our exploded scheme for beginning the life of Paradise anew.

Paradise, indeed! Nobody else in the world, I am bold to affirm,—nobody, at least, in our bleak little world of New England,—had dreamed of Paradise that day, except as the pole suggests the tropic. Nor, with such materials as were at hand, could the most skilful architect have constructed any better imitation of Eve's bower than might be seen in the snow-hut of an Esquimaux. But we made a summer of it, in spite of the wild drifts.

It was an April day, as already hinted, and well towards the middle of the month. When morning dawned upon me, in town, its temperature was mild enough to be pronounced even balmy, by a lodger, like myself, in one of the midmost houses of a brick block,—each house partaking of the warmth of all the rest, besides the sultriness of its individual furnace-heat. But, towards noon, there had come snow, driven along the street by a northeasterly blast, and whitening the roofs and side-walks with a business-like perseverance that would have done credit to our severest January tempest. It set about its task apparently as much in earnest as if it had been guaranteed from a thaw for months to come. The greater, surely, was my heroism, when, puffing out a final whiff of cigar-smoke, I quitted my cosey pair of bachelor-rooms,—with a good fire burning in the grate, and a closet right at hand, where there was still a bottle or two in the champagne-basket, and a residuum of claret in a box,—quitted, I say, these comfortable quarters, and plunged into the heart of the pitiless snowstorm, in quest of a better life.

The better life! Possibly, it would hardly look so, now; it is enough if it looked so then. The greatest obstacle to being heroic is the doubt whether one may not be going to prove one's self a fool; the truest heroism is, to resist the doubt; and the profoundest wisdom, to know when it ought to be resisted, and when to be obeyed.

Yet, after all, let us acknowledge it wiser, if not more sagacious, to follow out one's day-dream to its natural consummation, although, if the vision have been worth the having, it is certain never to be con-summated otherwise than by a failure. And what of that? Its airiest frag-ments, impalpable as they may be, will possess a value that lurks not in the most ponderous realities of any practicable scheme. They are not the rubbish of the mind. Whatever else I may repent of, therefore, let it be reckoned neither among my sins nor follies that I once had faith and force enough to form generous hopes of the world's destiny,— yes!—and to do what in me lay for their accomplishment; even to the extent of quitting a warm fireside, flinging away a freshly-lighted cigar, and travelling far beyond the strike of city clocks, through a drifting snow-storm.

There were four of us who rode together through the storm; and Hollingsworth, who had agreed to be of the number, was accidentally delayed, and set forth at a later hour alone. As we threaded the street, I remember how the buildings on either side seemed to press too closely upon us, insomuch that our mighty hearts found barely room enough to throb between them. The snowfall, too, looked inexpressibly dreary (I had almost called it dingy), coming down through an atmosphere of city smoke, and alighting on the side-walk only to be moulded into the impress of somebody's patched boot or overshoe. Thus the track of an old conventionalism was visible on what was freshest from the sky. But, when we left the pavements, and our muffled hoof-tramps beat upon a desolate extent of country road, and were effaced by the unfettered blast as soon as stamped, then there was better air to breathe. Air that had not been breathed once and again! air that had not been spoken into words of falsehood, formality and error, like all the air of the dusky city!

"How pleasant it is!" remarked I, while the snowflakes flew into my mouth the moment it was opened. "How very mild and balmy is this country air!"

"Ah, Coverdale, don't laugh at what little enthusiasm you have left!" said one of my companions. "I maintain that this nitrous atmosphere is really exhilarating; and, at any rate, we can never call ourselves regen-erated men till a February north-easter shall be as grateful to us as the softest breeze of June."

So we all of us took courage, riding fleetly and merrily along, by stone-fences that were half-buried in the wave-like drifts; and through patches of woodland, where the tree-trunks opposed a snow-encrusted side towards the north-east; and within ken of deserted villas, with no footprints in their avenues; and past scattered dwellings, whence puffed the smoke of country fires, strongly impregnated with the pungent aroma of burning peat. Sometimes, encountering a traveller, we shouted a friendly greeting; and he, unmuffling his ears to the bluster and the snow-spray, and listening eagerly, appeared to think our courtesy worth less than the trouble which it cost him. The churl! He understood the shrill whistle of the blast, but had no intelligence for our blithe tones of brotherhood. This lack of faith in our cordial sympathy, on the traveller's part, was one among the innumerable tokens how difficult a task we had in hand, for the reformation of the world. We rode on, however, with still unflagging spirits, and made such good companionship with the tempest that, at our journey's end, we professed ourselves almost loth to bid the rude blusterer good-by. But, to own the truth, I was little better than an icicle, and began to be suspicious that I had caught a fearful cold.

And now we were seated by the brisk fireside of the old farm-house, — the same fire that glimmers so faintly among my reminiscences at the beginning of this chapter. There we sat, with the snow melting out of our hair and beards, and our faces all a-blaze, what with the past inclemency and present warmth. It was, indeed, a right good fire that we found awaiting us, built up of great, rough logs, and knotty limbs, and splintered fragments, of an oak-tree, such as farmers are wont to keep for their own hearths, — since these crooked and unmanageable boughs could never be measured into merchantable cords for the market. A family of the old Pilgrims might have swung their kettle over precisely such a fire as this, only, no doubt, a bigger one; and, contrasting it with my coal-grate, I felt so much the more that we had transported ourselves a world-wide distance from the system of society that shackled us at breakfast-time.

Good, comfortable Mrs. Foster (the wife of stout Silas Foster, who was to manage the farm, at a fair stipend, and be our tutor in the art of husbandry) bade us a hearty welcome. At her back — a back of generous breadth — appeared two young women, smiling most hospitably, but looking rather awkward withal, as not well knowing what was to be their position in our new arrangement of the world. We shook hands affectionately, all round, and congratulated ourselves that the blessed state of brotherhood and sisterhood, at which we aimed, might fairly be dated from this moment. Our greetings were hardly concluded, when the door opened, and Zenobia, — whom I had never before seen, important as was her place in our enterprise, — Zenobia entered the parlor.

This (as the reader, if at all acquainted with our literary biography, need scarcely be told) was not her real name. She had assumed it, in the first instance, as her magazine signature; and, as it accorded well with something imperial which her friends attributed to this lady's figure and deportment, they, half-laughingly, adopted it in their familiar intercourse with her. She took the appellation in good part, and even encouraged its constant use; which, in fact, was thus far appropriate, that our Zenobia — however humble looked her new philosophy — had as much native pride as any queen would have known what to do with.

III.

A KNOT OF DREAMERS

ZENOBIA bade us welcome, in a fine, frank, mellow voice, and gave each of us her hand, which was very soft and warm. She had something appropriate, I recollect, to say to every individual; and what she said to myself was this:

"I have long wished to know you, Mr. Coverdale, and to thank you for your beautiful poetry, some of which I have learned by heart; or, rather, it has stolen into my memory, without my exercising any choice or volition about the matter. Of course—permit me to say—you do not think of relinquishing an occupation in which you have done yourself so much credit. I would almost rather give you up as an associate, than that the world should lose one of its true poets!"

"Ah, no; there will not be the slightest danger of that, especially after this inestimable praise from Zenobia," said I, smiling, and blushing, no doubt, with excess of pleasure. "I hope, on the contrary, now to produce something that shall really deserve to be called poetry,—true, strong, natural, and sweet, as is the life which we are going to lead,—something that shall have the notes of wild birds twittering through it, or a strain like the wind-anthems in the woods, as the case may be."

"Is it irksome to you to hear your own verses sung?" asked Zenobia, with a gracious smile. "If so, I am very sorry, for you will certainly hear me singing them, sometimes, in the summer evenings."

"Of all things," answered I, "that is what will delight me most."

While this passed, and while she spoke to my companions, I was taking note of Zenobia's aspect; and it impressed itself on me so distinctly, that I can now summon her up, like a ghost, a little wanner than the life, but otherwise identical with it. She was dressed as simply as possible, in an American print (I think the dry goods people call it so), but with a silken kerchief, between which and her gown there was one glimpse of a white shoulder. It struck me as a great piece of good fortune that there should be just that glimpse. Her hair, which was dark, glossy, and of singular abundance, was put up rather soberly and primly, without curls, or other ornament, except a single flower. It was an exotic, of rare beauty, and as fresh as if the hot-house gardener had just clipt it from the stem. That flower has struck deep root into my memory. I can both see it and smell it, at this moment. So brilliant, so rare, so costly, as it must have been, and yet enduring only for a day, it was more indicative of the pride and pomp which had a luxuriant growth in Zenobia's character than if a great diamond had sparkled among her hair.

Her hand, though very soft, was larger than most women would like to have, or than they could afford to have, though not a whit too large in proportion with the spacious plan of Zenobia's entire development. It did one good to see a fine intellect (as hers really was, although its natural tendency lay in another direction than towards literature) so fitly cased. She was, indeed, an admirable figure of a woman, just on the hither verge of her richest maturity, with a combination of features which it is safe to call remarkably beautiful, even if some fastidious persons might pronounce them a little deficient in softness and delicacy. But we find enough of those attributes everywhere. Preferable—by way of variety, at least—was Zenobia's bloom, health, and vigor, which she possessed in such overflow that a man might well have fallen in love with her for their sake only. In her quiet moods, she seemed rather indolent; but when really in earnest, particularly if there were a spice of bitter feeling, she grew all alive, to her fingertips.

"I am the first comer," Zenobia went on to say, while her smile beamed warmth upon us all; "so I take the part of hostess, for to-day, and welcome you as if to my own fireside. You shall be my guests, too, at supper. To-morrow, if you please, we will be brethren and sisters, and begin our new life from daybreak."

"Have we our various parts assigned?" asked some one.

"O, we of the softer sex," responded Zenobia, with her mellow, almost broad laugh,—most delectable to hear, but not in the least like an ordinary woman's laugh,—"we women (there are four of us here already) will take the domestic and indoor part of the business, as a matter of course. To bake, to boil, to roast, to fry, to stew,—to wash, and iron, and scrub, and sweep,—and, at our idler intervals, to repose ourselves on knitting and sewing,—these, I suppose, must be feminine occupations, for the present. By and by, perhaps, when our individual adaptations begin to develop themselves, it may be that some of us who wear the petticoat will go a-field, and leave the weaker brethren to take our places in the kitchen."

"What a pity," I remarked, "that the kitchen, and the house-work generally, cannot be left out of our system altogether! It is odd enough that the kind of labor which falls to the lot of women is just that which chiefly distinguishes artificial life—the life of degenerated mortals—from the life of Paradise. Eve had no dinner-pot, and no clothes to mend, and no washing-day."

"I am afraid," said Zenobia, with mirth gleaming out of her eyes, "we shall find some difficulty in adopting the Paradisiacal system for at least a month to come. Look at that snow-drift sweeping past the window! Are there any figs ripe, do you think? Have the pine-apples been gathered, to-day? Would you like a breadfruit, or a cocoanut? Shall I run out and pluck you some roses? No, no, Mr. Coverdale; the only flower hereabouts is the one in my hair, which I got out of a green-house this morning. As for the garb of Eden," added she, shivering playfully, "I shall not assume it till after May-day!"

Assuredly, Zenobia could not have intended it; — the fault must have been entirely in my imagination. But these last words, together with something in her manner, irresistibly brought up a picture of that fine, perfectly developed figure, in Eve's earliest garment. Her free, careless, generous modes of expression, often had this effect, of creating images, which, though pure, are hardly felt to be quite decorous when born of a thought that passes between man and woman. I imputed it, at that time, to Zenobia's noble courage, conscious of no harm, and scorning the petty restraints which take the life and color out of other women's conversation. There was another peculiarity about her. We seldom meet with women, now-a-days, and in this country, who impress us as being women at all; — their sex fades away, and goes for nothing, in ordinary intercourse. Not so with Zenobia. One felt an influence breathing out of her such as we might suppose to come from Eve, when she was just made, and her Creator brought her to Adam, saying, "Behold! here is a woman!" Not that I would convey the idea of especial gentleness, grace, modesty and shyness, but of a certain warm and rich characteristic, which seems, for the most part, to have been refined away out of the feminine system.

"And now," continued Zenobia, "I must go and help get supper. Do you think you can be content, instead of figs, pine-apples, and all the other delicacies of Adam's supper-table, with tea and toast, and a certain modest supply of ham and tongue, which, with the instinct of a housewife, I brought hither in a basket? And there shall be bread and milk, too, if the innocence of your taste demands it."

The whole sisterhood now went about their domestic avocations, utterly declining our offers to assist, further than by bringing wood, for the kitchen-fire, from a huge pile in the back yard. After heaping up more than a sufficient quantity, we returned to the sitting-room, drew our chairs close to the hearth, and began to talk over our prospects. Soon, with a tremendous stamping in the entry, appeared Silas Foster, lank, stalwart, uncouth, and grisly-bearded. He came from foddering the cattle in the barn, and from the field, where he had been ploughing, until the depth of the snow rendered it impossible to draw a furrow. He greeted us in pretty much the same tone as if he were speaking to his oxen, took a quid from his iron tobacco-box, pulled off his wet cowhide boots, and sat down before the fire in his stocking-feet. The steam arose from his soaked garments, so that the stout yeoman looked vaporous and spectre-like.

"Well, folks," remarked Silas, "you'll be wishing yourselves back to town again, if this weather holds."

And, true enough, there was a look of gloom, as the twilight fell silently and sadly out of the sky, its gray or sable flakes intermingling themselves with the fast descending snow. The storm, in its evening aspect, was decidedly dreary. It seemed to have arisen for our especial behoof,—a symbol of the cold, desolate, distrustful phantoms that invariably haunt the mind, on the eve of adventurous enterprises, to warn us back within the boundaries of ordinary life.

But our courage did not quail. We would not allow ourselves to be depressed by the snow-drift trailing past the window, any more than if it had been the sigh of a summer wind among rustling boughs. There have been few brighter seasons for us than that. If ever men might lawfully dream awake, and give utterance to their wildest visions without dread of laughter or scorn on the part of the audience,—yes, and speak of earthly happiness, for themselves and mankind, as an object to be hopefully striven for, and probably attained,—we, who made that little semi-circle round the blazing fire, were those very men. We had left the rusty iron frame-work of society behind us; we had broken through many hindrances that are powerful enough to keep most people on the weary treadmill of the established system, even while they feel its irksomeness almost as intolerable as we did. We had stept down from the pulpit; we had flung aside the pen; we had shut up the ledger; we had thrown off that sweet, bewitching, enervating indolence, which is better, after all, than most of the enjoyments within mortal grasp. It was our purpose—a generous one, certainly, and absurd, no doubt, in full proportion with its generosity—to give up whatever we had heretofore attained, for the sake of showing mankind the example of a life governed by other than the false and cruel principles on which human society has all along been based.

And, first of all, we had divorced ourselves from pride, and were striving to supply its place with familiar love. We meant to lessen the laboring man's great burthen of toil, by performing our due share of it at the cost of our own thews and sinews. We sought our profit by mutual aid, instead of wresting it by the strong hand from an enemy, or filching it craftily from those less shrewd than ourselves (if, indeed, there were any such in New England), or winning it by selfish competition with a neighbor; in one or another of which fashions every son of woman both perpetrates and suffers his share of the common evil, whether he chooses it or no. And, as the basis of our institution, we purposed to offer up the earnest toil of our bodies, as a prayer no less than an effort for the advancement of our race.

Therefore, if we built splendid castles (phalansteries, perhaps they might be more fitly called), and pictured beautiful scenes, among the fervid coals of the hearth around which we were clustering, and if all went to rack with the crumbling embers, and have never since arisen out of the ashes, let us take to ourselves no shame. In my own behalf, I rejoice that I could once think better of the world's improvability than it deserved. It is a mistake into which men seldom fall twice in a life-time; or, if so, the rarer and higher is the nature that can thus mag-nanimously persist in error.

Stout Silas Foster mingled little in our conversation; but when he did speak, it was very much to some practical purpose. For instance:

"Which man among you," quoth he, "is the best judge of swine? Some of us must go to the next Brighton fair, and buy half a dozen pigs."

Pigs! Good heavens! had we come out from among the swinish multi-tude for this? And, again, in reference to some discussion about raising early vegetables for the market:

"We shall never make any hand at market-gardening," said Silas Foster, "unless the women folks will undertake to do all the weeding. We haven't team enough for that and the regular farm-work, reckoning three of you city folks as worth one common field-hand. No, no; I tell you, we should have to get up a little too early in the morning, to compete with the market-gardeners round Boston."

It struck me as rather odd, that one of the first questions raised, after our separation from the greedy, struggling, self-seeking world, should relate to the possibility of getting the advantage over the outside barbar-ians in their own field of labor. But, to own the truth, I very soon became sensible that, as regarded society at large, we stood in a position of new hostility, rather than new brotherhood. Nor could this fail to be the case, in some degree, until the bigger and better half of society should range itself on our side. Constituting so pitiful a minority as now, we were inevitably estranged from the rest of mankind in pretty fair proportion with the strictness of our mutual bond among ourselves.

This dawning idea, however, was driven back into my inner con-sciousness by the entrance of Zenobia. She came with the welcome intelligence that supper was on the table. Looking at herself in the glass, and perceiving that her one magnificent flower had grown rather languid (probably by being exposed to the fervency of the kitchen fire), she flung it on the floor, as unconcernedly as a village girl would throw away a faded violet. The action seemed proper to her character, although, methought, it would still more have befitted the bounteous nature of this beautiful woman to scatter fresh flowers from her hand, and to revive faded ones by her touch. Nevertheless, it was a singular but irresistible effect; the presence of Zenobia caused our heroic enter-prise to show like an illusion, a masquerade, a pastoral, a counter-feit Arcadia, in which we grown-up men and women were making a play-day of the years that were given us to live in. I tried to analyze this impression, but not with much success.

"It really vexes me," observed Zenobia, as we left the room, "that Mr. Hollingsworth should be such a laggard. I should not have thought him at all the sort of person to be turned back by a puff of contrary wind, or a few snow-flakes drifting into his face."

"Do you know Hollingsworth personally?" I inquired.

"No; only as an auditor—auditress, I mean—of some of his lectures," said she. "What a voice he has! and what a man he is! Yet not so much an intellectual man, I should say, as a great heart; at least, he moved me more deeply than I think myself capable of being moved, except by the stroke of a true, strong heart against my own. It is a sad pity that he should have devoted his glorious powers to such a grimy, unbeautiful and positively hopeless object as this reformation of criminals, about which he makes himself and his wretchedly small audiences so very miserable. To tell you a secret, I never could tolerate a philanthropist before. Could you?"

"By no means," I answered; "neither can I now."

"They are, indeed, an odiously disagreeable set of mortals," continued Zenobia. "I should like Mr. Hollingsworth a great deal better, if the philanthropy had been left out. At all events, as a mere matter of taste, I wish he would let the bad people alone, and try to benefit those who are not already past his help. Do you suppose he will be content to spend his life, or even a few months of it, among tolerably virtuous and comfortable individuals, like ourselves?"

"Upon my word, I doubt it," said I. "If we wish to keep him with us, we must systematically commit, at least, one crime apiece! Mere peccadilloes will not satisfy him."

Zenobia turned, sidelong, a strange kind of a glance upon me; but, before I could make out what it meant, we had entered the kitchen, where, in accordance with the rustic simplicity of our new life, the supper-table was spread.

IV.

THE SUPPER-TABLE

THE pleasant fire-light! I must still keep harping on it.

The kitchen-hearth had an old-fashioned breadth, depth and spaciousness, far within which lay what seemed the butt of a good-sized oak-tree, with the moisture bubbling merrily out of both ends. It was now half an hour beyond dusk. The blaze from an armful of substantial sticks, rendered more combustible by brushwood and pine, flickered powerfully on the smoke-blackened walls, and so cheered our spirits that we cared not what inclemency might rage and roar on the other side of our illuminated windows. A yet sultrier warmth was bestowed by a goodly quantity of peat, which was crumbling to white ashes among the burning brands, and incensed the kitchen with its not ungrateful fragrance. The exuberance of this household fire would alone have sufficed to bespeak us no true farmers; for the New England yeoman, if he have the misfortune to dwell within practicable distance of a wood-market, is as niggardly of each stick as if it were a bar of California gold.

But it was fortunate for us, on that wintry eve of our untried life, to enjoy the warm and radiant luxury of a somewhat too abundant fire. If it served no other purpose, it made the men look so full of youth, warm blood, and hope, and the women—such of them, at least, as were anywise convertible by its magic—so very beautiful, that I would cheerfully have spent my last dollar to prolong the blaze. As for Zenobia, there was a glow in her cheeks that made me think of Pandora, fresh from Vulcan's workshop, and full of the celestial warmth by dint of which he had tempered and moulded her.

"Take your places, my dear friends all," cried she; "seat yourselves without ceremony, and you shall be made happy with such tea as not many of the world's working-people, except yourselves, will find in their cups to-night. After this one supper, you may drink buttermilk, if you please. To-night we will quaff this nectar, which, I assure you, could not be bought with gold."

We all sat down,—grisly Silas Foster, his rotund helpmate, and the two bouncing handmaidens, included,—and looked at one another in a friendly but rather awkward way. It was the first practical trial of our theories of equal brotherhood and sisterhood; and we people of superior cultivation and refinement (for as such, I presume, we unhesitatingly reckoned ourselves) felt as if something were already accomplished towards the millennium of love. The truth is, however, that the laboring-oar was with our unpolished companions; it being far easier to condescend than to accept of condescension. Neither did I refrain from questioning, in secret, whether some of us—and Zenobia among the rest—would so quietly have taken our places among these good people, save for the cherished consciousness that it was not by necessity, but choice. Though we saw fit to drink our tea out of earthen cups to-night, and in earthen company, it was at our own option to use pictured porcelain and handle silver forks again to-morrow: This same salvo, as to the power of regaining our former position, contributed much, I fear, to the equanimity with which we subsequently bore many of the hardships and humiliations of a life of toil. If ever I have deserved (which has not often been the case, and, I think, never), but if ever I did deserve to be soundly cuffed by a fellow-mortal, for secretly putting weight upon some imaginary social advantage, it must have been while I was striving to prove myself ostentatiously his equal, and no more. It was while I sat beside him on his cobbler's bench, or clinked my hoe against his own in the cornfield, or broke the same crust of bread, my earth-grimed hand to his, at our noon-tide lunch. The poor, proud man should look at both sides of sympathy like this.

The silence which followed upon our sitting down to table grew rather oppressive; indeed, it was hardly broken by a word, during the first round of Zenobia's fragrant tea.

"I hope," said I, at last, "that our blazing windows will be visible a great way off. There is nothing so pleasant and encouraging to a solitary traveller, on a stormy night, as a flood of fire-light seen amid the gloom. These ruddy window-panes cannot fail to cheer the hearts of all that look at them. Are they not warm and bright with the beacon-fire which we have kindled for humanity?"

"The blaze of that brush-wood will only last a minute or two longer," observed Silas Foster; but whether he meant to insinuate that our moral illumination would have as brief a term, I cannot say.

"Meantime," said Zenobia, "it may serve to guide some wayfarer to a shelter."

And, just as she said this, there came a knock at the house-door.

"There is one of the world's wayfarers," said I.

"Ay, ay, just so!" quoth Silas Foster. "Our firelight will draw stragglers, just as a candle draws dor-bugs, on a summer night."

Whether to enjoy a dramatic suspense, or that we were selfishly contrasting our own comfort with the chill and dreary situation of the unknown person at the threshold, or that some of us city-folk felt a little startled at the knock which came so unseasonably, through night and storm, to the door of the lonely farmhouse,—so it happened, that nobody, for an instant or two, arose to answer the summons. Pretty soon, there came another knock. The first had been moderately loud; the second was smitten so forcibly that the knuckles of the applicant must have left their mark in the door-panel.

"He knocks as if he had a right to come in," said Zenobia, laughing. "And what are we thinking of? It must be Mr. Hollingsworth!"

Hereupon, I went to the door, unbolted, and flung it wide open. There, sure enough, stood Hollingsworth, his shaggy great-coat all covered with snow, so that he looked quite as much like a polar bear as a modern philanthropist.

"Sluggish hospitality this!" said he, in those deep tones of his, which seemed to come out of a chest as capacious as a barrel. "It would have served you right if I had lain down and spent the night on the doorstep, just for the sake of putting you to shame. But here is a guest who will need a warmer and softer bed."

And, stepping back to the wagon in which he had journeyed hither, Hollingsworth received into his arms and deposited on the door-step a figure enveloped in a cloak. It was evidently a woman; or, rather,—judging from the ease with which he lifted her, and the little space which she seemed to fill in his arms,—a slim and unsubstantial girl. As she showed some hesitation about entering the door, Hollingsworth, with his usual directness and lack of ceremony, urged her forward, not merely within the entry, but into the warm and strongly-lighted kitchen.

"Who is this?" whispered I, remaining behind with him while he was taking off his great-coat.

"Who? Really, I don't know," answered Hollingsworth, looking at me with some surprise. "It is a young person who belongs here, however; and, no doubt, she has been expected. Zenobia, or some of the women-folks, can tell you all about it."

"I think not," said I, glancing towards the new comer and the other occupants of the kitchen. "Nobody seems to welcome her. I should hardly judge that she was an expected guest."

"Well, well," said Hollingsworth, quietly. "We'll make it right."

The stranger, or whatever she were, remained standing precisely on that spot of the kitchen floor to which Hollingsworth's kindly hand had impelled her. The cloak falling partly off, she was seen to be a very young woman, dressed in a poor but decent gown, made high in the neck, and without any regard to fashion or smartness. Her brown hair fell down from beneath a hood, not in curls, but with only a slight wave; her face was of a wan, almost sickly hue, betokening habitual seclusion from the sun and free atmosphere, like a flower-shrub that had done its best to blossom in too scanty light. To complete the pitiableness of her aspect, she shivered, either with cold, or fear, or nervous excitement, so that you might have beheld her shadow vibrating on the fire-lighted wall. In short, there has seldom been seen so depressed and sad a figure as this young girl's; and it was hardly possible to help being angry with her, from mere despair of doing anything for her comfort. The fantasy occurred to me that she was some desolate kind of a creature, doomed to wander about in snow-storms; and that, though the ruddiness of our window-panes had tempted her into a human dwelling, she would not remain long enough to melt the icicles out of her hair.

Another conjecture likewise came into my mind. Recollecting Hollingsworth's sphere of philanthropic action, I deemed it possible that he might have brought one of his guilty patients, to be wrought upon, and restored to spiritual health, by the pure influences which our mode of life would create.

As yet, the girl had not stirred. She stood near the door, fixing a pair of large, brown, melancholy eyes upon Zenobia,—only upon Zenobia!—she evidently saw nothing else in the room, save that bright, fair, rosy, beautiful woman. It was the strangest look I ever witnessed; long a mystery to me, and forever a memory. Once she seemed about to move forward and greet her,—I know not with what warmth, or with what words;—but, finally, instead of doing so, she dropped down upon her knees, clasped her hands, and gazed piteously into Zenobia's face. Meeting no kindly reception, her head fell on her bosom.

I never thoroughly forgave Zenobia for her conduct on this occasion. But women are always more cautious in their casual hospitalities than men.

"What does the girl mean?" cried she, in rather a sharp tone. "Is she crazy? Has she no tongue?"

And here Hollingsworth stepped forward.

"No wonder if the poor child's tongue is frozen in her mouth," said he,—and I think he positively frowned at Zenobia. "The very heart will be frozen in her bosom, unless you women can warm it, among you, with the warmth that ought to be in your own!"

Hollingsworth's appearance was very striking at this moment. He was then about thirty years old, but looked several years older, with his great shaggy head, his heavy brow, his dark complexion, his abundant beard, and the rude strength with which his features seemed to have been hammered out of iron, rather than chiselled or moulded from any finer or softer material. His figure was not tall, but massive and brawny, and well befitting his original occupation, which—as the reader probably knows— was that of a blacksmith. As for external polish, or mere courtesy of manner, he never possessed more than a tolerably educated bear; although, in his gentler moods, there was a tenderness in his voice, eyes, mouth, in his gesture, and in every indescribable manifestation, which few men could resist, and no woman. But he now looked stern and reproachful; and it was with that inauspicious meaning in his glance that Hollingsworth first met Zenobia's eyes, and began his influence upon her life.

To my surprise, Zenobia—of whose haughty spirit I had been told so many examples—absolutely changed color, and seemed mortified and confused.

"You do not quite do me justice, Mr. Hollingsworth," said she, almost humbly. "I am willing to be kind to the poor girl. Is she a protegée of yours? What can I do for her?"

"Have you anything to ask of this lady?" said Hollingsworth, kindly, to the girl. "I remember you mentioned her name before we left town."

"Only that she will shelter me," replied the girl, tremulously. "Only that she will let me be always near her."

"Well, indeed," exclaimed Zenobia, recovering herself, and laughing, "this is an adventure, and well worthy to be the first incident in our life of love and free-heartedness! But I accept it, for the present, without further question,—only," added she, "it would be a convenience if we knew your name."

"Priscilla," said the girl; and it appeared to me that she hesitated whether to add anything more, and decided in the negative. "Pray do not ask me my other name,—at least, not yet,—if you will be so kind to a forlorn creature."

Priscilla!—Priscilla! I repeated the name to myself, three or four times; and, in that little space, this quaint and prim cognomen had so amalgamated itself with my idea of the girl, that it seemed as if no other name could have adhered to her for a moment. Heretofore, the poor thing had not shed any tears; but now that she found herself received, and at least temporarily established, the big drops began to ooze out from beneath her eyelids, as if she were full of them. Perhaps it showed the iron substance of my heart, that I could not help smiling at this odd scene of unknown and unaccountable calamity, into which our cheerful party had been entrapped, without the liberty of choosing whether to sympathize or no. Hollingsworth's behavior was certainly a great deal more creditable than mine.

"Let us not pry further into her secrets," he said to Zenobia and the rest of us, apart,—and his dark, shaggy face looked really beautiful with its expression of thoughtful benevolence. "Let us conclude that Providence has sent her to us, as the first fruits of the world, which we have undertaken to make happier than we find it. Let us warm her poor, shivering body with this good fire, and her poor, shivering heart with our best kindness. Let us feed her, and make her one of us. As we do by this friendless girl, so shall we prosper. And, in good time, whatever is desirable for us to know will be melted out of her, as inevitably as those tears which we see now."

"At least," remarked I, "you may tell us how and where you met with her."

"An old man brought her to my lodgings," answered Hollingsworth, "and begged me to convey her to Blithedale, where—so I understood him—she had friends; and this is positively all I know about the matter."

Grim Silas Foster, all this while, had been busy at the supper-table, pouring out his own tea, and gulping it down with no more sense of its exquisiteness than if it were a decoction of catnip; helping himself to pieces of dipt toast on the flat of his knife-blade, and dropping half of it on the table-cloth; using the same serviceable implement to cut slice after slice of ham; perpetrating terrible enormities with the butter-plate; and, in all other respects, behaving less like a civilized Christian than the worst kind of an ogre. Being by this time fully gorged, he crowned his amiable exploits with a draught from the water pitcher, and then favored us with his opinion about the business in hand. And, certainly, though they proceeded out of an unwiped mouth, his expressions did him honor.

"Give the girl a hot cup of tea, and a thick slice of this first-rate bacon," said Silas, like a sensible man as he was. "That's what she wants. Let her stay with us as long as she likes, and help in the kitchen, and take the cow-breath at milking-time; and, in a week or two, she'll begin to look like a creature of this world."

So we sat down again to supper, and Priscilla along with us.

V.

UNTIL BED-TIME

SILAS Foster, by the time we concluded our meal, had stript off his coat, and planted himself on a low chair by the kitchen fire, with a lapstone, a hammer, a piece of sole-leather, and some waxed ends, in order to cobble an old pair of cow-hide boots; he being, in his own phrase, "something of a dab" (whatever degree of skill that may imply) at the shoemaking business. We heard the tap of his hammer, at intervals, for the rest of the evening. The remainder of the party adjourned to the sitting-room. Good Mrs. Foster took her knitting-work, and soon fell fast asleep, still keeping her needles in brisk movement, and, to the best of my observation, absolutely footing a stocking out of the texture of a dream. And a very substantial stocking it seemed to be. One of the two handmaidens hemmed a towel, and the other appeared to be making a ruffle, for her Sunday's wear, out of a little bit of embroidered muslin, which Zenobia had probably given her.

It was curious to observe how trustingly, and yet how timidly, our poor Priscilla betook herself into the shadow of Zenobia's protection. She sat beside her on a stool, looking up, every now and then, with an expression of humble delight, at her new friend's beauty. A brilliant woman is often an object of the devoted admiration — it might almost be termed worship, or idolatry — of some young girl, who perhaps beholds the cynosure only at an awful distance, and has as little hope of personal intercourse as of climbing among the stars of heaven. We men are too gross to comprehend it. Even a woman, of mature age, despises or laughs at such a passion. There occurred to me no mode of accounting for Priscilla's behavior, except by supposing that she had read some of Zenobia's stories (as such literature goes everywhere), or her

tracts in defence of the sex, and had come hither with the one purpose
of being her slave. There is nothing parallel to this, I believe,—nothing
so foolishly disinterested, and hardly anything so beautiful,—in the masculine nature, at whatever epoch of life; or, if there be, a fine and rare
development of character might reasonably be looked for from the youth
who should prove himself capable of such self-forgetful affection.

Zenobia happening to change her seat, I took the opportunity, in an
under tone, to suggest some such notion as the above.

"Since you see the young woman in so poetical a light," replied she,
in the same tone, "you had better turn the affair into a ballad. It is a
grand subject, and worthy of supernatural machinery. The storm, the
startling knock at the door, the entrance of the sable knight
Hollingsworth and this shadowy snow-maiden, who, precisely at the
stroke of midnight, shall melt away at my feet in a pool of ice-cold
water, and give me my death with a pair of wet slippers! And when the
verses are written, and polished quite to your mind, I will favor you with
my idea as to what the girl really is."

"Pray let me have it now," said I; "it shall be woven into the ballad."

"She is neither more nor less," answered Zenobia, "than a seamstress
from the city; and she has probably no more transcendental purpose
than to do my miscellaneous sewing, for I suppose she will hardly
expect to make my dresses."

"How can you decide upon her so easily?" I inquired.

"O, we women judge one another by tokens that escape the obtuse-
ness of masculine perceptions," said Zenobia. "There is no proof which
you would be likely to appreciate, except the needle-marks on the tip of
her fore-finger. Then, my supposition perfectly accounts for her paleness,
her nervousness, and her wretched fragility. Poor thing! She has been stifled with the heat of a salamander-stove, in a small, close room, and has
drunk coffee, and fed upon dough-nuts, raisins, candy, and all such trash,
till she is scarcely half alive; and so, as she has hardly any physique, a
poet, like Mr. Miles Coverdale, may be allowed to think her spiritual."

"Look at her now!" whispered I.

Priscilla was gazing towards us, with an inexpressible sorrow in her
wan face, and great tears running down her cheeks. It was difficult to
resist the impression that, cautiously as we had lowered our voices, she
must have overheard and been wounded by Zenobia's scornful estimate of her character and purposes.

"What ears the girl must have!" whispered Zenobia, with a look of
vexation, partly comic, and partly real. "I will confess to you that I cannot quite make her out. However, I am positively not an ill-natured person, unless when very grievously provoked; and as you, and especially
Mr. Hollingsworth, take so much interest in this odd creature,—and as
she knocks, with a very slight tap, against my own heart, likewise,—why,

I mean to let her in. From this moment, I will be reasonably kind to her. There is no pleasure in tormenting a person of one's own sex, even if she do favor one with a little more love than one can conveniently dispose of;—and that, let me say, Mr. Coverdale, is the most troublesome offence you can offer to a woman."

"Thank you," said I, smiling; "I don't mean to be guilty of it."

She went towards Priscilla, took her hand, and passed her own rosy finger-tips, with a pretty, caressing movement, over the girl's hair. The touch had a magical effect. So vivid a look of joy flushed up beneath those fingers, that it seemed as if the sad and wan Priscilla had been snatched away, and another kind of creature substituted in her place. This one caress, bestowed voluntarily by Zenobia, was evidently received as a pledge of all that the stranger sought from her, whatever the unuttered boon might be. From that instant, too, she melted in quietly amongst us, and was no longer a foreign element. Though always an object of peculiar interest, a riddle, and a theme of frequent discussion, her tenure at Blithedale was thenceforth fixed. We no more thought of questioning it, than if Priscilla had been recognized as a domestic sprite, who had haunted the rustic fireside, of old, before we had ever been warmed by its blaze.

She now produced, out of a work-bag that she had with her, some little wooden instruments (what they are called, I never knew), and proceeded to knit, or net, an article which ultimately took the shape of a silk purse. As the work went on, I remembered to have seen just such purses before; indeed, I was the possessor of one. Their peculiar excellence, besides the great delicacy and beauty of the manufacture, lay in the almost impossibility that any uninitiated person should discover the aperture; although, to a practised touch, they would open as wide as charity or prodigality might wish. I wondered if it were not a symbol of Priscilla's own mystery.

Notwithstanding the new confidence with which Zenobia had inspired her, our guest showed herself disquieted by the storm. When the strong puffs of wind spattered the snow against the windows, and made the oaken frame of the farm-house creak, she looked at us apprehensively, as if to inquire whether these tempestuous outbreaks did not betoken some unusual mischief in the shrieking blast. She had been bred up, no doubt, in some close nook, some inauspiciously sheltered court of the city, where the uttermost rage of a tempest, though it might scatter down the slates of the roof into the bricked area, could not shake the casement of her little room. The sense of vast, undefined space, pressing from the outside against the black panes of our uncurtained windows, was fearful to the poor girl, heretofore accustomed to the narrowness of human limits, with the lamps of neighboring tenements glimmering across the street. The house probably seemed to her adrift on the great ocean of the night. A little parallelogram of sky was all that she had hitherto known of nature, so that she felt the awfulness that really exists in its limitless extent. Once, while the blast was bellowing, she caught hold of Zenobia's robe, with precisely the air of one who hears her own name spoken at a distance, but is unutterably reluctant to obey the call.

We spent rather an incommunicative evening. Hollingsworth hardly said a word, unless when repeatedly and pertinaciously addressed. Then, indeed, he would glare upon us from the thick shrubbery of his meditations like a tiger out of a jungle, make the briefest reply possible, and betake himself back into the solitude of his heart and mind. The poor fellow had contracted this ungracious habit from the intensity with which he contemplated his own ideas, and the infrequent sympathy which they met with from his auditors,—a circumstance that seemed only to strengthen the implicit confidence that he awarded to them. His heart, I imagine, was never really interested in our socialist scheme, but was forever busy with his strange, and, as most people thought it, impracticable plan, for the reformation of criminals through an appeal to their higher instincts. Much as I liked Hollingsworth, it cost me many a groan to tolerate him on this point. He ought to have commenced his investigation of the subject by perpetrating some huge sin in his proper person, and examining the condition of his higher instincts afterwards.

The rest of us formed ourselves into a committee for providing our infant community with an appropriate name,—a matter of greatly more difficulty than the uninitiated reader would suppose. Blithedale was neither good nor bad. We should have resumed the old Indian name of the premises, had it possessed the oil-and-honey flow which the aborigines were so often happy in communicating to their local appellations; but it chanced to be a harsh, ill-connected, and interminable word, which seemed to fill the mouth with a mixture of very stiff clay and very crumbly pebbles. Zenobia suggested "Sunny Glimpse," as expressive of a vista into a better system of society. This we turned over and over, for a while, acknowledging its prettiness, but concluded it to be rather too fine and sentimental a name (a fault inevitable by literary ladies, in such attempts) for sunburnt men to work under. I ventured to whisper "Utopia," which, however, was unanimously scouted down, and the proposer very harshly maltreated, as if he had intended a latent satire. Some were for calling our institution "The Oasis," in view of its being the one green spot in the moral sand-waste of the world; but others insisted on a proviso for reconsidering the matter at a twelve-month's end, when a final decision might be had, whether to name it "The Oasis," or "Sahara." So, at last, finding it impracticable to hammer out anything better, we resolved that the spot should still be Blithedale, as being of good augury enough.

The evening wore on, and the outer solitude looked in upon us through the windows, gloomy, wild, and vague, like another state of existence, close beside the little sphere of warmth and light in which we were the prattlers and bustlers of a moment. By and by, the door was opened by Silas Foster, with a cotton handkerchief about his head, and a tallow candle in his hand.

"Take my advice, brother farmers," said he, with a great, broad, bottomless yawn, "and get to bed as soon as you can. I shall sound the horn at daybreak; and we've got the cattle to fodder, and nine cows to milk, and a dozen other things to do, before breakfast."

Thus ended the first evening at Blithedale. I went shivering to my fireless chamber, with the miserable consciousness (which had been growing upon me for several hours past) that I had caught a tremendous cold, and should probably awaken, at the blast of the horn, a fit subject for a hospital. The night proved a feverish one. During the greater part of it, I was in that vilest of states when a fixed idea remains in the mind, like the nail in Sisera's brain, while innumerable other ideas go and come, and flutter to and fro, combining constant transition with intolerable sameness. Had I made a record of that night's half-waking dreams, it is my belief that it would have anticipated several of the chief incidents of this narrative, including a dim shadow of its catastrophe. Starting up in bed, at length, I saw that the storm was past, and the moon was shining on the snowy landscape, which looked like a lifeless copy of the world in marble.

From the bank of the distant river, which was shimmering in the moonlight, came the black shadow of the only cloud in heaven, driven swiftly by the wind, and passing over meadow and hillock, vanishing amid tufts of leafless trees, but reappearing on the hither side, until it swept across our door-step.

How cold an Arcadia was this!

VI.

COVERDALE'S SICK-CHAMBER

THE horn sounded at daybreak, as Silas Foster had forewarned us, harsh, uproarious, inexorably drawn out, and as sleep-dispelling as if this hard-hearted old yeoman had got hold of the trump of doom.

On all sides I could hear the creaking of the bedsteads, as the brethren of Blithedale started from slumber, and thrust themselves into their habiliments, all awry, no doubt, in their haste to begin the reformation of the world. Zenobia put her head into the entry, and besought Silas Foster to cease his clamor, and to be kind enough to leave an armful of firewood and a pail of water at her chamber-door. Of the whole household,—unless, indeed, it were Priscilla, for whose habits, in this particular, I cannot vouch,—of all our apostolic society, whose mission was to bless mankind, Hollingsworth, I apprehend, was the only one who began the enterprise with prayer. My sleeping-room being but thinly partitioned from his, the solemn murmur of his voice made its way to my ears, compelling me to be an auditor of his awful privacy with the Creator. It affected me with a deep reverence for Hollingsworth, which no familiarity then existing, or that afterwards grew more intimate between us,—no, nor my subsequent perception of his own great errors,—ever quite effaced. It is so rare, in these times, to meet with a man of prayerful habits (except, of course, in the pulpit), that such an one is decidedly marked out by a light of transfiguration, shed upon him in the divine interview from which he passes into his daily life.

As for me, I lay abed; and if I said my prayers, it was backward, cursing my day as bitterly as patient Job himself. The truth was, the hothouse warmth of a town-residence, and the luxurious life in which I indulged myself, had taken much of the pith out of my physical system; and the wintry blast of the preceding day, together with the general chill of our airy old farmhouse, had got fairly into my heart and the marrow of my bones. In this predicament, I seriously wished—selfish as it may appear—that the reformation of society had been postponed about half a century, or, at all events, to such a date as should have put my intermeddling with it entirely out of the question.

What, in the name of common sense, had I to do with any better society than I had always lived in? It had satisfied me well enough. My pleasant bachelor-parlor, sunny and shadowy, curtained and carpeted, with the bed-chamber adjoining; my centre-table, strewn with books and periodicals; my writing-desk, with a half-finished poem, in a stanza of my own contrivance; my morning lounge at the reading-room or picture-gallery; my noontide walk along the cheery pavement, with the suggestive succession of human faces, and the brisk throb of human life, in which I shared; my dinner at the Albion, where I had a hundred dishes at command, and could banquet as delicately as the wizard Michael Scott when the devil fed him from the King of France's kitchen; my evening at the billiard-club, the concert, the theatre, or at somebody's party, if I pleased;—what could be better than all this? Was it better to hoe, to mow, to toil and moil amidst the accumulations of a barn-yard; to be the chamber-maid of two yoke of oxen and a dozen cows; to eat salt beef, and earn it with the sweat of my brow, and thereby take the tough morsel out of some wretch's mouth, into whose vocation I had thrust myself? Above all, was it better to have a fever, and die blaspheming, as I was like to do?

In this wretched plight, with a furnace in my heart, and another in my head, by the heat of which I was kept constantly at the boiling point, yet shivering at the bare idea of extruding so much as a finger into the icy atmosphere of the room, I kept my bed until breakfast-time, when Hollingsworth knocked at the door, and entered.

"Well, Coverdale," cried he, "you bid fair to make an admirable farmer! Don't you mean to get up to-day?"

"Neither to-day nor to-morrow," said I, hopelessly. "I doubt if I ever rise again!"

"What is the matter, now?" he asked.

I told him my piteous case, and besought him to send me back to town in a close carriage.

"No, no!" said Hollingsworth, with kindly seriousness. "If you are really sick, we must take care of you."

Accordingly, he built a fire in my chamber, and, having little else to do while the snow lay on the ground, established himself as my nurse. A doctor was sent for, who, being homoeopathic, gave me as much medicine, in the course of a fortnight's attendance, as would have lain on the point of a needle. They fed me on water-gruel, and I speedily became a skeleton above ground. But, after all, I have many precious recollections connected with that fit of sickness.

Hollingsworth's more than brotherly attendance gave me inexpressible comfort. Most men—and certainly I could not always claim to be one of the exceptions—have a natural indifference, if not an absolutely hostile feeling, towards those whom disease, or weakness, or calamity of any kind, causes to falter and faint amid the rude jostle of our selfish existence. The education of Christianity, it is true, the sympathy of a like experience, and the example of women, may soften, and, possibly, subvert, this ugly characteristic of our sex; but it is originally there, and has likewise its analogy in the practice of our brute brethren, who hunt the sick or disabled member of the herd from among them, as an enemy. It is for this reason that the stricken deer goes apart, and the sick lion grimly withdraws himself into his den. Except in love, or the attachments of kindred, or other very long and habitual affection, we really have no tenderness. But there was something of the woman moulded into the great, stalwart frame of Hollingsworth; nor was he ashamed of it, as men often are of what is best in them, nor seemed ever to know that there was such a soft place in his heart. I knew it well, however, at that time, although afterwards it came nigh to be forgotten. Methought there could not be two such men alive as Hollingsworth. There never was any blaze of a fireside that warmed and cheered me, in the down-sinkings and shiverings of my spirit, so effectually as did the light out of those eyes, which lay so deep and dark under his shaggy brows.

Happy the man that has such a friend beside him when he comes to die! and unless a friend like Hollingsworth be at hand,—as most probably there will not,—he had better make up his mind to die alone. How many men, I wonder, does one meet with, in a lifetime, whom he would choose for his death-bed companions! At the crisis of my fever, I besought Hollingsworth to let nobody else enter the room, but continually to make me sensible of his own presence, by a grasp of the hand, a word, a prayer, if he thought good to utter it; and that then he should be the witness how courageously I would encounter the worst. It still impresses me as almost a matter of regret, that I did not die then, when I had tolerably made up my mind to it; for Hollingsworth would have gone with me to the hither verge of life, and have sent his friendly and hopeful accents far over on the other side, while I should be treading the unknown path. Now, were I to send for him, he would hardly come to my bed-side, nor should I depart the easier for his presence.

"You are not going to die, this time," said he, gravely smiling. "You know nothing about sickness, and think your case a great deal more desperate than it is."

"Death should take me while I am in the mood," replied I, with a little of my customary levity.

"Have you nothing to do in life," asked Hollingsworth, "that you fancy yourself so ready to leave it?"

"Nothing," answered I; "nothing, that I know of, unless to make pretty verses, and play a part, with Zenobia and the rest of the amateurs, in our pastoral. It seems but an unsubstantial sort of business, as viewed through a mist of fever. But, dear Hollingsworth, your own vocation is evidently to be a priest, and to spend your days and nights in helping your fellow-creatures to draw peaceful dying breaths."

"And by which of my qualities," inquired he, "can you suppose me fitted for this awful ministry?"

"By your tenderness," I said. "It seems to me the reflection of God's own love."

"And you call me tender!" repeated Hollingsworth, thoughtfully. "I should rather say that the most marked trait in my character is an inflexible severity of purpose. Mortal man has no right to be so inflexible as it is my nature and necessity to be."

"I do not believe it," I replied.

But, in due time, I remembered what he said.

Probably, as Hollingsworth suggested, my disorder was never so serious as, in my ignorance of such matters, I was inclined to consider it. After so much tragical preparation, it was positively rather mortifying to find myself on the mending hand.

All the other members of the Community showed me kindness

according to the full measure of their capacity. Zenobia brought me my gruel, every day, made by her own hands (not very skilfully, if the truth must be told); and whenever I seemed inclined to converse, would sit by my bed-side, and talk with so much vivacity as to add several gratu-itous throbs to my pulse. Her poor little stories and tracts never half did justice to her intellect. It was only the lack of a fitter avenue that drove her to seek development in literature. She was made (among a thousand other things that she might have been) for a stump-oratress. I recognized no severe culture in Zenobia; her mind was full of weeds. It startled me, sometimes, in my state of moral as well as bodily faint-heartedness, to observe the hardihood of her philosophy. She made no scruple of oversetting all human institutions, and scattering them as with a breeze from her fan. A female reformer, in her attacks upon society, has an instinctive sense of where the life lies, and is inclined to aim directly at that spot. Especially the relation between the sexes is naturally among the earliest to attract her notice.

Zenobia was truly a magnificent woman. The homely simplicity of her dress could not conceal, nor scarcely diminish, the queenliness of her presence. The image of her form and face should have been multiplied all over the earth. It was wronging the rest of mankind to retain her as the spectacle of only a few. The stage would have been her proper sphere. She should have made it a point of duty, moreover, to sit endlessly to painters and sculptors, and preferably to the latter; because the cold decorum of the marble would consist with the utmost scantiness of drapery, so that the eye might chastely be gladdened with her material perfection in its entireness. I know not well how to express, that the native glow of coloring in her cheeks, and even the flesh-warmth over her round arms, and what was visible of her full bust,—in a word, her womanliness incarnated,—compelled me sometimes to close my eyes, as if it were not quite the privilege of modesty to gaze at her. Illness and exhaustion, no doubt, had made me morbidly sensitive.

I noticed—and wondered how Zenobia contrived it—that she had always a new flower in her hair. And still it was a hot-house flower,—an outlandish flower,—a flower of the tropics, such as appeared to have sprung passionately out of a soil the very weeds of which would be fervid and spicy. Unlike as was the flower of each successive day to the preceding one, it yet so assimilated its richness to the rich beauty of the woman, that I thought it the only flower fit to be worn; so fit, indeed, that Nature had evidently created this floral gem, in a happy exuberance, for the one purpose of worthily adorning Zenobia's head. It might be that my feverish fantasies clustered themselves about this peculiarity, and caused it to look more gorgeous and wonderful than if beheld with temperate eyes. In the height of my illness, as I well recollect, I went so far as to pronounce it preternatural.

"Zenobia is an enchantress!" whispered I once to Hollingsworth. "She is a sister of the Veiled Lady. That flower in her hair is a talisman. If you were to snatch it away, she would vanish, or be transformed into something else."

"What does he say?" asked Zenobia.

"Nothing that has an atom of sense in it," answered Hollingsworth. "He is a little beside himself, I believe, and talks about your being a witch, and of some magical property in the flower that you wear in your hair."

"It is an idea worthy of a feverish poet," said she, laughing rather compassionately, and taking out the flower. "I scorn to owe anything to magic. Here, Mr. Hollingsworth, you may keep the spell while it has any virtue in it; but I cannot promise you not to appear with a new one to-morrow. It is the one relic of my more brilliant, my happier days!"

The most curious part of the matter was, that long after my slight delirium had passed away,—as long, indeed, as I continued to know this remarkable woman,—her daily flower affected my imagination, though more slightly, yet in very much the same way. The reason must have been that, whether intentionally on her part or not, this favorite ornament was actually a subtile expression of Zenobia's character.

One subject, about which—very impertinently, moreover—I perplexed myself with a great many conjectures, was, whether Zenobia had ever been married. The idea, it must be understood, was unauthorized by any circumstance or suggestion that had made its way to my ears. So young as I beheld her, and the freshest and rosiest woman of a thousand, there was certainly no need of imputing to her a destiny already accomplished; the probability was far greater that her coming years had all life's richest gifts to bring. If the great event of a woman's existence had been consummated, the world knew nothing of it, although the world seemed to know Zenobia well. It was a ridiculous piece of romance, undoubtedly, to imagine that this beautiful personage, wealthy as she was, and holding a position that might fairly enough be called distinguished, could have given herself away so privately, but that some whisper and suspicion, and, by degrees, a full understanding of the fact, would eventually be blown abroad. But then, as I failed not to consider, her original home was at a distance of many hundred miles. Rumors might fill the social atmosphere, or might once have filled it, there, which would travel but slowly, against the wind, towards our north-eastern metropolis, and perhaps melt into thin air before reaching it.

There was not—and I distinctly repeat it—the slightest foundation in my knowledge for any surmise of the kind. But there is a species of intuition,—either a spiritual lie, or the subtile recognition of a fact,—which comes to us in a reduced state of the corporeal system. The soul gets the better of the body, after wasting illness, or when a vegetable diet may have mingled too much ether in the blood. Vapors then rise up to the brain, and take shapes that often image falsehood, but sometimes truth. The spheres of our companions have, at such periods, a vastly greater influence upon our own than when robust health gives us a repellent and self-defensive energy. Zenobia's sphere, I imagine, impressed itself powerfully on mine, and transformed me, during this period of my weakness, into something like a mesmerical clairvoyant.

Then, also, as anybody could observe, the freedom of her deportment (though, to some tastes, it might commend itself as the utmost perfection of manner in a youthful widow or a blooming matron) was not exactly maiden-like. What girl had ever laughed as Zenobia did? What girl had ever spoken in her mellow tones? Her unconstrained and inevitable manifestation, I said often to myself, was that of a woman to whom wedlock had thrown wide the gates of mystery. Yet sometimes I strove to be ashamed of these conjectures. I acknowledged it as a masculine grossness,—a sin of wicked interpretation, of which man is often guilty towards the other sex,—thus to mistake the sweet, liberal, but womanly frankness of a noble and generous disposition. Still, it was of no avail to reason with myself, nor to upbraid myself. Pertinaciously the thought, "Zenobia is a wife,—Zenobia has lived and loved! There is no folded petal, no latent dewdrop, in this perfectly-developed rose!"—irresistibly that thought drove out all other conclusions, as often as my mind reverted to the subject.

Zenobia was conscious of my observation, though not, I presume, of the point to which it led me.

"Mr. Coverdale," said she, one day, as she saw me watching her, while she arranged my gruel on the table, "I have been exposed to a great deal of eye-shot in the few years of my mixing in the world, but never, I think, to precisely such glances as you are in the habit of favoring me with. I seem to interest you very much; and yet—or else a woman's instinct is for once deceived—I cannot reckon you as an admirer. What are you seeking to discover in me?"

"The mystery of your life," answered I, surprised into the truth by the unexpectedness of her attack. "And you will never tell me."

She bent her head towards me, and let me look into her eyes, as if challenging me to drop a plummet-line down into the depths of her consciousness.

"I see nothing now," said I, closing my own eyes, "unless it be the face of a sprite laughing at me from the bottom of a deep well."

A bachelor always feels himself defrauded, when he knows, or suspects, that any woman of his acquaintance has given herself away. Otherwise, the matter could have been no concern of mine. It was purely speculative; for I should not, under any circumstances, have fallen in love with Zenobia. The riddle made me so nervous, however, in my sensitive condition of mind and body, that I most ungratefully began to wish that she would let me alone. Then, too, her gruel was very wretched stuff, with almost invariably the smell of pine smoke upon it, like the evil taste that is said to mix itself up with a witch's best concocted dainties. Why could not she have allowed one of the other women to take the gruel in charge? Whatever else might be her gifts, Nature certainly never intended Zenobia for a cook. Or, if so, she should have meddled only with the richest and spiciest dishes, and such as are to be tasted at banquets, between draughts of intoxicating wine.

VII.

THE CONVALESCENT

As soon as my incommodities allowed me to think of past occurrences, I failed not to inquire what had become of the odd little guest whom Hollingsworth had been the medium of introducing among us. It now appeared that poor Priscilla had not so literally fallen out of the clouds as we were at first inclined to suppose. A letter, which should have introduced her, had since been received from one of the city missionaries, containing a certificate of character, and an allusion to circumstances which, in the writer's judgment, made it especially desirable that she should find shelter in our Community. There was a hint, not very intelligible, implying either that Priscilla had recently escaped from some particular peril or irksomeness of position, or else that she was still liable to this danger or difficulty, whatever it might be. We should ill have deserved the reputation of a benevolent fraternity, had we hesitated to entertain a petitioner in such need, and so strongly recommended to our kindness; not to mention, moreover, that the strange maiden had set herself diligently to work, and was doing good service with her needle. But a slight mist of uncertainty still floated about Priscilla, and kept her, as yet, from taking a very decided place among creatures of flesh and blood.

The mysterious attraction, which, from her first entrance on our scene, she evinced for Zenobia, had lost nothing of its force. I often heard her footsteps, soft and low, accompanying the light but decided tread of the latter up the staircase, stealing along the passage-way by her new friend's side, and pausing while Zenobia entered my chamber. Occasionally, Zenobia would be a little annoyed by Priscilla's too close attendance. In an authoritative and not very kindly tone, she would advise her to breathe the pleasant air in a walk, or to go with her work into the barn, holding out half a promise to come and sit on the hay with her, when at leisure. Evidently, Priscilla found but scanty requital for her love. Hollingsworth was likewise a great favorite with her. For several minutes together, sometimes, while my auditory nerves retained the susceptibility of delicate health, I used to hear a low, pleasant murmur, ascending from the room below; and at last ascertained it to be Priscilla's voice, babbling like a little brook to Hollingsworth. She talked more largely and freely with him than with Zenobia, towards whom, indeed, her feelings seemed not so much to be confidence as involuntary affection. I should have thought all the better of my own qualities, had Priscilla marked me out for the third place in her regards. But, though she appeared to like me tolerably well, I could never flatter myself with being distinguished by her as Hollingsworth and Zenobia were.

One forenoon, during my convalescence, there came a gentle tap at my chamber-door. I immediately said, "Come in, Priscilla!" with an acute sense of the applicant's identity. Nor was I deceived. It was really Priscilla,—a pale, large-eyed little woman (for she had gone far enough into her teens to be, at least, on the outer limit of girlhood), but much less wan than at my previous view of her, and far better conditioned both as to health and spirits. As I first saw her, she had reminded me of plants that one sometimes observes doing their best to vegetate among the bricks of an enclosed court, where there is scanty soil, and never any sunshine. At present, though with no approach to bloom, there were indications that the girl had human blood in her veins.

Priscilla came softly to my bed-side, and held out an article of snow-white linen, very carefully and smoothly ironed. She did not seem bashful, nor anywise embarrassed. My weakly condition, I suppose, supplied a medium in which she could approach me.

"Do not you need this?" asked she. "I have made it for you."

It was a night-cap!

"My dear Priscilla," said I, smiling, "I never had on a night-cap in my life! But perhaps it will be better for me to wear one, now that I am a miserable invalid. How admirably you have done it! No, no; I never can think of wearing such an exquisitely wrought night-cap as this, unless it be in the day-time, when I sit up to receive company."

"It is for use, not beauty," answered Priscilla. "I could have embroidered it, and made it much prettier, if I pleased."

While holding up the night-cap, and admiring the fine needle-work, I perceived that Priscilla had a sealed letter, which she was waiting for me to take. It had arrived from the village post-office that morning. As

I did not immediately offer to receive the letter, she drew it back, and held it against her bosom, with both hands clasped over it, in a way that had probably grown habitual to her. Now, on turning my eyes from the night-cap to Priscilla, it forcibly struck me that her air, though not her figure, and the expression of her face, but not its features, had a resemblance to what I had often seen in a friend of mine, one of the most gifted women of the age. I cannot describe it. The points easiest to convey to the reader were, a certain curve of the shoulders, and a partial closing of the eyes, which seemed to look more penetratingly into my own eyes, through the narrowed apertures, than if they had been open at full width. It was a singular anomaly of likeness coëxisting with perfect dissimilitude.

"Will you give me the letter, Priscilla?" said I.

She started, put the letter into my hand, and quite lost the look that had drawn my notice.

"Priscilla," I inquired, "did you ever see Miss Margaret Fuller?"

"No," she answered.

"Because," said I, "you reminded me of her, just now; and it happens, strangely enough, that this very letter is from her."

Priscilla, for whatever reason, looked very much discomposed.

"I wish people would not fancy such odd things in me!" she said, rather petulantly. "How could I possibly make myself resemble this lady, merely by holding her letter in my hand?"

"Certainly, Priscilla, it would puzzle me to explain it," I replied; "nor do I suppose that the letter had anything to do with it. It was just a coincidence, nothing more."

She hastened out of the room, and this was the last that I saw of Priscilla until I ceased to be an invalid.

Being much alone during my recovery, I read interminably in Mr. Emerson's Essays, the Dial, Carlyle's works, George Sand's romances (lent me by Zenobia), and other books which one or another of the brethren or sisterhood had brought with them. Agreeing in little else, most of these utterances were like the cry of some solitary sentinel, whose station was on the outposts of the advance-guard of human progression; or, sometimes, the voice came sadly from among the shattered ruins of the past, but yet had a hopeful echo in the future. They were well adapted (better, at least, than any other intellectual products, the volatile essence of which had heretofore tinctured a printed page) to pilgrims like ourselves, whose present bivouac was considerably further into the waste of chaos than any mortal army of crusaders had ever marched before. Fourier's works, also, in a series of horribly tedious volumes, attracted a good deal of my attention, from the analogy which I could not but recognize between his system and our own. There was far less resemblance, it is true, than the world chose to imagine, inasmuch as the two theories differed, as widely as the zenith from the nadir, in their main principles.

I talked about Fourier to Hollingsworth, and translated, for his benefit, some of the passages that chiefly impressed me.

"When, as a consequence of human improvement," said I, "the globe shall arrive at its final perfection, the great ocean is to be converted into a particular kind of lemonade, such as was fashionable at Paris in Fourier's time. He calls it *limonade a cédre*. It is positively a fact! Just imagine the city-docks filled, every day, with a floodtide of this delectable beverage!"

"Why did not the Frenchman make punch of it, at once?" asked Hollingsworth. "The jack-tars would be delighted to go down in ships and do business in such an element."

I further proceeded to explain, as well as I modestly could, several points of Fourier's system, illustrating them with here and there a page or two, and asking Hollingsworth's opinion as to the expediency of introducing these beautiful peculiarities into our own practice.

"Let me hear no more of it!" cried he, in utter disgust. "I never will forgive this fellow! He has committed the unpardonable sin; for what more monstrous iniquity could the devil himself contrive than to choose the selfish principle,—the principle of all human wrong, the very blackness of man's heart, the portion of ourselves which we shudder at, and which it is the whole aim of spiritual discipline to eradicate,—to choose it as the master-workman of his system? To seize upon and foster whatever vile, petty, sordid, filthy, bestial and abominable corruptions have cankered into our nature, to be the efficient instruments of his infernal regeneration! And his consummated Paradise, as he pictures it, would be worthy of the agency which he counts upon for establishing it. The nauseous villain!"

"Nevertheless," remarked I, "in consideration of the promised delights of his system,—so very proper, as they certainly are, to be appreciated by Fourier's countrymen,—I cannot but wonder that universal France did not adopt his theory, at a moment's warning. But is there not something very characteristic of his nation in Fourier's manner of putting forth his views? He makes no claim to inspiration. He has not persuaded himself—as Swedenborg did, and as any other than a Frenchman would, with a mission of like importance to communicate—that he speaks with authority from above. He promulgates his system, so far as I can perceive, entirely on his own responsibility. He has searched out and discovered the whole counsel of the Almighty, in respect to mankind, past, present, and for exactly seventy thousand years to come, by the mere force and cunning of his individual intellect!"

"Take the book out of my sight," said Hollingsworth, with great virulence of expression, "or, I tell you fairly, I shall fling it in the fire! And as for Fourier, let him make a Paradise, if he can, of Gehenna, where, as I conscientiously believe, he is floundering at this moment!"

"And bellowing, I suppose," said I, — not that I felt any ill-will towards Fourier, but merely wanted to give the finishing touch to Hollingsworth's image, — "bellowing for the least drop of his beloved *limonade a cédre!*"

There is but little profit to be expected in attempting to argue with a man who allows himself to declaim in this manner; so I dropt the subject, and never took it up again.

But had the system at which he was so enraged combined almost any amount of human wisdom, spiritual insight, and imaginative beauty, I question whether Hollingsworth's mind was in a fit condition to receive it. I began to discern that he had come among us actuated by no real sympathy with our feelings and our hopes, but chiefly because we were estranging ourselves from the world, with which his lonely and exclusive object in life had already put him at odds. Hollingsworth must have been originally endowed with a great spirit of benevolence, deep enough and warm enough to be the source of as much disinterested good as Providence often allows a human being the privilege of conferring upon his fellows. This native instinct yet lived within him. I myself had profited by it, in my necessity. It was seen, too, in his treatment of Priscilla. Such casual circumstances as were here involved would quicken his divine power of sympathy, and make him seem, while their influence lasted, the tenderest man and the truest friend on earth. But, by and by, you missed the tenderness of yesterday, and grew drearily conscious that Hollingsworth had a closer friend than ever you could be; and this friend was the cold, spectral monster which he had himself conjured up, and on which he was wasting all the warmth of his heart, and of which, at last, — as these men of a mighty purpose so invariably do, — he had grown to be the bond-slave. It was his philanthropic theory.

This was a result exceedingly sad to contemplate, considering that it had been mainly brought about by the very ardor and exuberance of his philanthropy. Sad, indeed, but by no means unusual. He had taught his benevolence to pour its warm tide exclusively through one channel; so that there was nothing to spare for other great manifestations of love to man, nor scarcely for the nutriment of individual attachments, unless they could minister, in some way, to the terrible egotism which he mistook for an angel of God. Had Hollingsworth's

education been more enlarged, he might not so inevitably have stumbled into this pit-fall. But this identical pursuit had educated him. He
knew absolutely nothing, except in a single direction, where he had
thought so energetically, and felt to such a depth, that, no doubt, the
entire reason and justice of the universe appeared to be concentrated
thitherward.

It is my private opinion that, at this period of his life, Hollingsworth
was fast going mad; and, as with other crazy people (among whom I
include humorists of every degree), it required all the constancy of
friendship to restrain his associates from pronouncing him an intolerable bore. Such prolonged fiddling upon one string, —such multi-
form presentation of one idea! His specific object (of which he made
the public more than sufficiently aware, through the medium of lectures and pamphlets) was to obtain funds for the construction of an
edifice, with a sort of collegiate endowment. On this foundation, he
purposed to devote himself and a few disciples to the reform and
mental culture of our criminal brethren. His visionary edifice was
Hollingsworth's one castle in the air; it was the material type in which
his philanthropic dream strove to embody itself; and he made the
scheme more definite, and caught hold of it the more strongly, and
kept his clutch the more pertinaciously, by rendering it visible to the
bodily eye. I have seen him, a hundred times, with a pencil and sheet
of paper, sketching the façade, the sideview, or the rear of the struc-
ture, or planning the internal arrangements, as lovingly as another
man might plan those of the projected home where he meant to be
happy with his wife and children. I have known him to begin a model
of the building with little stones, gathered at the brook-side, whither
we had gone to cool ourselves in the sultry noon of haying-time.
Unlike all other ghosts, his spirit haunted an edifice which, instead of
being time-worn, and full of storied love, and joy, and sorrow, had
never yet come into existence.

"Dear friend," said I, once, to Hollingsworth, before leaving my sick-
chamber, "I heartily wish that I could make your schemes my schemes,
because it would be so great a happiness to find myself treading the
same path with you. But I am afraid there is not stuff in me stern
enough for a philanthropist, —or not in this peculiar direction, —or, at
all events, not solely in this. Can you bear with me, if such should
prove to be the case?"

"I will, at least, wait a while," answered Hollingsworth, gazing at me
sternly and gloomily. "But how can you be my life-long friend, except
you strive with me towards the great object of my life?"

Heaven forgive me! A horrible suspicion crept into my heart, and
stung the very core of it as with the fangs of an adder. I wondered

whether it were possible that Hollingsworth could have watched by my bed-side, with all that devoted care, only for the ulterior purpose of making me a proselyte to his views!

VIII.

A MODERN ARCADIA

MAY-DAY—I forget whether by Zenobia's sole decree, or by the unanimous vote of our Community—had been declared a movable festival. It was deferred until the sun should have had a reasonable time to clear away the snow-drifts along the lee of the stone walls, and bring out a few of the readiest wild-flowers. On the forenoon of the substituted day, after admitting some of the balmy air into my chamber, I decided that it was nonsense and effeminacy to keep myself a prisoner any longer. So I descended to the sitting-room, and finding nobody there, proceeded to the barn, whence I had already heard Zenobia's voice, and along with it a girlish laugh, which was not so certainly recognizable. Arriving at the spot, it a little surprised me to discover that these merry outbreaks came from Priscilla.

The two had been a-Maying together. They had found anemones in abundance, housatonias by the handful, some columbines, a few long-stalked violets, and a quantity of white everlasting-flowers, and had filled up their basket with the delicate spray of shrubs and trees. None were prettier than the maple-twigs, the leaf of which looks like a scarlet bud in May, and like a plate of vegetable gold in October. Zenobia, who showed no conscience in such matters, had also rifled a cherry-tree of one of its blossomed boughs, and, with all this variety of sylvan ornament, had been decking out Priscilla. Being done with a good deal of taste, it made her look more charming than I should have thought possible, with my recollection of the wan, frost-nipt girl, as heretofore described. Nevertheless, among those fragrant blossoms, and conspicuously, too, had been stuck a weed of evil odor and ugly aspect, which, as soon as I detected it, destroyed the effect of all the rest. There was a gleam of latent mischief—not to call it deviltry—in Zenobia's eye, which seemed to indicate a slightly malicious purpose in the arrangement.

As for herself, she scorned the rural buds and leaflets, and wore nothing but her invariable flower of the tropics.

"What do you think of Priscilla now, Mr. Coverdale?" asked she, surveying her as a child does its doll. "Is not she worth a verse or two?"

"There is only one thing amiss," answered I.

Zenobia laughed, and flung the malignant weed away.

"Yes; she deserves some verses now," said I, "and from a better poet than myself. She is the very picture of the New England spring; subdued in tint, and rather cool, but with a capacity of sunshine, and bringing us a few Alpine blossoms, as earnest of something richer, though hardly more beautiful, hereafter. The best type of her is one of those anemones."

"What I find most singular in Priscilla, as her health improves," observed Zenobia, "is her wildness. Such a quiet little body as she seemed, one would not have expected that. Why, as we strolled the woods together, I could hardly keep her from scrambling up the trees, like a squirrel! She has never before known what it is to live in the free air, and so it intoxicates her as if she were sipping wine. And she thinks it such a paradise here, and all of us, particularly Mr. Hollingsworth and myself, such angels! It is quite ridiculous, and provokes one's malice almost, to see a creature so happy, — especially a feminine creature."

"They are always happier than male creatures," said I.

"You must correct that opinion, Mr. Coverdale," replied Zenobia, contemptuously, "or I shall think you lack the poetic insight. Did you ever see a happy woman in your life? Of course, I do not mean a girl, like Priscilla, and a thousand others, — for they are all alike, while on the sunny side of experience, — but a grown woman. How can she be happy, after discovering that fate has assigned her but one single event, which she must contrive to make the substance of her whole life? A man has his choice of innumerable events."

"A woman, I suppose," answered I, "by constant repetition of her one event, may compensate for the lack of variety."

"Indeed!" said Zenobia.

While we were talking, Priscilla caught sight of Hollingsworth, at a distance, in a blue frock, and with a hoe over his shoulder, returning from the field. She immediately set out to meet him, running and skipping, with spirits as light as the breeze of the May morning, but with limbs too little exercised to be quite responsive; she clapped her hands, too, with great exuberance of gesture, as is the custom of young girls when their electricity overcharges them. But, all at once, midway to Hollingsworth, she paused, looked round about her, towards the river, the road, the woods, and back towards us, appearing to listen, as if she heard some one calling her name, and knew not precisely in what direction.

"Have you bewitched her?" I exclaimed.

"It is no sorcery of mine," said Zenobia; "but I have seen the girl do that identical thing once or twice before. Can you imagine what is the matter with her?"

"No; unless," said I, "she has the gift of hearing those 'airy tongues that syllable men's names,' which Milton tells about."

From whatever cause, Priscilla's animation seemed entirely to have deserted her. She seated herself on a rock, and remained there until Hollingsworth came up; and when he took her hand and led her back to us, she rather resembled my original image of the wan and spiritless Priscilla than the flowery May-queen of a few moments ago. These sudden transformations, only to be accounted for by an extreme nervous susceptibility, always continued to characterize the girl, though with diminished frequency as her health progressively grew more robust.

I was now on my legs again. My fit of illness had been an avenue between two existences; the low-arched and darksome doorway, through which I crept out of a life of old conventionalisms, on my hands and knees, as it were, and gained admittance into the freer region that lay beyond. In this respect, it was like death. And, as with death, too, it was good to have gone through it. No otherwise could I have rid myself of a thousand follies, fripperies, prejudices, habits, and other such worldly dust as inevitably settles upon the crowd along the broad highway, giving them all one sordid aspect before noontime, however freshly they may have begun their pilgrimage in the dewy morning. The very substance upon my bones had not been fit to live with in any better, truer, or more energetic mode than that to which I was accustomed. So it was taken off me and flung aside, like any other worn-out or unseasonable garment; and, after shivering a little while in my skeleton, I began to be clothed anew, and much more satisfactorily than in my previous suit. In literal and physical truth, I was quite another man. I had a lively sense of the exultation with which the spirit will enter on the next stage of its eternal progress, after leaving the heavy burthen of its mortality in an earthly grave, with as little concern for what may become of it as now affected me for the flesh which I had lost.

Emerging into the genial sunshine, I half fancied that the labors of the brotherhood had already realized some of Fourier's predictions. Their enlightened culture of the soil, and the virtues with which they sanctified their life, had begun to produce an effect upon the material world and its climate. In my new enthusiasm, man looked strong and stately,—and woman, O, how beautiful!—and the earth a green garden, blossoming with many-colored delights. Thus Nature, whose laws I had broken in various artificial ways, comported herself towards me as a strict but loving mother, who uses the rod upon her little boy for his naughtiness, and then gives him a smile, a kiss, and some pretty playthings, to console the urchin for her severity.

In the interval of my seclusion, there had been a number of recruits to our little army of saints and martyrs. They were mostly individuals who had gone through such an experience as to disgust them with ordinary pursuits, but who were not yet so old, nor had suffered so deeply, as to lose their faith in the better time to come. On comparing their minds one with another, they often discovered that this idea of a Community had been growing up, in silent and unknown sympathy, for years. Thoughtful, strongly-lined faces were among them; sombre brows, but eyes that did not require spectacles, unless prematurely dimmed by the student's lamplight, and hair that seldom showed a thread of silver. Age, wedded to the past, incrusted over with a stony layer of habits, and retaining nothing fluid in its possibilities, would have been absurdly out of place in an enterprise like this. Youth, too, in its early dawn, was hardly more adapted to our purpose; for it would behold the morning radiance of its own spirit beaming over the very same spots of withered grass and barren sand whence most of us had seen it vanish. We had very young people with us, it is true—downy lads, rosy girls in their first teens, and children of all heights above one's knee—but these had chiefly been sent hither for education, which it was one of the objects and methods of our institution to supply. Then we had boarders, from town and elsewhere, who lived with us in a familiar way, sympathized more or less in our theories, and sometimes shared in our labors.

On the whole, it was a society such as has seldom met together; nor, perhaps, could it reasonably be expected to hold together long. Persons of marked individuality—crooked sticks, as some of us might be called—are not exactly the easiest to bind up into a fagot. But, so long as our union should subsist, a man of intellect and feeling, with a free nature in him, might have sought far and near without finding so many points of attraction as would allure him hitherward. We were of all creeds and opinions, and generally tolerant of all, on every imaginable subject. Our bond, it seems to me, was not affirmative, but negative. We had individually found one thing or another to quarrel with in our past life, and were pretty well agreed as to the inexpediency of lumbering along with the old system any further. As to what should be substituted, there was much less unanimity. We did not greatly care—at least, I never did—for the written constitution under which our millennium had commenced. My hope was, that, between theory and practice, a true and available mode of life might be struck out; and that, even should we ultimately fail, the months or years spent in the trial would not have been wasted, either as regarded passing enjoyment, or the experience which makes men wise.

Arcadians though we were, our costume bore no resemblance to the be-ribboned doublets, silk breeches and stockings, and slippers fastened with artificial roses, that distinguished the pastoral people of poetry and the stage. In outward show, I humbly conceive, we looked rather like a gang of beggars, or banditti, than either a company of honest laboring men, or a conclave of philosophers. Whatever might be our points of difference, we all of us seemed to have come to Blithedale with the one thrifty and laudable idea of wearing out our old clothes. Such garments as had an airing, whenever we strode a-field! Coats with high collars and with no collars, broad-skirted or swallow-tailed, and with the waist at every point between the hip and armpit; pantaloons of a dozen successive epochs, and greatly defaced at the knees by the humiliations of the wearer before his lady-love;—in short, we were a living epitome of defunct fashions, and the very raggedest presentment of men who had seen better days. It was gentility in tatters. Often retaining a scholarlike or clerical air, you might have taken us for the denizens of Grub-street, intent on getting a comfortable livelihood by agricultural labor; or, Coleridge's projected Pantisocracy in full experiment; or, Candide and his motley associates, at work in their cabbage-garden; or anything else that was miserably out at elbows, and most clumsily patched in the rear. We might have been sworn comrades to Falstaff's ragged regiment. Little skill as we boasted in other points of husbandry, every mother's son of us would have served admirably to stick up for a scarecrow. And the worst of the matter was, that the first energetic movement essential to one downright stroke of real labor was sure to put a finish to these poor habiliments. So we gradually flung them all aside, and took to honest homespun and linsey-woolsey, as preferable, on the whole, to the plan recommended, I think, by Virgil,—"Ara nudus; sere nudus," —which, as Silas Foster remarked, when I translated the maxim, would be apt to astonish the women-folks.

After a reasonable training, the yeoman life throve well with us. Our faces took the sunburn kindly; our chests gained in compass, and our shoulders in breadth and squareness; our great brown fists looked as if they had never been capable of kid gloves. The plough, the hoe, the scythe, and the hay-fork, grew familiar to our grasp. The oxen responded to our voices. We could do almost as fair a day's work as Silas Foster himself, sleep dreamlessly after it, and awake at daybreak with only a little stiffness of the joints, which was usually quite gone by breakfast-time.

To be sure, our next neighbors pretended to be incredulous as to our real proficiency in the business which we had taken in hand. They told slanderous fables about our inability to yoke our own oxen, or to drive them a-field when yoked, or to release the poor brutes from their conjugal bond at night-fall. They had the face to say, too, that the cows laughed at our awkwardness at milking-time, and invariably kicked over the pails; partly in consequence of our putting the stool on the wrong side, and partly because, taking offence at the whisking of their tails, we were in the habit of holding these natural fly-flappers with one hand, and milking with the other. They further averred that we hoed up whole acres of Indian corn and other crops, and drew the earth carefully about the weeds; and that, we raised five hundred tufts of burdock, mistaking them for cabbages; and that, by dint of unskilful planting, few of our seeds ever came up at all, or, if they did come up, it was stern-foremost; and that we spent the better part of the month of June in reversing a field of beans, which had thrust themselves out of the ground in this unseemly way. They quoted it as nothing more than an ordinary occurrence for one or other of us to crop off two or three fingers, of a morning, by our clumsy use of the hay-cutter. Finally, and as an ultimate catastrophe, these mendacious rogues circulated a report that we communitarians were exterminated, to the last man, by severing ourselves asunder with the sweep of our own scythes! — and that the world had lost nothing by this little accident.

But this was pure envy and malice on the part of the neighboring farmers. The peril of our new way of life was not lest we should fail in becoming practical agriculturists, but that we should probably cease to be anything else. While our enterprise lay all in theory, we had pleased ourselves with delectable visions of the spiritualization of labor. It was to be our form of prayer and ceremonial of worship. Each stroke of the hoe was to uncover some aromatic root of wisdom, heretofore hidden from the sun. Pausing in the field, to let the wind exhale the moisture from our foreheads, we were to look upward, and catch glimpses into the far-off soul of truth. In this point of view, matters did not turn out quite so well as we anticipated. It is very true that, sometimes, gazing casually around me, out of the midst of my toil, I used to discern a richer picturesqueness in the visible scene of earth and sky. There was, at such moments, a novelty, an unwonted aspect, on the face of Nature, as if she had been taken by surprise and seen at unawares, with no opportunity to put off her real look, and assume the mask with which she mysteriously hides herself from mortals. But this was all. The clods of earth, which we so constantly belabored and turned over and over, were never etherealized into thought. Our thoughts, on the contrary, were fast becoming cloddish. Our labor symbolized nothing, and left us mentally sluggish in the dusk of the evening. Intellectual activity is incompatible with any large amount of bodily exercise. The yeoman and the scholar — the yeoman and the man of finest moral culture, though not the man of sturdiest sense and integrity — are two distinct individuals, and can never be melted or welded into one substance.

Zenobia soon saw this truth, and gibed me about it, one evening, as Hollingsworth and I lay on the grass, after a hard day's work.

"I am afraid you did not make a song, to-day, while loading the hay-cart," said she, "as Burns did, when he was reaping barley."

"Burns never made a song in haying-time," I answered, very positively. "He was no poet while a farmer, and no farmer while a poet."

"And, on the whole, which of the two characters do you like best?" asked Zenobia. "For I have an idea that you cannot combine them any better than Burns did. Ah, I see, in my mind's eye, what sort of an individual you are to be, two or three years hence. Grim Silas Foster is your prototype, with his palm of sole-leather and his joints of rusty iron (which all through summer keep the stiffness of what he calls his winter's rheumatize), and his brain of—I don't know what his brain is made of, unless it be a Savoy cabbage; but yours may be cauliflower, as a rather more delicate variety. Your physical man will be transmuted into salt beef and fried pork, at the rate, I should imagine, of a pound and a half a day; that being about the average which we find necessary in the kitchen. You will make your toilet for the day (still like this delightful Silas Foster) by rinsing your fingers and the front part of your face in a little tin-pan of water at the door-step, and teasing your hair with a wooden pocket-comb before a seven-by-nine-inch looking-glass. Your only pastime will be to smoke some very vile tobacco in the black stump of a pipe."

"Pray, spare me!" cried I. "But the pipe is not Silas's only mode of solacing himself with the weed."

"Your literature," continued Zenobia, apparently delighted with her description, "will be the Farmer's Almanac; for I observe our friend Foster never gets so far as the newspaper. When you happen to sit down, at odd moments, you will fall asleep, and make nasal proclamation of the fact, as he does; and invariably you must be jogged out of a nap, after supper, by the future Mrs. Coverdale, and persuaded to go regularly to bed. And on Sundays, when you put on a blue coat with brass buttons, you will think of nothing else to do, but to go and lounge over the stone walls and rail fences, and stare at the corn growing. And you will look with a knowing eye at oxen, and will have a tendency to clamber over into pig-sties, and feel of the hogs, and give a guess how much they will weigh after you shall have stuck and dressed them. Already I have noticed you begin to speak through your nose, and with a drawl. Pray, if you really did make any poetry to-day, let us hear it in that kind of utterance!"

"Coverdale has given up making verses now," said Hollingsworth, who never had the slightest appreciation of my poetry. "Just think of him penning a sonnet with a fist like that! There is at least this good in a life of toil, that it takes the nonsense and fancy-work out of a man, and leaves nothing but what truly belongs to him. If a farmer can make poetry at the plough-tail, it must be because his nature insists on it; and if that be the case, let him make it, in Heaven's name!"

"And how is it with you?" asked Zenobia, in a different voice; for she never laughed at Hollingsworth, as she often did at me. "You, I think, cannot have ceased to live a life of thought and feeling."

"I have always been in earnest," answered Hollingsworth. "I have hammered thought out of iron, after heating the iron in my heart! It matters little what my outward toil may be. Were I a slave at the bottom of a mine, I should keep the same purpose, the same faith in its ultimate accomplishment, that I do now. Miles Coverdale is not in earnest, either as a poet or a laborer."

"You give me hard measure, Hollingsworth," said I, a little hurt. "I have kept pace with you in the field; and my bones feel as if I had been in earnest, whatever may be the case with my brain!"

"I cannot conceive," observed Zenobia, with great emphasis,—and, no doubt, she spoke fairly the feeling of the moment,—"I cannot conceive of being so continually as Mr. Coverdale is within the sphere of a strong and noble nature, without being strengthened and ennobled by its influence!"

This amiable remark of the fair Zenobia confirmed me in what I had already begun to suspect, that Hollingsworth, like many other illustrious prophets, reformers, and philanthropists, was likely to make at least two proselytes among the women to one among the men. Zenobia and Priscilla! These, I believe (unless my unworthy self might be reckoned for a third), were the only disciples of his mission; and I spent a great deal of time, uselessly, in trying to conjecture what Hollingsworth meant to do with them—and they with him!

IX.

HOLLINGSWORTH, ZENOBIA, PRISCILLA

It is not, I apprehend, a healthy kind of mental occupation, to devote ourselves too exclusively to the study of individual men and women. If the person under examination be one's self, the result is pretty certain to be diseased action of the heart, almost before we can snatch a second glance. Or, if we take the freedom to put a friend under our microscope, we thereby insulate him from many of his true relations, magnify his peculiarities, inevitably tear him into parts, and, of course, patch him very clumsily together again. What wonder, then, should we be frightened by the aspect of a monster, which, after all,—though we can point to every feature of his deformity in the real personage,—may be said to have been created mainly by ourselves.

Thus, as my conscience has often whispered me, I did Hollingsworth a great wrong by prying into his character; and am perhaps doing him as great a one, at this moment, by putting faith in the discoveries which I seemed to make. But I could not help it. Had I loved him less, I might have used him better. He—and Zenobia and Priscilla, both for their own sakes and as connected with him—were separated from the rest of the Community, to my imagination, and stood forth as the indices of a problem which it was my business to solve. Other associates had a portion of my time; other matters amused me; passing occurrences carried me along with them, while they lasted. But here was the vortex of my meditations around which they revolved, and whitherward they too continually tended. In the midst of cheerful society, I had often a feeling of loneliness. For it was impossible not to be sensible that, while these three characters figured so largely on my private theatre, I— though probably reckoned as a friend by all—was at best but a secondary or tertiary personage with either of them.

I loved Hollingsworth, as has already been enough expressed. But it impressed me, more and more, that there was a stern and dreadful peculiarity in this man, such as could not prove otherwise than pernicious to the happiness of those who should be drawn into too intimate a connection with him. He was not altogether human. There was something else in Hollingsworth besides flesh and blood, and sympathies and affections, and celestial spirit.

This is always true of those men who have surrendered themselves to an overruling purpose. It does not so much impel them from without, nor even operate as a motive power within, but grows incorporate with all that they think and feel, and finally converts them into little else save that one principle. When such begins to be the predicament, it is not cowardice, but wisdom, to avoid these victims. They have no heart, no sympathy, no reason, no conscience. They will keep no friend, unless he make himself the mirror of their purpose; they will smite and slay you, and trample your dead corpse under foot, all the more readily, if you take the first step with them, and cannot take the second, and the third, and every other step of their terribly straight path. They have an idol, to which they consecrate themselves high-priest, and deem it holy work to offer sacrifices of whatever is most precious; and never once seem to suspect—so cunning has the Devil been with them—that this false deity, in whose iron features, immitigable to all the rest of mankind, they see only benignity and love, is but a spectrum of the very priest himself, projected upon the surrounding darkness. And the higher and purer the original object, and the more unselfishly it may have been taken up, the slighter is the probability that they can be led to recognize the process by which godlike benevolence has been debased into all-devouring egotism.

Of course, I am perfectly aware that the above statement is exaggerated, in the attempt to make it adequate. Professed philanthropists have gone far; but no originally good man, I presume, ever went quite so far as this. Let the reader abate whatever he deems fit. The paragraph may remain, however, both for its truth and its exaggeration, as strongly expressive of the tendencies which were really operative in Hollingsworth, and as exemplifying the kind of error into which my mode of observation was calculated to lead me. The issue was, that in solitude I often shuddered at my friend. In my recollection of his dark and impressive countenance, the features grew more sternly prominent than the reality, duskier in their depth and shadow, and more lurid in their light; the frown, that had merely flitted across his brow, seemed to have contorted it with an adamantine wrinkle. On meeting him again, I was often filled with remorse, when his deep eyes beamed kindly upon me, as with the glow of a household fire that was burning in a cave. "He is a man, after all," thought I; "his Maker's own truest image, a philanthropic man!—not that steel engine of the devil's contrivance, a philanthropist!" But in my wood-walks, and in my silent chamber, the dark face frowned at me again.

When a young girl comes within the sphere of such a man, she is as perilously situated as the maiden whom, in the old classical myths, the people used to expose to a dragon. If I had any duty whatever, in reference to Hollingsworth, it was to endeavor to save Priscilla from that kind of personal worship which her sex is generally prone to lavish upon saints and heroes. It often requires but one smile out of the hero's eyes into the girl's or woman's heart, to transform this devotion, from a sentiment of the highest approval and confidence, into passionate love. Now, Hollingsworth smiled much upon Priscilla,—more than upon any other person. If she thought him beautiful, it was no wonder. I often thought him so, with the expression of tender human care and gentlest sympathy which she alone seemed to have power to call out upon his features. Zenobia, I suspect, would have given her eyes, bright as they were, for such a look;—it was the least that our poor Priscilla could do, to give her heart for a great many of them. There was the more danger of this, inasmuch as the footing on which we all associated at Blithedale was widely different from that of conventional society. While inclining us to the soft affections of the golden age, it seemed to authorize any individual, of either sex, to fall in love with any other, regardless of what would elsewhere be judged suitable and prudent. Accordingly, the tender passion was very rife among us, in various degrees of mildness or virulence, but mostly passing away with the state of things that had given it origin. This was all well enough; but, for a girl like Priscilla and a woman like Zenobia to jostle one another in their love of a man like Hollingsworth, was likely to be no child's play.

Had I been as cold-hearted as I sometimes thought myself, nothing would have interested me more than to witness the play of passions that must thus have been evolved. But, in honest truth, I would really have gone far to save Priscilla, at least, from the catastrophe in which such a drama would be apt to terminate.

Priscilla had now grown to be a very pretty girl, and still kept budding and blossoming, and daily putting on some new charm, which you no sooner became sensible of than you thought it worth all that she had previously possessed. So unformed, vague, and without substance, as she had come to us, it seemed as if we could see Nature shaping out a woman before our very eyes, and yet had only a more reverential sense of the mystery of a woman's soul and frame. Yesterday, her cheek was pale,—to-day, it had a bloom. Priscilla's smile, like a baby's first one, was a wondrous novelty. Her imperfections and short-comings affected me with a kind of playful pathos, which was as absolutely bewitching a sensation as ever I experienced. After she had been a month or two at Blithedale, her animal spirits waxed high, and kept her pretty constantly in a state of bubble and ferment, impelling her to far more bodily activity than she had yet strength to endure. She was very fond of playing with the other girls out of doors. There is hardly another sight in the world so pretty as that of a company of young girls, almost women grown, at play, and so giving themselves up to their airy impulse that their tiptoes barely touch the ground.

Girls are incomparably wilder and more effervescent than boys, more untamable, and regardless of rule and limit, with an ever-shifting variety, breaking continually into new modes of fun, yet with a harmonious propriety through all. Their steps, their voices, appear free as the wind, but keep consonance with a strain of music inaudible to us. Young men and boys, on the other hand, play, according to recognized law, old, traditionary games, permitting no caprioles of fancy, but with scope enough for the outbreak of savage instincts. For, young or old, in play or in earnest, man is prone to be a brute.

Especially is it delightful to see a vigorous young girl run a race, with her head thrown back, her limbs moving more friskily than they need, and an air between that of a bird and a young colt. But Priscilla's peculiar charm, in a foot-race, was the weakness and irregularity with which she ran. Growing up without exercise, except to her poor little fingers, she had never yet acquired the perfect use of her legs. Setting buoyantly

forth, therefore, as if no rival less swift than Atalanta could compete with
her, she ran falteringly, and often tumbled on the grass. Such an incident—
though it seems too slight to think of—was a thing to laugh at, but which
brought the water into one's eyes, and lingered in the memory after far
greater joys and sorrows were swept out of it, as antiquated trash. Priscilla's
life, as I beheld it, was full of trifles that affected me in just this way.

When she had come to be quite at home among us, I used to fancy
that Priscilla played more pranks, and perpetrated more mischief, than
any other girl in the Community. For example, I once heard Silas
Foster, in a very gruff voice, threatening to rivet three horseshoes round
Priscilla's neck and chain her to a post, because she, with some other
young people, had clambered upon a load of hay, and caused it to slide
off the cart. How she made her peace I never knew; but very soon afterwards I saw old Silas, with his brawny hands round Priscilla's waist,
swinging her to and fro, and finally depositing her on one of the oxen,
to take her first lessons in riding. She met with terrible mishaps in her
efforts to milk a cow; she let the poultry into the garden; she generally
spoilt whatever part of the dinner she took in charge; she broke crock-
ery; she dropt our biggest pitcher into the well; and—except with her
needle, and those little wooden instruments for pursemaking—was as
unserviceable a member of society as any young lady in the land. There
was no other sort of efficiency about her. Yet everybody was kind to
Priscilla; everybody loved her and laughed at her to her face, and did
not laugh behind her back; everybody would have given her half of his
last crust, or the bigger share of his plum-cake. These were pretty certain indications that we were all conscious of a pleasant weakness in the
girl, and considered her not quite able to look after her own interests,
or fight her battle with the world. And Hollingsworth—perhaps because
he had been the means of introducing Priscilla to her new abode—
appeared to recognize her as his own especial charge.

Her simple, careless, childish flow of spirits often made me sad. She
seemed to me like a butterfly at play in a flickering bit of sunshine, and
mistaking it for a broad and eternal summer. We sometimes hold mirth
to a stricter accountability than sorrow;—it must show good cause, or
the echo of its laughter comes back drearily. Priscilla's gayety, moreover, was of a nature that showed me how delicate an instrument she
was, and what fragile harp-strings were her nerves. As they made sweet
music at the airiest touch, it would require but a stronger one to burst
them all asunder. Absurd as it might be, I tried to reason with her, and
persuade her not to be so joyous, thinking that, if she would draw less
lavishly upon her fund of happiness, it would last the longer. I remember doing so, one summer evening, when we tired laborers sat looking
on, like Goldsmith's old folks under the village thorn-tree, while the
young people were at their sports.

"What is the use or sense of being so very gay?" I said to Priscilla, while she was taking breath, after a great frolic. "I love to see a sufficient cause for everything; and I can see none for this. Pray tell me, now, what kind of a world you imagine this to be, which you are so merry in."

"I never think about it at all," answered Priscilla, laughing. "But this I am sure of, that it is a world where everybody is kind to me, and where I love everybody. My heart keeps dancing within me, and all the foolish things which you see me do are only the motions of my heart. How can I be dismal, if my heart will not let me?"

"Have you nothing dismal to remember?" I suggested. "If not, then, indeed, you are very fortunate!"

"Ah!" said Priscilla, slowly.

And then came that unintelligible gesture, when she seemed to be listening to a distant voice.

"For my part," I continued, beneficently seeking to overshadow her with my own sombre humor, "my past life has been a tiresome one enough; yet I would rather look backward ten times than forward once. For, little as we know of our life to come, we may be very sure, for one thing, that the good we aim at will not be attained. People never do get just the good they seek. If it come at all, it is something else, which they never dreamed of, and did not particularly want. Then, again, we may rest certain that our friends of to-day will not be our friends of a few years hence; but, if we keep one of them, it will be at the expense of the others; and, most probably, we shall keep none. To be sure, there are more to be had; but who cares about making a new set of friends, even should they be better than those around us?"

"Not I!" said Priscilla. "I will live and die with these!"

"Well; but let the future go," resumed I. "As for the present moment, if we could look into the hearts where we wish to be most valued, what should you expect to see? One's own likeness, in the innermost, holiest niche? Ah! I don't know! It may not be there at all. It may be a dusty image, thrust aside into a corner, and by and by to be flung out of doors, where any foot may trample upon it. If not to-day, then to-morrow! And so, Priscilla, I do not see much wisdom in being so very merry in this kind of a world."

It had taken me nearly seven years of worldly life to hive up the bitter honey which I here offered to Priscilla. And she rejected it!

"I don't believe one word of what you say!" she replied, laughing anew. "You made me sad, for a minute, by talking about the past; but the past never comes back again. Do we dream the same dream twice? There is nothing else that I am afraid of."

So away she ran, and fell down on the green grass, as it was often her luck to do, but got up again, without any harm.

"Priscilla, Priscilla!" cried Hollingsworth, who was sitting on the door-step; "you had better not run any more to-night. You will weary yourself too much. And do not sit down out of doors, for there is a heavy dew beginning to fall."

At his first word, she went and sat down under the porch, at Hollingsworth's feet, entirely contented and happy. What charm was there in his rude massiveness that so attracted and soothed this shadow-like girl? It appeared to me, who have always been curious in such matters, that Priscilla's vague and seemingly causeless flow of felicitous feeling was that with which love blesses inexperienced hearts, before they begin to suspect what is going on within them. It transports them to the seventh heaven; and, if you ask what brought them thither, they neither can tell nor care to learn, but cherish an ecstatic faith that there they shall abide forever.

Zenobia was in the door-way, not far from Hollingsworth. She gazed at Priscilla in a very singular way. Indeed, it was a sight worth gazing at, and a beautiful sight, too, as the fair girl sat at the feet of that dark, powerful figure. Her air, while perfectly modest, delicate and virgin-like, denoted her as swayed by Hollingsworth, attracted to him, and unconsciously seeking to rest upon his strength. I could not turn away my own eyes, but hoped that nobody, save Zenobia and myself, were witnessing this picture. It is before me now, with the evening twilight a little deepened by the dusk of memory.

"Come hither, Priscilla," said Zenobia. "I have something to say to you."

She spoke in little more than a whisper. But it is strange how expressive of moods a whisper may often be. Priscilla felt at once that something had gone wrong.

"Are you angry with me?" she asked, rising slowly, and standing before Zenobia in a drooping attitude. "What have I done? I hope you are not angry!"

"No, no, Priscilla!" said Hollingsworth, smiling. "I will answer for it, she is not. You are the one little person in the world with whom nobody can be angry!"

"Angry with you, child? What a silly idea!" exclaimed Zenobia, laughing. "No, indeed! But, my dear Priscilla, you are getting to be so very pretty that you absolutely need a duenna; and, as I am older than you, and have had my own little experience of life, and think myself exceedingly sage, I intend to fill the place of a maiden aunt. Every day, I shall give you a lecture, a quarter of an hour in length, on the morals, manners, and proprieties of social life. When our pastoral shall be quite played out, Priscilla, my worldly wisdom may stand you in good stead."

"I am afraid you are angry with me!" repeated Priscilla, sadly; for, while she seemed as impressible as wax, the girl often showed a persistency in her own ideas as stubborn as it was gentle.

"Dear me, what can I say to the child!" cried Zenobia, in a tone of humorous vexation. "Well, well; since you insist on my being angry, come to my room, this moment, and let me beat you!"

Zenobia bade Hollingsworth good-night very sweetly, and nodded to me with a smile. But, just as she turned aside with Priscilla into the dimness of the porch, I caught another glance at her countenance. It would have made the fortune of a tragic actress, could she have borrowed it for the moment when she fumbles in her bosom for the concealed dagger, or the exceedingly sharp bodkin, or mingles the ratsbane in her lover's bowl of wine or her rival's cup of tea. Not that I in the least anticipated any such catastrophe,—it being a remarkable truth that custom has in no one point a greater sway than over our modes of wreaking our wild passions. And, besides, had we been in Italy, instead of New England, it was hardly yet a crisis for the dagger or the bowl.

It often amazed me, however, that Hollingsworth should show himself so recklessly tender towards Priscilla, and never once seem to think of the effect which it might have upon her heart. But the man, as I have endeavored to explain, was thrown completely off his moral balance, and quite bewildered as to his personal relations, by his great excrescence of a philanthropic scheme. I used to see, or fancy, indications that he was not altogether obtuse to Zenobia's influence as a woman. No doubt, however, he had a still more exquisite enjoyment of Priscilla's silent sympathy with his purposes, so unalloyed with criticism, and therefore more grateful than any intellectual approbation, which always involves a possible reserve of latent censure. A man— poet, prophet, or whatever he may be—readily persuades himself of his right to all the worship that is voluntarily tendered. In requital of so rich benefits as he was to confer upon mankind, it would have been hard to deny Hollingsworth the simple solace of a young girl's heart, which he held in his hand, and smelled to, like a rosebud. But what if, while pressing out its fragrance, he should crush the tender rosebud in his grasp!

As for Zenobia, I saw no occasion to give myself any trouble. With her native strength, and her experience of the world, she could not be supposed to need any help of mine. Nevertheless, I was really generous enough to feel some little interest likewise for Zenobia. With all her faults (which might have been a great many, besides the abundance that I knew of), she possessed noble traits, and a heart which must at least have been valuable while new. And she seemed ready to fling it away as uncalculatingly as Priscilla herself. I could not but suspect that, if merely at play with Hollingsworth, she was sporting with a power which she did not fully estimate. Or, if in earnest, it might chance, between Zenobia's passionate force, and his dark, self-delusive egotism, to turn out such earnest as would develop itself in some sufficiently tragic catastrophe, though the dagger and the bowl should go for nothing in it.

Meantime, the gossip of the Community set them down as a pair of lovers. They took walks together, and were not seldom encountered in the wood-paths; Hollingsworth deeply discoursing, in tones solemn and sternly pathetic. Zenobia, with a rich glow on her cheeks, and her eyes softened from their ordinary brightness, looked so beautiful, that, had her companion been ten times a philanthropist, it seemed impossible but that one glance should melt him back into a man. Oftener than anywhere else, they went to a certain point on the slope of a pasture, commanding nearly the whole of our own domain, besides a view of the river, and an airy prospect of many distant hills. The bond of our Community was such, that the members had the privilege of building cottages for their own residence within our precincts, thus laying a hearth-stone and fencing in a home private and peculiar to all desirable extent, while yet the inhabitants should continue to share the advantages of an associated life. It was inferred that Hollingsworth and Zenobia intended to rear their dwelling on this favorite spot.

I mentioned those rumors to Hollingsworth, in a playful way.

"Had you consulted me," I went on to observe, "I should have recommended a site further to the left, just a little withdrawn into the wood, with two or three peeps at the prospect, among the trees. You will be in the shady vale of years, long before you can raise any better kind of shade around your cottage, if you build it on this bare slope."

"But I offer my edifice as a spectacle to the world," said Hollingsworth, "that it may take example and build many another like it. Therefore, I mean to set it on the open hill-side."

Twist these words how I might, they offered no very satisfactory import. It seemed hardly probable that Hollingsworth should care about educating the public taste in the department of cottage architecture, desirable as such improvement certainly was.

X.

A VISITOR FROM TOWN

HOLLINGSWORTH and I—we had been hoeing potatoes, that forenoon, while the rest of the fraternity were engaged in a distant quarter of the farm—sat under a clump of maples, eating our eleven o'clock lunch, when we saw a stranger approaching along the edge of the field. He had admitted himself from the road-side through a turnstile, and seemed to have a purpose of speaking with us.

And, by the by, we were favored with many visits at Blithedale, especially from people who sympathized with our theories, and perhaps held themselves ready to unite in our actual experiment as soon as there should appear a reliable promise of its success. It was rather ludicrous, indeed—(to me, at least, whose enthusiasm had insensibly been exhaled, together with the perspiration of many a hard day's toil),—it was absolutely funny, therefore, to observe what a glory was shed about our life and labors, in the imagination of these longing proselytes. In their view, we were as poetical as Arcadians, besides being as practical as the hardest-fisted husbandmen in Massachusetts. We did not, it is true, spend much time in piping to our sheep, or warbling our innocent loves to the sisterhood. But they gave us credit for imbuing the ordinary rustic occupations with a kind of religious poetry, insomuch that our very cow-yards and pig-sties were as delightfully fragrant as a flower-garden. Nothing used to please me more than to see one of these lay enthusiasts snatch up a hoe, as they were very prone to do, and set to work with a vigor that perhaps carried him through about a dozen ill-directed strokes. Men are wonderfully soon satisfied, in this day of shameful bodily enervation, when, from one end of life to the other, such multitudes never taste the sweet weariness that follows accustomed toil. I seldom saw the new enthusiasm that did not grow as flimsy and flaccid as the proselyte's moistened shirt-collar, with a quarter of an hour's active labor under a July sun.

But the person now at hand had not at all the air of one of these amiable visionaries. He was an elderly man, dressed rather shabbily, yet decently enough, in a gray frock-coat, faded towards a brown hue, and wore a broad-brimmed white hat, of the fashion of several years gone by. His hair was perfect silver, without a dark thread in the whole of it; his nose, though it had a scarlet tip, by no means indicated the jollity of which a red nose is the generally admitted symbol. He was a subdued, undemonstrative old man, who would doubtless drink a glass of liquor, now and then, and probably more than was good for him;—not, however, with a purpose of undue exhilaration, but in the hope of bringing his spirits up to the ordinary level of the world's cheerfulness. Drawing nearer, there was a shy look about him, as if he were ashamed of his poverty; or, at any rate, for some reason or other, would rather have us glance at him sidelong than take a full front view. He had a queer appearance of hiding himself behind the patch on his left eye.

"I know this old gentleman," said I to Hollingsworth, as we sat observing him; "that is, I have met him a hundred times in town, and have often amused my fancy with wondering what he was before he came to be what he is. He haunts restaurants and such places, and has an odd way of lurking in corners or getting behind a door, whenever practicable, and holding out his hand, with some little article in it which he wishes you to buy. The eye of the world seems to trouble him, although he necessarily lives so much in it. I never expected to see him in an open field."

"Have you learned anything of his history?" asked Hollingsworth.

"Not a circumstance," I answered; "but there must be something curious in it. I take him to be a harmless sort of a person, and a tolerably honest one; but his manners, being so furtive, remind me of those of a rat,— a rat without the mischief, the fierce eye, the teeth to bite with, or the desire to bite. See, now! He means to skulk along that fringe of bushes, and approach us on the other side of our clump of maples."

We soon heard the old man's velvet tread on the grass, indicating that he had arrived within a few feet of where we sat.

"Good-morning, Mr. Moodie," said Hollingsworth, addressing the stranger as an acquaintance; "you must have had a hot and tiresome walk from the city. Sit down, and take a morsel of our bread and cheese."

The visitor made a grateful little murmur of acquiescence, and sat down in a spot somewhat removed; so that, glancing round, I could see his gray pantaloons and dusty shoes, while his upper part was mostly hidden behind the shrubbery. Nor did he come forth from this retirement during the whole of the interview that followed. We handed him such food as we had, together with a brown jug of molasses and water (would that it had been brandy, or something better, for the sake of his chill old heart!), like priests offering dainty sacrifice to an enshrined and invisible idol. I have no idea that he really lacked sustenance; but it was quite touching, nevertheless, to hear him nibbling away at our crusts.

"Mr. Moodie," said I, "do you remember selling me one of those very pretty little silk purses, of which you seem to have a monopoly in the market? I keep it to this day, I can assure you."

"Ah, thank you," said our guest. "Yes, Mr. Coverdale, I used to sell a good many of those little purses."

He spoke languidly, and only those few words, like a watch with an inelastic spring, that just ticks a moment or two, and stops again. He seemed a very forlorn old man. In the wantonness of youth, strength, and comfortable condition,—making my prey of people's individualities, as my custom was,—I tried to identify my mind with the old fellow's, and take his view of the world, as if looking through a smoke-blackened glass at the sun. It robbed the landscape of all its life. Those pleasantly swelling slopes of our farm, descending towards the wide meadows, through which sluggishly circled the brimful tide of the Charles, bathing the long sedges on its hither and further shores; the broad, sunny gleam over the winding water; that peculiar picturesqueness of the scene where capes and headlands put themselves boldly forth upon the perfect level of the meadow, as into a green lake, with inlets between the promontories; the shadowy woodland, with twinkling showers of light falling into its depths; the sultry heat-vapor, which rose everywhere like incense, and in which my soul delighted, as indicating so rich a fervor in the passionate day, and in the earth that was burning with its love;—I beheld all these things as through old Moodie's eyes. When my eyes are dimmer than they have yet come to be, I will go thither again, and see if I did not catch the tone of his mind aright, and if the cold and lifeless tint of his perceptions be not then repeated in my own.

Yet it was unaccountable to myself, the interest that I felt in him.

"Have you any objection," said I, "to telling me who made those little purses?"

"Gentlemen have often asked me that," said Moodie, slowly; "but I shake my head, and say little or nothing, and creep out of the way as well as I can. I am a man of few words; and if gentlemen were to be told one thing, they would be very apt, I suppose, to ask me another. But it happens, just now, Mr. Coverdale, that you can tell me more about the maker of those little purses than I can tell you."

"Why do you trouble him with needless questions, Coverdale?" interrupted Hollingsworth. "You must have known, long ago, that it was Priscilla. And so, my good friend, you have come to see her? Well, I am glad of it. You will find her altered very much for the better, since that winter evening when you put her into my charge. Why, Priscilla has a bloom in her cheeks, now!"

"Has my pale little girl a bloom?" repeated Moodie, with a kind of slow wonder. "Priscilla with a bloom in her cheeks! Ah, I am afraid I shall not know my little girl. And is she happy?"

"Just as happy as a bird," answered Hollingsworth.

"Then, gentlemen," said our guest, apprehensively, "I don't think it well for me to go any further. I crept hitherward only to ask about Priscilla; and now that you have told me such good news, perhaps I can do no better than to creep back again. If she were to see this old face of mine, the child would remember some very sad times which we have spent together. Some very sad times, indeed! She has forgotten them, I know,—them and me,—else she could not be so happy, nor have a bloom in her cheeks. Yes—yes—yes," continued he, still with the same torpid utterance; "with many thanks to you, Mr. Hollingsworth, I will creep back to town again."

"You shall do no such thing, Mr. Moodie," said Hollingsworth, bluffly. "Priscilla often speaks of you; and if there lacks anything to make her cheeks bloom like two damask roses, I'll venture to say it is just the sight of your face. Come,—we will go and find her."

"Mr. Hollingsworth!" said the old man, in his hesitating way.

"Well," answered Hollingsworth.

"Has there been any call for Priscilla?" asked Moodie; and though his face was hidden from us, his tone gave a sure indication of the mysterious nod and wink with which he put the question. "You know, I think, sir, what I mean."

"I have not the remotest suspicion what you mean, Mr. Moodie," replied Hollingsworth; "nobody, to my knowledge, has called for Priscilla, except yourself. But, come; we are losing time, and I have several things to say to you by the way."

"And, Mr. Hollingsworth!" repeated Moodie.

"Well, again!" cried my friend, rather impatiently. "What now?"

"There is a lady here," said the old man; and his voice lost some of its wearisome hesitation. "You will account it a very strange matter for me to talk about; but I chanced to know this lady when she was but a little child. If I am rightly informed, she has grown to be a very fine woman, and makes a brilliant figure in the world, with her beauty, and her talents, and her noble way of spending her riches. I should recognize this lady, so people tell me, by a magnificent flower in her hair."

"What a rich tinge it gives to his colorless ideas, when he speaks of Zenobia!" I whispered to Hollingsworth. "But how can there possibly be any interest or connecting link between him and her?"

"The old man, for years past," whispered Hollingsworth, "has been a little out of his right mind, as you probably see."

"What I would inquire," resumed Moodie, "is whether this beautiful lady is kind to my poor Priscilla."

"Very kind," said Hollingsworth.

"Does she love her?" asked Moodie.

"It should seem so," answered my friend. "They are always together."

"Like a gentlewoman and her maid-servant, I fancy?" suggested the old man.

There was something so singular in his way of saying this, that I could not resist the impulse to turn quite round, so as to catch a glimpse of his face, almost imagining that I should see another person than old Moodie. But there he sat, with the patched side of his face towards me.

"Like an elder and younger sister, rather," replied Hollingsworth.

"Ah!" said Moodie, more complacently,—for his latter tones had harshness and acidity in them,—"it would gladden my old heart to witness that. If one thing would make me happier than another, Mr. Hollingsworth, it would be to see that beautiful lady holding my little girl by the hand."

"Come along," said Hollingsworth, "and perhaps you may."

After a little more delay on the part of our freakish visitor, they set forth together, old Moodie keeping a step or two behind Hollingsworth,

so that the latter could not very conveniently look him in the face. I
remained under the tuft of maples, doing my utmost to draw an infer-
ence from the scene that had just passed. In spite of Hollingsworth's off-
hand explanation, it did not strike me that our strange guest was really
beside himself, but only that his mind needed screwing up, like an
instrument long out of tune, the strings of which have ceased to vibrate
smartly and sharply. Methought it would be profitable for us, projectors
of a happy life, to welcome this old gray shadow, and cherish him as
one of us, and let him creep about our domain, in order that he might
be a little merrier for our sakes, and we, sometimes, a little sadder for
his. Human destinies look ominous without some perceptible inter-
mixture of the sable or the gray. And then, too, should any of our fraternity grow feverish with an over-exulting sense of prosperity, it would
be a sort of cooling regimen to slink off into the woods, and spend an
hour, or a day, or as many days as might be requisite to the cure, in
uninterrupted communion with this deplorable old Moodie!

Going homeward to dinner, I had a glimpse of him, behind the
trunk of a tree, gazing earnestly towards a particular window of the
farm-house; and, by and by, Priscilla appeared at this window, playfully
drawing along Zenobia, who looked as bright as the very day that was
blazing down upon us, only not, by many degrees, so well advanced
towards her noon. I was convinced that this pretty sight must have been
purposely arranged by Priscilla for the old man to see. But either the
girl held her too long, or her fondness was resented as too great a freedom; for Zenobia suddenly put Priscilla decidedly away, and gave her
a haughty look, as from a mistress to a dependant. Old Moodie shook
his head; and again and again I saw him shake it, as he withdrew along
the road; and, at the last point whence the farm-house was visible, he
turned, and shook his uplifted staff.

XI.

THE WOOD-PATH

NOT long after the preceding incident, in order to get the ache of too
constant labor out of my bones, and to relieve my spirit of the irksomeness of a settled routine, I took a holiday. It was my purpose to
spend it, all alone, from breakfast-time till twilight, in the deepest
wood-seclusion that lay anywhere around us. Though fond of society, I
was so constituted as to need these occasional retirements, even in a

life like that of Blithedale, which was itself characterized by a remoteness from the world. Unless renewed by a yet further withdrawal towards the inner circle of self-communion, I lost the better part of my individuality. My thoughts became of little worth, and my sensibilities grew as arid as a tuft of moss (a thing whose life is in the shade, the rain, or the noontide dew), crumbling in the sunshine, after long expectance of a shower. So, with my heart full of a drowsy pleasure, and cautious not to dissipate my mood by previous intercourse with any one, I hurried away, and was soon pacing a wood-path, arched over head with boughs, and dusky-brown beneath my feet.

At first, I walked very swiftly, as if the heavy floodtide of social life were roaring at my heels, and would outstrip and overwhelm me, without all the better diligence in my escape. But, threading the more distant windings of the track, I abated my pace, and looked about me for some side-aisle, that should admit me into the innermost sanctuary of this green cathedral, just as, in human acquaintanceship, a casual opening sometimes lets us, all of a sudden, into the long-sought intimacy of a mysterious heart. So much was I absorbed in my reflections,— or, rather, in my mood, the substance of which was as yet too shapeless to be called thought,— that footsteps rustled on the leaves, and a figure passed me by, almost without impressing either the sound or sight upon my consciousness.

A moment afterwards, I heard a voice at a little distance behind me, speaking so sharply and impertinently that it made a complete discord with my spiritual state, and caused the latter to vanish as abruptly as when you thrust a finger into a soap-bubble.

"Halloo, friend!" cried this most unseasonable voice. "Stop a moment, I say! I must have a word with you!"

I turned about, in a humor ludicrously irate. In the first place, the interruption, at any rate, was a grievous injury; then, the tone displeased me. And, finally, unless there be real affection in his heart, a man cannot,—such is the bad state to which the world has brought itself,—cannot more effectually show his contempt for a brother-mortal, nor more gallingly assume a position of superiority, than by addressing him as "friend." Especially does the misapplication of this phrase bring out that latent hostility which is sure to animate peculiar sects, and those who, with however generous a purpose, have sequestered themselves from the crowd; a feeling, it is true, which may be hidden in some dog-kennel of the heart, grumbling there in the darkness, but is never quite extinct, until the dissenting party have gained power and scope enough to treat the world generously. For my part, I should have taken it as far less an insult to be styled "fellow," "clown," or "bumpkin." To either of these appellations my rustic garb (it was a linen blouse, with checked shirt and striped pantaloons, a chip-hat on my head, and a rough hickory-stick in my hand) very fairly entitled me. As the case stood, my temper darted at once to the opposite pole; not friend, but enemy!

"What do you want with me?" said I, facing about.

"Come a little nearer, friend," said the stranger, beckoning.

"No," answered I. "If I can do anything for you, without too much trouble to myself, say so. But recollect, if you please, that you are not speaking to an acquaintance, much less a friend!"

"Upon my word, I believe not!" retorted he, looking at me with some curiosity; and, lifting his hat, he made me a salute which had enough of sarcasm to be offensive, and just enough of doubtful courtesy to render any resentment of it absurd. "But I ask your pardon! I recognize a little mistake. If I may take the liberty to suppose it, you, sir, are probably one of the aesthetic—or shall I rather say ecstatic?—laborers, who have planted themselves hereabouts. This is your forest of Arden; and you are either the banished Duke in person, or one of the chief nobles in his train. The melancholy Jacques, perhaps? Be it so. In that case, you can probably do me a favor."

I never, in my life, felt less inclined to confer a favor on any man.

"I am busy," said I.

So unexpectedly had the stranger made me sensible of his presence, that he had almost the effect of an apparition; and certainly a less appropriate one (taking into view the dim woodland solitude about us) than if the salvage man of antiquity, hirsute and cinctured with a leafy girdle, had started out of a thicket. He was still young, seemingly a little under thirty, of a tall and well-developed figure, and as handsome a man as ever I beheld. The style of his beauty, however, though a masculine style, did not at all commend itself to my taste. His countenance—I hardly know how to describe the peculiarity—had an indecorum in it, a kind of rudeness, a hard, coarse, forth-putting freedom of expression, which no degree of external polish could have abated one single jot. Not that it was vulgar. But he had no fineness of nature; there was in his eyes (although they might have artifice enough of another sort) the naked exposure of something that ought not to be left prominent. With these vague allusions to what I have seen in other faces, as well as his, I leave the quality to be comprehended best—because with an intuitive repugnance—by those who possess least of it.

His hair, as well as his beard and mustache, was coal-black; his eyes, too, were black and sparkling, and his teeth remarkably brilliant. He was rather carelessly but well and fashionably dressed, in a summer-morning costume. There was a gold chain, exquisitely wrought, across his vest. I never saw a smoother or whiter gloss than that upon his shirt-bosom, which had a pin in it, set with a gem that glimmered, in the leafy shadow where he stood, like a living tip of fire. He carried a stick with a wooden head, carved in vivid imitation of that of a serpent. I hated him, partly, I do believe, from a comparison of my own homely garb with his well-ordered foppishness.

"Well, sir," said I, a little ashamed of my first irritation, but still with no waste of civility, "be pleased to speak at once, as I have my own business in hand."

"I regret that my mode of addressing you was a little unfortunate," said the stranger, smiling; for he seemed a very acute sort of person, and saw, in some degree, how I stood affected towards him. "I intended no offence, and shall certainly comport myself with due ceremony hereafter. I merely wish to make a few inquiries respecting a lady, formerly of my acquaintance, who is now resident in your Community, and, I believe, largely concerned in your social enterprise. You call her, I think, Zenobia."

"That is her name in literature," observed I; "a name, too, which possibly she may permit her private friends to know and address her by, — but not one which they feel at liberty to recognize when used of her, personally, by a stranger or casual acquaintance."

"Indeed!" answered this disagreeable person; and he turned aside his face for an instant with a brief laugh, which struck me as a note-worthy expression of his character. "Perhaps I might put forward a claim, on your own grounds, to call the lady by a name so appropriate to her splendid qualities. But I am willing to know her by any cognomen that you may suggest."

Heartily wishing that he would be either a little more offensive, or a good deal less so, or break off our intercourse altogether, I mentioned Zenobia's real name.

"True," said he; "and, in general society, I have never heard her called otherwise. And, after all, our discussion of the point has been gratuitous. My object is only to inquire when, where and how, this lady may most conveniently be seen."

"At her present residence, of course," I replied. "You have but to go thither and ask for her. This very path will lead you within sight of the house; so I wish you good-morning."

"One moment, if you please," said the stranger. "The course you indicate would certainly be the proper one, in an ordinary morning call. But my business is private, personal, and somewhat peculiar. Now, in a community like this, I should judge that any little occurrence is likely to be discussed rather more minutely than would quite suit my views. I refer solely to myself, you understand, and without intimating that it would be other than a matter of entire indifference to the lady. In short, I especially desire to see her in private. If her habits are such as I have known them, she is probably often to be met with in the woods, or by the river-side; and I think you could do me the favor to point out some favorite walk where, about this hour, I might be fortunate enough to gain an interview."

I reflected that it would be quite a supererogatory piece of Quixotism in me to undertake the guardianship of Zenobia, who, for my pains, would only make me the butt of endless ridicule, should the fact ever come to her knowledge. I therefore described a spot which, as often as any other, was Zenobia's resort at this period of the day; nor was it so remote from the farm-house as to leave her in much peril, whatever might be the stranger's character.

"A single word more," said he; and his black eyes sparkled at me, whether with fun or malice I knew not, but certainly as if the devil were peeping out of them. "Among your fraternity, I understand, there is a certain holy and benevolent blacksmith; a man of iron, in more senses than one; a rough, cross-grained, well-meaning individual, rather boorish in his manners, as might be expected, and by no means of the highest intellectual cultivation. He is a philanthropical lecturer, with two or three disciples, and a scheme of his own, the preliminary step in which involves a large purchase of land, and the erection of a spacious edifice, at an expense considerably beyond his means; inasmuch as these are to be reckoned in copper or old iron much more conveniently than in gold or silver. He hammers away upon his one topic as lustily as ever he did upon a horse-shoe! Do you know such a person?"

I shook my head, and was turning away.

"Our friend," he continued, "is described to me as a brawny, shaggy, grim, and ill-favored personage, not particularly well calculated, one would say, to insinuate himself with the softer sex. Yet, so far has this honest fellow succeeded with one lady whom we wot of, that he anticipates, from her abundant resources, the necessary funds for realizing his plan in brick and mortar!"

Here the stranger seemed to be so much amused with his sketch of Hollingsworth's character and purposes, that he burst into a fit of merriment, of the same nature as the brief, metallic laugh, already alluded to, but immensely prolonged and enlarged. In the excess of his delight, he opened his mouth wide, and disclosed a gold band around the upper part of his teeth, thereby making it apparent that every one of his brilliant grinders and incisors was a sham. This discovery affected me very oddly. I felt as if the whole man were a moral and physical humbug; his wonderful beauty of face, for aught I knew, might be removable like a mask; and, tall and comely as his figure looked, he was perhaps but a wizened little elf, gray and decrepit, with nothing genuine about him, save the wicked expression of his grin. The fantasy of his spectral character so wrought upon me, together with the contagion of his strange mirth on my sympathies, that I soon began to laugh as loudly as himself.

By and by, he paused all at once; so suddenly, indeed, that my own cachinnation lasted a moment longer.

"Ah, excuse me!" said he. "Our interview seems to proceed more merrily than it began."

"It ends here," answered I. "And I take shame to myself, that my folly has lost me the right of resenting your ridicule of a friend."

"Pray allow me," said the stranger, approaching a step nearer, and laying his gloved hand on my sleeve. "One other favor I must ask of you. You have a young person, here at Blithedale, of whom I have heard,—whom, perhaps, I have known,—and in whom, at all events, I take a peculiar interest. She is one of those delicate, nervous young creatures, not uncommon in New England, and whom I suppose to have become what we find them by the gradual refining away of the physical system among your women. Some philosophers choose to glorify this habit of body by terming it spiritual; but, in my opinion, it is rather the effect of unwholesome food, bad air, lack of out-door exercise, and neglect of bathing, on the part of these damsels and their female progenitors, all resulting in a kind of hereditary dyspepsia. Zenobia, even with her uncomfortable surplus of vitality, is far the better model of womanhood. But—to revert again to this young person—she goes among you by the name of Priscilla. Could you possibly afford me the means of speaking with her?"

"You have made so many inquiries of me," I observed, "that I may at least trouble you with one. What is your name?"

He offered me a card, with "Professor Westervelt" engraved on it. At the same time, as if to vindicate his claim to the professional dignity, so often assumed on very questionable grounds, he put on a pair of spectacles, which so altered the character of his face that I hardly knew him again. But I liked the present aspect no better than the former one.

"I must decline any further connection with your affairs," said I, drawing back. "I have told you where to find Zenobia. As for Priscilla, she has closer friends than myself, through whom, if they see fit, you can gain access to her."

"In that case," returned the Professor, ceremoniously raising his hat, "good-morning to you."

He took his departure, and was soon out of sight among the windings of the wood-path. But, after a little reflection, I could not help regretting that I had so peremptorily broken off the interview, while the stranger seemed inclined to continue it. His evident knowledge of matters affecting my three friends might have led to disclosures, or inferences, that would perhaps have been serviceable. I was particularly struck with the fact that, ever since the appearance of Priscilla, it had been the tendency of events to suggest and establish a connection between Zenobia and her. She had come, in the first instance, as if with the sole purpose of claiming Zenobia's protection. Old Moodie's visit, it appeared, was chiefly to ascertain whether this object had been accomplished. And here, to-day, was the questionable Professor, linking one with the other in his inquiries, and seeking communication with both.

Meanwhile, my inclination for a ramble having been balked, I lingered in the vicinity of the farm, with perhaps a vague idea that some new event would grow out of Westervelt's proposed interview with Zenobia. My own part in these transactions was singularly subordinate. It resembled that of the Chorus in a classic play, which seems to be set aloof from the possibility of personal concernment, and bestows the whole measure of its hope or fear, its exultation or sorrow, on the fortunes of others, between whom and itself this sympathy is the only bond. Destiny, it may be,—the most skilful of stage-managers,—seldom chooses to arrange its scenes, and carry forward its drama, without securing the presence of at least one calm observer. It is his office to give applause when due, and sometimes an inevitable tear, to detect the final fitness of incident to character, and distil in his long-brooding thought the whole morality of the performance.

Not to be out of the way, in case there were need of me in my vocation, and, at the same time, to avoid thrusting myself where neither destiny nor mortals might desire my presence, I remained pretty near the verge of the woodlands. My position was off the track of Zenobia's customary walk, yet not so remote but that a recognized occasion might speedily have brought me thither.

XII.

COVERDALE'S HERMITAGE

LONG since, in this part of our circumjacent wood, I had found out for myself a little hermitage. It was a kind of leafy cave, high upward into the air, among the midmost branches of a white-pine tree. A wild grapevine, of unusual size and luxuriance, had twined and twisted itself up into the tree, and, after wreathing the entanglement of its tendrils almost around every bough, had caught hold of three or four neighboring trees, and married the whole clump with a perfectly inextricable knot of polygamy. Once, while sheltering myself from a summer shower, the fancy had taken me to clamber up into this seemingly impervious mass of foliage. The branches yielded me a passage, and closed again beneath, as if only a squirrel or a bird had passed. Far aloft, around the stem of the central pine, behold a perfect nest for Robinson Crusoe or King Charles! A hollow chamber of rare seclusion had been formed by the decay of some of the pine branches, which the vine had lovingly strangled with its embrace, burying them from the light of day in an aërial sepulchre of its own leaves. It cost me but little ingenuity to enlarge the interior, and open loop-holes through the verdant walls. Had it ever been my fortune to spend a honey-moon, I should have thought seriously of inviting my bride up thither, where our next neighbors would have been two orioles in another part of the clump.

It was an admirable place to make verses, tuning the rhythm to the breezy symphony that so often stirred among the vine-leaves; or to meditate an essay for the Dial, in which the many tongues of Nature whispered mysteries, and seemed to ask only a little stronger puff of wind to speak out the solution of its riddle. Being so pervious to air-currents, it was just the nook, too, for the enjoyment of a cigar. This hermitage was my one exclusive possession while I counted myself a brother of the socialists. It symbolized my individuality, and aided me in keeping it inviolate. None ever found me out in it, except, once, a squirrel. I brought thither no guest, because, after Hollingsworth failed me, there was no longer the man alive with whom I could think of sharing all. So there I used to sit, owl-like, yet not without liberal and hospitable thoughts. I counted the innumerable clusters of my vine, and fore-reckoned the abundance of my vintage. It gladdened me to anticipate the surprise of the Community, when, like an allegorical figure of rich October, I should make my appearance, with shoulders bent beneath the burthen of ripe grapes, and some of the crushed ones crimsoning my brow as with a bloodstain.

Ascending into this natural turret, I peeped in turn out of several of its small windows. The pine-tree, being ancient, rose high above the rest of the wood, which was of comparatively recent growth. Even where I sat, about midway between the root and the topmost bough, my position was lofty enough to serve as an observatory, not for starry investigations, but for those sublunary matters in which lay a lore as infinite as that of the planets. Through one loop-hole I saw the river lapsing calmly onward, while in the meadow, near its brink, a few of the brethren were digging peat for our winter's fuel. On the interior cart-road of our farm, I discerned Hollingsworth, with a yoke of oxen hitched to a drag of stones, that were to be piled into a fence, on which we employed ourselves at the odd intervals of other labor. The harsh tones of his voice, shouting to the sluggish steers, made me sensible, even at such a distance, that he was ill at ease, and that the balked philanthropist had the battle-spirit in his heart.

"Haw, Buck!" quoth he. "Come along there, ye lazy ones! What are ye about, now? Gee!"

"Mankind, in Hollingsworth's opinion," thought I, "is but another yoke of oxen, as stubborn, stupid, and sluggish, as our old Brown and Bright. He vituperates us aloud, and curses us in his heart, and will begin to prick us with the goad-stick, by and by. But are we his oxen? And what right has he to be the driver? And why, when there is enough else to do, should we waste our strength in dragging home the ponderous load of his philanthropic absurdities? At my height above the earth, the whole matter looks ridiculous!"

Turning towards the farm-house, I saw Priscilla (for, though a great way off, the eye of faith assured me that it was she) sitting at Zenobia's window, and making little purses, I suppose; or, perhaps, mending the Community's old linen. A bird flew past my tree; and, as it clove its way onward into the sunny atmosphere, I flung it a message for Priscilla.

"Tell her," said I, "that her fragile thread of life has inextricably knotted itself with other and tougher threads, and most likely it will be broken. Tell her that Zenobia will not be long her friend. Say that Hollingsworth's heart is on fire with his own purpose, but icy for all human affection; and that, if she has given him her love, it is like casting a flower into a sepulchre. And say that if any mortal really cares for her, it is myself; and not even I, for her realities, — poor little seamstress, as Zenobia rightly called her! — but for the fancy-work with which I have idly decked her out!"

The pleasant scent of the wood, evolved by the hot sun, stole up to my nostrils, as if I had been an idol in its niche. Many trees mingled their fragrance into a thousand-fold odor. Possibly there was a sensual influence in the broad light of noon that lay beneath me. It may have been the cause, in part, that I suddenly found myself possessed by a mood of disbelief in moral beauty or heroism, and a conviction of the folly of attempting to benefit the world. Our especial scheme of reform, which, from my observatory, I could take in with the bodily eye, looked so ridiculous that it was impossible not to laugh aloud.

"But the joke is a little too heavy," thought I. "If I were wise, I should get out of the scrape with all diligence, and then laugh at my companions for remaining in it."

While thus musing, I heard, with perfect distinctness, somewhere in the wood beneath, the peculiar laugh which I have described as one of the disagreeable characteristics of Professor Westervelt. It brought my thoughts back to our recent interview. I recognized as chiefly due to this man's influence the sceptical and sneering view which, just now, had filled my mental vision, in regard to all life's better purposes. And it was through his eyes, more than my own, that I was looking at Hollingsworth, with his glorious, if impracticable dream, and at the noble

earthliness of Zenobia's character, and even at Priscilla, whose impalpable grace lay so singularly between disease and beauty. The essential
charm of each had vanished. There are some spheres the contact with
which inevitably degrades the high, debases the pure, deforms the
beautiful. It must be a mind of uncommon strength, and little impress-
ibility, that can permit itself the habit of such intercourse, and not be
permanently deteriorated; and yet the Professor's tone represented that
of worldly society at large, where a cold scepticism smothers what it can
of our spiritual aspirations, and makes the rest ridiculous. I detested this
kind of man; and all the more because a part of my own nature showed
itself responsive to him.

Voices were now approaching through the region of the wood which
lay in the vicinity of my tree. Soon I caught glimpses of two figures—a
woman and a man—Zenobia and the stranger—earnestly talking
together as they advanced.

Zenobia had a rich, though varying color. It was, most of the while,
a flame, and anon a sudden paleness. Her eyes glowed, so that their
light sometimes flashed upward to me, as when the sun throws a daz-
zle from some bright object on the ground. Her gestures were free, and
strikingly impressive. The whole woman was alive with a passionate
intensity, which I now perceived to be the phase in which her beauty
culminated. Any passion would have become her well; and passionate
love, perhaps, the best of all. This was not love, but anger, largely inter-
mixed with scorn. Yet the idea strangely forced itself upon me, that
there was a sort of familiarity between these two companions, necessarily the result of an intimate love,—on Zenobia's part, at least,—in
days gone by, but which had prolonged itself into as intimate a hatred,
for all futurity. As they passed among the trees, reckless as her movement was, she took good heed that even the hem of her garment should
not brush against the stranger's person. I wondered whether there had
always been a chasm, guarded so religiously, betwixt these two.

As for Westervelt, he was not a whit more warmed by Zenobia's passion than a salamander by the heat of its native furnace. He would have
been absolutely statuesque, save for a look of slight perplexity, tinctured
strongly with derision. It was a crisis in which his intellectual perceptions could not altogether help him out. He failed to comprehend, and
cared but little for comprehending, why Zenobia should put herself
into such a fume; but satisfied his mind that it was all folly, and only
another shape of a woman's manifold absurdity, which men can never
understand. How many a woman's evil fate has yoked her with a man like
this! Nature thrusts some of us into the world miserably incomplete on
the emotional side, with hardly any sensibilities except what pertain to us
as animals. No passion, save of the senses; no holy tenderness, nor the

delicacy that results from this. Externally they bear a close resemblance to other men, and have perhaps all save the finest grace; but when a woman wrecks herself on such a being, she ultimately finds that the real womanhood within her has no corresponding part in him. Her deepest voice lacks a response; the deeper her cry, the more dead his silence. The fault may be none of his; he cannot give her what never lived within his soul. But the wretchedness on her side, and the moral deterioration attendant on a false and shallow life, without strength enough to keep itself sweet, are among the most pitiable wrongs that mortals suffer.

Now, as I looked down from my upper region at this man and woman,—outwardly so fair a sight, and wandering like two lovers in the wood,—I imagined that Zenobia, at an earlier period of youth, might have fallen into the misfortune above indicated. And when her passionate womanhood, as was inevitable, had discovered its mistake, there had ensued the character of eccentricity and defiance which distinguished the more public portion of her life.

Seeing how aptly matters had chanced thus far, I began to think it the design of fate to let me into all Zenobia's secrets, and that therefore the couple would sit down beneath my tree, and carry on a conversation which would leave me nothing to inquire. No doubt, however, had it so happened, I should have deemed myself honorably bound to warn them of a listener's presence, by flinging down a handful of unripe grapes, or by sending an unearthly groan out of my hiding-place, as if this were one of the trees of Dante's ghostly forest. But real life never arranges itself exactly like a romance. In the first place, they did not sit down at all. Secondly, even while they passed beneath the tree, Zenobia's utterance was so hasty and broken, and Westervelt's so cool and low, that I hardly could make out an intelligible sentence, on either side. What I seem to remember, I yet suspect, may have been patched together by my fancy, in brooding over the matter, afterwards.

"Why not fling the girl off," said Westervelt, "and let her go?"

"She clung to me from the first," replied Zenobia. "I neither know nor care what it is in me that so attaches her. But she loves me, and I will not fail her."

"She will plague you, then," said he, "in more ways than one."

"The poor child!" exclaimed Zenobia. "She can do me neither good nor harm. How should she?"

I know not what reply Westervelt whispered; nor did Zenobia's subsequent exclamation give me any clue, except that it evidently inspired her with horror and disgust.

"With what kind of a being am I linked?" cried she. "If my Creator cares aught for my soul, let him release me from this miserable bond!"

"I did not think it weighed so heavily," said her companion.

"Nevertheless," answered Zenobia, "it will strangle me, at last!"

And then I heard her utter a helpless sort of moan; a sound which, struggling out of the heart of a person of her pride and strength, affected me more than if she had made the wood dolorously vocal with a thousand shrieks and wails.

Other mysterious words, besides what are above written, they spoke together; but I understood no more, and even question whether I fairly understood so much as this. By long brooding over our recollections, we subtilize them into something akin to imaginary stuff, and hardly capable of being distinguished from it. In a few moments, they were completely beyond ear-shot. A breeze stirred after them, and awoke the leafy tongues of the surrounding trees, which forthwith began to babble, as if innumerable gossips had all at once got wind of Zenobia's secret. But, as the breeze grew stronger, its voice among the branches was as if it said, "Hush! Hush!" and I resolved that to no mortal would I disclose what I had heard. And, though there might be room for casuistry, such, I conceive, is the most equitable rule in all similar conjunctures.

XIII.

ZENOBIA'S LEGEND

THE illustrious Society of Blithedale, though it toiled in downright earnest for the good of mankind, yet not unfrequently illuminated its laborious life with an afternoon or evening of pastime. Picnics under the trees were considerably in vogue; and, within doors, fragmentary bits of theatrical performance, such as single acts of tragedy or comedy, or dramatic proverbs and charades. Zenobia, besides, was fond of giving us readings from Shakespeare, and often with a depth of tragic power, or breadth of comic effect, that made one feel it an intolerable wrong to the world that she did not at once go upon the stage. Tableaux vivants were another of our occasional modes of amusement, in which scarlet shawls, old silken robes, ruffs, velvets, furs, and all kinds of miscellaneous trumpery, converted our familiar companions into the people of a pictorial world. We had been thus engaged on the evening after the incident narrated in the last chapter. Several splendid works of art— either arranged after engravings from the old masters, or original illustrations of scenes in history or romance—had been presented, and we were earnestly entreating Zenobia for more.

She stood, with a meditative air, holding a large piece of gauze, or

some such ethereal stuff, as if considering what picture should next
occupy the frame; while at her feet lay a heap of many-colored garments, which her quick fancy and magic skill could so easily convert
into gorgeous draperies for heroes and princesses.

"I am getting weary of this," said she, after a moment's thought. "Our
own features, and our own figures and airs, show a little too intrusively
through all the characters we assume. We have so much familiarity
with one another's realities, that we cannot remove ourselves, at pleasure, into an imaginary sphere. Let us have no more pictures to-night;
but, to make you what poor amends I can, how would you like to have
me trump up a wild, spectral legend, on the spur of the moment?"

Zenobia had the gift of telling a fanciful little story, off-hand, in a
way that made it greatly more effective than it was usually found to be
when she afterwards elaborated the same production with her pen. Her
proposal, therefore, was greeted with acclamation.

"O, a story, a story, by all means!" cried the young girls. "No matter
how marvellous; we will believe it, every word. And let it be a ghost-
story, if you please."

"No, not exactly a ghost-story," answered Zenobia; "but something so
nearly like it that you shall hardly tell the difference. And, Priscilla,
stand you before me, where I may look at you, and get my inspiration
out of your eyes. They are very deep and dreamy to-night."

I know not whether the following version of her story will retain any
portion of its pristine character; but, as Zenobia told it wildly and rapidly,
hesitating at no extravagance, and dashing at absurdities which I am too
timorous to repeat,—giving it the varied emphasis of her inimitable voice,
and the pictorial illustration of her mobile face, while through it all we
caught the freshest aroma of the thoughts, as they came bubbling out of
her mind,—thus narrated, and thus heard, the legend seemed quite a
remarkable affair. I scarcely knew, at the time, whether she intended us to
laugh or be more seriously impressed. From beginning to end, it was
undeniable nonsense, but not necessarily the worse for that.

THE SILVERY VEIL

You have heard, my dear friends, of the Veiled Lady, who grew suddenly so very famous, a few months ago. And have you never thought
how remarkable it was that this marvellous creature should vanish, all
at once, while her renown was on the increase, before the public had
grown weary of her, and when the enigma of her character, instead of
being solved, presented itself more mystically at every exhibition? Her
last appearance, as you know, was before a crowded audience. The next
evening,—although the bills had announced her, at the corner of every

street, in red letters of a gigantic size, — there was no Veiled Lady to be seen! Now, listen to my simple little tale, and you shall hear the very latest incident in the known life — (if life it may be called, which seemed to have no more reality than the candle-light image of one's self which peeps at us outside of a dark window-pane) — the life of this shadowy phenomenon.

A party of young gentlemen, you are to understand, were enjoying themselves, one afternoon, — as young gentlemen are sometimes fond of doing, — over a bottle or two of champagne; and, among other ladies less mysterious, the subject of the Veiled Lady, as was very natural, happened to come up before them for discussion. She rose, as it were, with the sparkling effervescence of their wine, and appeared in a more airy and fantastic light on account of the medium through which they saw her. They repeated to one another, between jest and earnest, all the wild stories that were in vogue; nor, I presume, did they hesitate to add any small circumstance that the inventive whim of the moment might suggest, to heighten the marvellousness of their theme.

"But what an audacious report was that," observed one, "which pretended to assert the identity of this strange creature with a young lady," — and here he mentioned her name, — "the daughter of one of our most distinguished families!"

"Ah, there is more in that story than can well be accounted for," remarked another. "I have it on good authority, that the young lady in question is invariably out of sight, and not to be traced, even by her own family, at the hours when the Veiled Lady is before the public; nor can any satisfactory explanation be given of her disappearance. And just look at the thing: Her brother is a young fellow of spirit. He cannot but be aware of these rumors in reference to his sister. Why, then, does he not come forward to defend her character, unless he is conscious that an investigation would only make the matter worse?"

It is essential to the purposes of my legend to distinguish one of these young gentlemen from his companions; so, for the sake of a soft and pretty name (such as we of the literary sisterhood invariably bestow upon our heroes), I deem it fit to call him Theodore.

"Pshaw!" exclaimed Theodore; "her brother is no such fool! Nobody, unless his brain be as full of bubbles as this wine, can seriously think of crediting that ridiculous rumor. Why, if my senses did not play me false (which never was the case yet), I affirm that I saw that very lady, last evening, at the exhibition, while this veiled phenomenon was playing off her juggling tricks! What can you say to that?"

"O, it was a spectral illusion that you saw," replied his friends, with a general laugh. "The Veiled Lady is quite up to such a thing."

However, as the above-mentioned fable could not hold its ground against Theodore's downright refutation, they went on to speak of other stories which the wild babble of the town had set afloat. Some upheld that the veil covered the most beautiful countenance in the world; others,—and certainly with more reason, considering the sex of the Veiled Lady,—that the face was the most hideous and horrible, and that this was her sole motive for hiding it. It was the face of a corpse; it was the head of a skeleton; it was a monstrous visage, with snaky locks, like Medusa's, and one great red eye in the centre of the forehead. Again, it was affirmed that there was no single and unchangeable set of features beneath the veil; but that whosoever should be bold enough to lift it would behold the features of that person, in all the world, who was destined to be his fate; perhaps he would be greeted by the tender smile of the woman whom he loved, or, quite as probably, the deadly scowl of his bitterest enemy would throw a blight over his life. They quoted, moreover, this startling explanation of the whole affair: that the magician who exhibited the Veiled Lady—and who, by the by, was the handsomest man in the whole world—had bartered his own soul for seven years' possession of a familiar fiend, and that the last year of the contract was wearing towards its close.

If it were worth our while, I could keep you till an hour beyond midnight listening to a thousand such absurdities as these. But finally our friend Theodore, who prided himself upon his common sense, found the matter getting quite beyond his patience.

"I offer any wager you like," cried he, setting down his glass so forcibly as to break the stem of it, "that this very evening I find out the mystery of the Veiled Lady!"

Young men, I am told, boggle at nothing, over their wine; so, after a little more talk, a wager of considerable amount was actually laid, the money staked, and Theodore left to choose his own method of settling the dispute.

How he managed it I know not, nor is it of any great importance to this veracious legend. The most natural way, to be sure, was by bribing the door-keeper,—or possibly he preferred clambering in at the window. But, at any rate, that very evening, while the exhibition was going forward in the hall, Theodore contrived to gain admittance into the private withdrawing-room whither the Veiled Lady was accustomed to retire at the close of her performances. There he waited, listening, I suppose, to the stifled hum of the great audience; and no doubt he could distinguish the deep tones of the magician, causing the wonders that he wrought to appear more dark and intricate, by his mystic pretence of an explanation. Perhaps, too, in the intervals of the wild, breezy music which accompanied the exhibition, he might hear the low voice of the Veiled Lady, conveying her sibylline responses. Firm as Theodore's nerves might be, and much as he prided himself on his sturdy perception of realities, I should not be surprised if his heart throbbed at a little more than its ordinary rate.

Theodore concealed himself behind a screen. In due time, the performance was brought to a close, and whether the door was softly opened, or whether her bodiless presence came through the wall, is more than I can say, but, all at once, without the young man's knowing how it happened, a veiled figure stood in the centre of the room. It was one thing to be in presence of this mystery in the hall of exhibition, where the warm, dense life of hundreds of other mortals kept up the beholder's courage, and distributed her influence among so many; it was another thing to be quite alone with her, and that, too, with a hostile, or, at least, an unauthorized and unjustifiable purpose. I rather imagine that Theodore now began to be sensible of something more serious in his enterprise than he had been quite aware of, while he sat with his boon-companions over their sparkling wine.

Very strange, it must be confessed, was the movement with which the figure floated to and fro over the carpet, with the silvery veil covering her from head to foot; so impalpable, so ethereal, so without substance, as the texture seemed, yet hiding her every outline in an impenetrability like that of midnight. Surely, she did not walk! She floated, and flitted, and hovered about the room;—no sound of a footstep, no perceptible motion of a limb;—it was as if a wandering breeze wafted her before it, at its own wild and gentle pleasure. But, by and by, a purpose began to be discernible, throughout the seeming vagueness of her unrest. She was in quest of something. Could it be that a subtile presentiment had informed her of the young man's presence? And if so, did the Veiled Lady seek or did she shun him? The doubt in Theodore's mind was speedily resolved; for, after a moment or two of these erratic flutterings, she advanced more decidedly, and stood motionless before the screen.

"Thou art here!" said a soft, low voice. "Come forth, Theodore!"

Thus summoned by his name, Theodore, as a man of courage, had no choice. He emerged from his concealment, and presented himself before the Veiled Lady, with the wine-flush, it may be, quite gone out of his cheeks.

"What wouldst thou with me?" she inquired, with the same gentle composure that was in her former utterance.

"Mysterious creature," replied Theodore, "I would know who and what you are!"

"My lips are forbidden to betray the secret," said the Veiled Lady.

"At whatever risk, I must discover it," rejoined Theodore.

"Then," said the Mystery, "there is no way, save to lift my veil."

And Theodore, partly recovering his audacity, stept forward on the instant, to do as the Veiled Lady had suggested. But she floated backward to the opposite side of the room, as if the young man's breath had possessed power enough to waft her away.

"Pause, one little instant," said the soft, low voice, "and learn the conditions of what thou art so bold to undertake! Thou canst go hence, and think of me no more; or, at thy option, thou canst lift this mysterious veil, beneath which I am a sad and lonely prisoner, in a bondage which is worse to me than death. But, before raising it, I entreat thee, in all maiden modesty, to bend forward and impress a kiss where my breath stirs the veil; and my virgin lips shall come forward to meet thy lips; and from that instant, Theodore, thou shalt be mine, and I thine, with never more a veil between us. And all the felicity of earth and of the future world shall be thine and mine together. So much may a maiden say behind the veil. If thou shrinkest from this, there is yet another way."

"And what is that?" asked Theodore.

"Dost thou hesitate," said the Veiled Lady, "to pledge thyself to me, by meeting these lips of mine, while the veil yet hides my face? Has not thy heart recognized me? Dost thou come hither, not in holy faith, nor with a pure and generous purpose, but in scornful scepticism and idle curiosity? Still, thou mayest lift the veil! But, from that instant, Theodore, I am doomed to be thy evil fate; nor wilt thou ever taste another breath of happiness!"

There was a shade of inexpressible sadness in the utterance of these last words. But Theodore, whose natural tendency was towards scepticism, felt himself almost injured and insulted by the Veiled Lady's proposal that he should pledge himself, for life and eternity, to so questionable a creature as herself; or even that she should suggest an inconsequential kiss, taking into view the probability that her face was none of the most bewitching. A delightful idea, truly, that he should salute the lips of a dead girl, or the jaws of a skeleton, or the grinning cavity of a monster's mouth! Even should she prove a comely maiden enough in other respects, the odds were ten to one that her teeth were defective; a terrible drawback on the delectableness of a kiss.

"Excuse me, fair lady," said Theodore,—and I think he nearly burst into a laugh,—"if I prefer to lift the veil first; and for this affair of the kiss, we may decide upon it afterwards."

"Thou hast made thy choice," said the sweet, sad voice behind the veil; and there seemed a tender but unresentful sense of wrong done to womanhood by the young man's contemptuous interpretation of her offer. "I must not counsel thee to pause, although thy fate is still in thine own hand!"

Grasping at the veil, he flung it upward, and caught a glimpse of a pale, lovely face beneath; just one momentary glimpse, and then the apparition vanished, and the silvery veil fluttered slowly down and lay upon the floor. Theodore was alone. Our legend leaves him there. His retribution was, to pine for ever and ever for another sight of that dim, mournful face,— which might have been his life-long household fireside joy,—to desire, and waste life in a feverish quest, and never meet it more.

But what, in good sooth, had become of the Veiled Lady? Had all her existence been comprehended within that mysterious veil, and was she now annihilated? Or was she a spirit, with a heavenly essence, but which might have been tamed down to human bliss, had Theodore been brave and true enough to claim her? Hearken, my sweet friends,—and hearken, dear Priscilla,—and you shall learn the little more that Zenobia can tell you.

Just at the moment, so far as can be ascertained, when the Veiled Lady vanished, a maiden, pale and shadowy, rose up amid a knot of visionary people, who were seeking for the better life. She was so gentle and so sad,— a nameless melancholy gave her such hold upon their sympathies,—that they never thought of questioning whence she came. She might have heretofore existed, or her thin substance might have been moulded out of air at the very instant when they first beheld her. It was all one to them; they took her to their hearts. Among them was a lady, to whom, more than to all the rest, this pale, mysterious girl attached herself.

But one morning the lady was wandering in the woods, and there met her a figure in an oriental robe, with a dark beard, and holding in his hand a silvery veil. He motioned her to stay. Being a woman of some nerve, she did not shriek, nor run away, nor faint, as many ladies would have been apt to do, but stood quietly, and bade him speak. The truth was, she had seen his face before, but had never feared it, although she knew him to be a terrible magician.

"Lady," said he, with a warning gesture, "you are in peril!"

"Peril!" she exclaimed. "And of what nature?"

"There is a certain maiden," replied the magician, "who has come out of the realm of mystery, and made herself your most intimate companion. Now, the fates have so ordained it, that, whether by her own will or no, this stranger is your deadliest enemy. In love, in worldly fortune, in all your pursuit of happiness, she is doomed to fling a blight over your prospects. There is but one possibility of thwarting her disastrous influence."

"Then tell me that one method," said the lady.

"Take this veil," he answered, holding forth the silvery texture. "It is a spell; it is a powerful enchantment, which I wrought for her sake, and beneath which she was once my prisoner. Throw it, at unawares, over the head of this secret foe, stamp your foot, and cry, 'Arise, Magician, here is the Veiled Lady!' and immediately I will rise up through the earth, and seize her; and from that moment you are safe!"

So the lady took the silvery veil, which was like woven air, or like some substance airier than nothing, and that would float upward and be lost among the clouds, were she once to let it go. Returning homeward, she found the shadowy girl, amid the knot of visionary transcendentalists, who were still seeking for the better life. She was joyous now, and had a rosebloom in her cheeks, and was one of the prettiest creatures, and seemed one of the happiest, that the world could show. But the lady stole noiselessly behind her, and threw the veil over her head. As the slight, ethereal texture sank inevitably down over her figure, the poor girl strove to raise it, and met her dear friend's eyes with one glance of mortal terror, and deep, deep reproach. It could not change her purpose.

"Arise, Magician!" she exclaimed, stamping her foot upon the earth. "Here is the Veiled Lady!"

At the word, up rose the bearded man in the oriental robes,—the beautiful, the dark magician, who had bartered away his soul! He threw his arms around the Veiled Lady, and she was his bond-slave forevermore!

Zenobia, all this while, had been holding the piece of gauze, and so managed it as greatly to increase the dramatic effect of the legend at those points where the magic veil was to be described. Arriving at the catastrophe, and uttering the fatal words, she flung the gauze over Priscilla's head; and for an instant her auditors held their breath, half expecting, I verily believe, that the magician would start up through the floor, and carry off our poor little friend, before our eyes.

As for Priscilla, she stood droopingly in the midst of us, making no attempt to remove the veil.

"How do you find yourself, my love?" said Zenobia, lifting a corner of the gauze, and peeping beneath it, with a mischievous smile. "Ah, the dear little soul! Why, she is really going to faint! Mr. Coverdale, Mr. Coverdale, pray bring a glass of water!"

Her nerves being none of the strongest, Priscilla hardly recovered her equanimity during the rest of the evening. This, to be sure, was a great pity; but, nevertheless, we thought it a very bright idea of Zenobia's to bring her legend to so effective a conclusion.

XIV.

ELIOT'S PULPIT

OUR Sundays, at Blithedale, were not ordinarily kept with such rigid observance as might have befitted the descendants of the Pilgrims, whose high enterprise, as we sometimes flattered ourselves, we had taken up, and were carrying it onward and aloft, to a point which they never dreamed of attaining.

On that hallowed day, it is true, we rested from our labors. Our oxen, relieved from their week-day yoke, roamed at large through the pasture; each yoke-fellow, however, keeping close beside his mate, and continuing to acknowledge, from the force of habit and sluggish sympathy, the union which the taskmaster had imposed for his own hard ends. As for us human yoke-fellows, chosen companions of toil, whose hoes had clinked together throughout the week, we wandered off, in various directions, to enjoy our interval of repose. Some, I believe, went devoutly to the village church. Others, it may be, ascended a city or a country pulpit, wearing the clerical robe with so much dignity that you would scarcely have suspected the yeoman's frock to have been flung off only since milking-time. Others took long rambles among the rustic lanes and by-paths, pausing to look at black old farm-houses, with their sloping roofs; and at the modern cottage, so like a plaything that it seemed as if real joy or sorrow could have no scope within; and at the more pretending villa, with its range of wooden columns, supporting the needless insolence of a great portico. Some betook themselves into the wide, dusky barn, and lay there for hours together on the odorous hay; while the sunstreaks and the shadows strove together, — these to make the barn solemn, those to make it cheerful, — and both were conquerors; and the swallows twittered a cheery anthem, flashing into sight, or vanishing, as they darted to and fro among the golden rules of sunshine. And others went a little way into the woods, and threw themselves on mother earth, pillowing their heads on a heap of moss, the green decay of an old log; and, dropping asleep, the humblebees and mosquitoes sung and buzzed about their ears, causing the slumberers to twitch and start, without awakening.

With Hollingsworth, Zenobia, Priscilla and myself, it grew to be a custom to spend the Sabbath afternoon at a certain rock. It was known to us under the name of Eliot's pulpit, from a tradition that the venerable Apostle Eliot had preached there, two centuries gone by, to an Indian auditory. The old pine forest, through which the apostle's voice was wont to sound, had fallen, an immemorial time ago. But the soil, being of the rudest and most broken surface, had apparently never been brought under tillage; other growths, maple, and beech, and birch, had succeeded to the primeval trees; so that it was still as wild a tract of woodland as the great-great-great-great-grandson of one of Eliot's Indians (had any such posterity been in existence) could have desired, for the site and shelter of his wigwam. These aftergrowths, indeed, lose the stately solemnity of the original forest. If left in due neglect, however, they run into an entanglement of softer wildness, among the rustling leaves of which the sun can scatter cheerfulness as it never could among the dark-browed pines.

The rock itself rose some twenty or thirty feet, a shattered granite boulder, or heap of boulders, with an irregular outline and many fissures, out of which sprang shrubs, brushes, and even trees; as if the scanty soil within those crevices were sweeter to their roots than any other earth. At the base of the pulpit, the broken boulders inclined towards each other, so as to form a shallow cave, within which our little party had sometimes found protection from a summer shower. On the threshold, or just across it, grew a tuft of pale columbines, in their season, and violets, sad and shadowy recluses, such as Priscilla was when we first knew her; children of the sun, who had never seen their father, but dwelt among damp mosses, though not akin to them. At the summit, the rock was overshadowed by the canopy of a birch-tree, which served as a sounding-board for the pulpit. Beneath this shade (with my eyes of sense half shut, and those of the imagination widely opened) I used to see the holy Apostle of the Indians, with the sunlight flickering down upon him through the leaves, and glorifying his figure as with the half-perceptible glow of a transfiguration.

I the more minutely describe the rock, and this little Sabbath solitude, because Hollingsworth, at our solicitation, often ascended Eliot's pulpit, and not exactly preached, but talked to us, his few disciples, in a strain that rose and fell as naturally as the wind's breath among the leaves of the birch-tree. No other speech of man has ever moved me like some of those discourses. It seemed most pitiful—a positive calamity to the world—that a treasury of golden thoughts should thus be scattered, by the liberal handful, down among us three, when a thousand hearers might have been the richer for them; and Hollingsworth the richer, likewise, by the sympathy of multitudes. After speaking much or little, as might happen, he would descend from his gray pulpit, and generally fling himself at full length on the ground, face downward. Meanwhile, we talked around him, on such topics as were suggested by the discourse.

Since her interview with Westervelt, Zenobia's continual inequalities of temper had been rather difficult for her friends to bear. On the first Sunday after that incident, when Hollingsworth had clambered down from Eliot's pulpit, she declaimed with great earnestness and passion, nothing short of anger, on the injustice which the world did to women, and equally to itself, by not allowing them, in freedom and honor, and with the fullest welcome, their natural utterance in public.

"It shall not always be so!" cried she. "If I live another year, I will lift up my own voice in behalf of woman's wider liberty!"

She, perhaps, saw me smile.

"What matter of ridicule do you find in this, Miles Coverdale?" exclaimed Zenobia, with a flash of anger in her eyes. "That smile, permit me to say, makes me suspicious of a low tone of feeling and shallow thought. It is my belief—yes, and my prophecy, should I die before it happens—that, when my sex shall achieve its rights, there will be ten eloquent women where there is now one eloquent man. Thus far, no woman in the world has ever once spoken out her whole heart and her whole mind. The mistrust and disapproval of the vast bulk of society throttles us, as with two gigantic hands at our throats! We mumble a few weak words, and leave a thousand better ones unsaid. You let us write a little, it is true, on a limited range of subjects. But the pen is not for woman. Her power is too natural and immediate. It is with the living voice alone that she can compel the world to recognize the light of her intellect and the depth of her heart!"

Now,—though I could not well say so to Zenobia,—I had not smiled from any unworthy estimate of woman, or in denial of the claims which she is beginning to put forth. What amused and puzzled me was the fact, that women, however intellectually superior, so seldom disquiet themselves about the rights or wrongs of their sex, unless their own individual affections chance to lie in idleness, or to be ill at ease. They are not natural reformers, but become such by the pressure of exceptional misfortune. I could measure Zenobia's inward trouble by the animosity with which she now took up the general quarrel of woman against man.

"I will give you leave, Zenobia," replied I, "to fling your utmost scorn upon me, if you ever hear me utter a sentiment unfavorable to the widest liberty which woman has yet dreamed of. I would give her all she asks, and add a great deal more, which she will not be the party to demand, but which men, if they were generous and wise, would grant of their own free motion. For instance, I should love dearly,—for the next thousand years, at least,—to have all government devolve into the hands of women. I hate to be ruled by my own sex; it excites my jealousy, and wounds my pride. It is the iron sway of bodily force which abases us, in our compelled submission. But how sweet the free, generous courtesy, with which I would kneel before a woman-ruler!"

"Yes, if she were young and beautiful," said Zenobia, laughing. "But how if she were sixty, and a fright?"

"Ah! it is you that rate womanhood low," said I. "But let me go on. I have never found it possible to suffer a bearded priest so near my heart and conscience as to do me any spiritual good. I blush at the very thought! O, in the better order of things, Heaven grant that the ministry of souls may be left in charge of women! The gates of the Blessed City will be thronged with the multitude that enter in, when that day comes! The task belongs to woman. God meant it for her. He has endowed her with the religious sentiment in its utmost depth and purity, refined from that gross, intellectual alloy with which every masculine theologist—save only One, who merely veiled himself in mortal and masculine shape, but was, in truth, divine—has been prone to mingle it. I have always envied the Catholics their faith in that sweet, sacred Virgin Mother, who stands between them and the Deity, intercepting somewhat of his awful splendor, but permitting his love to stream upon the worshipper more intelligibly to human comprehension through the medium of a woman's tenderness. Have I not said enough, Zenobia?"

"I cannot think that this is true," observed Priscilla, who had been gazing at me with great, disapproving eyes. "And I am sure I do not wish it to be true!"

"Poor child!" exclaimed Zenobia, rather contemptuously. "She is the type of womanhood, such as man has spent centuries in making it. He is never content, unless he can degrade himself by stooping towards what he loves. In denying us our rights, he betrays even more blindness to his own interests than profligate disregard of ours!"

"Is this true?" asked Priscilla, with simplicity, turning to Hollingsworth. "Is it all true, that Mr. Coverdale and Zenobia have been saying?"

"No, Priscilla!" answered Hollingsworth, with his customary bluntness. "They have neither of them spoken one true word yet."

"Do you despise woman?" said Zenobia. "Ah, Hollingsworth, that would be most ungrateful!"

"Despise her? No!" cried Hollingsworth, lifting his great shaggy head and shaking it at us, while his eyes glowed almost fiercely. "She is the most admirable handiwork of God, in her true place and character. Her place is at man's side. Her office, that of the sympathizer; the unreserved, unquestioning believer; the recognition, withheld in every other manner, but given, in pity, through woman's heart, lest man should utterly lose faith in himself; the echo of God's own voice, pronouncing, 'It is well done!' All the separate action of woman is, and ever has been, and always shall be, false, foolish, vain, destructive of her own best and holiest qualities, void of every good effect, and productive of intolerable mischiefs! Man is a wretch without woman; but woman is a monster—and, thank Heaven, an almost impossible and hitherto imaginary monster—without man as her acknowledged principal! As true as I had once a mother whom I loved, were there any possible prospect of woman's taking the social stand which some of them—poor, miserable, abortive creatures, who only dream of such things because they have missed woman's peculiar happiness, or because nature made them really neither man nor woman!—if there were a chance of their attaining the end which these petticoated monstrosities have in view, I would call upon my own sex to use its physical force, that unmistakable evidence of sovereignty, to scourge them back within their proper bounds! But it will not be needful. The heart of true womanhood knows where its own sphere is, and never seeks to stray beyond it!"

Never was mortal blessed—if blessing it were—with a glance of such entire acquiescence and unquestioning faith, happy in its complete-ness, as our little Priscilla unconsciously bestowed on Hollingsworth. She seemed to take the sentiment from his lips into her heart, and brood over it in perfect content. The very woman whom he pictured—the gentle parasite, the soft reflection of a more powerful existence—sat there at his feet.

I looked at Zenobia, however, fully expecting her to resent—as I felt, by the indignant ebullition of my own blood, that she ought—this out-rageous affirmation of what struck me as the intensity of masculine egotism. It centred everything in itself, and deprived woman of her very soul, her inexpressible and unfathomable all, to make it a mere inci-dent in the great sum of man. Hollingsworth had boldly uttered what he, and millions of despots like him, really felt. Without intending it, he had disclosed the well-spring of all these troubled waters. Now, if ever, it surely behooved Zenobia to be the champion of her sex.

But, to my surprise, and indignation too, she only looked humbled. Some tears sparkled in her eyes, but they were wholly of grief, not anger.

"Well, be it so,"-was all she said. "I, at least, have deep cause to think you right. Let man be but manly and god-like, and woman is only too ready to become to him what you say!"

I smiled—somewhat bitterly, it is true—in contemplation of my own ill-luck. How little did these two women care for me, who had freely conceded all their claims, and a great deal more, out of the fulness of my heart; while Hollingsworth, by some necromancy of his horrible injustice, seemed to have brought them both to his feet!

"Women almost invariably behave thus," thought I. "What does the fact mean? Is it their nature? Or is it, at last, the result of ages of com-pelled degradation? And, in either case, will it be possible ever to redeem them?"

An intuition now appeared to possess all the party, that, for this time, at least, there was no more to be said. With one accord, we arose from the ground, and made our way through the tangled undergrowth towards one of those pleasant wood-paths that wound among the over-arching trees. Some of the branches hung so low as partly to conceal the figures that went before from those who followed. Priscilla had leaped up more lightly than the rest of us, and ran along in advance, with as much airy activity of spirit as was typified in the motion of a bird, which chanced to be flitting from tree to tree, in the same direc-tion as herself. Never did she seem so happy as that afternoon. She skipt, and could not help it, from very playfulness of heart.

Zenobia and Hollingsworth went next, in close contiguity, but not with arm in arm. Now, just when they had passed the impending bough of a birch-tree, I plainly saw Zenobia take the hand of Hollingsworth in both her own, press it to her bosom, and let it fall again!

The gesture was sudden, and full of passion; the impulse had evidently taken her by surprise; it expressed all! Had Zenobia knelt before him, or flung herself upon his breast, and gasped out, "I love you, Hollingsworth!" I could not have been more certain of what it meant. They then walked onward, as before. But, methought, as the declining sun threw Zenobia's magnified shadow along the path, I beheld it tremulous; and the delicate stem of the flower which she wore in her hair was likewise responsive to her agitation.

Priscilla—through the medium of her eyes, at least—could not possibly have been aware of the gesture above described. Yet, at that instant, I saw her droop. The buoyancy, which just before had been so bird-like, was utterly departed; the life seemed to pass out of her, and even the substance of her figure to grow thin and gray. I almost imagined her a shadow, fading gradually into the dimness of the wood. Her pace became so slow, that Hollingsworth and Zenobia passed by, and I, without hastening my footsteps, overtook her.

"Come, Priscilla," said I, looking her intently in the face, which was very pale and sorrowful, "we must make haste after our friends. Do you feel suddenly ill? A moment ago, you flitted along so lightly that I was comparing you to a bird. Now, on the contrary, it is as if you had a heavy heart, and very little strength to bear it with. Pray take my arm!"

"No," said Priscilla, "I do not think it would help me. It is my heart, as you say, that makes me heavy; and I know not why. Just now, I felt very happy."

No doubt it was a kind of sacrilege in me to attempt to come within her maidenly mystery; but, as she appeared to be tossed aside by her other friends, or carelessly let fall, like a flower which they had done with, I could not resist the impulse to take just one peep beneath her folded petals.

"Zenobia and yourself are dear friends, of late," I remarked. "At first,—that first evening when you came to us,—she did not receive you quite so warmly as might have been wished."

"I remember it," said Priscilla. "No wonder she hesitated to love me, who was then a stranger to her, and a girl of no grace or beauty,—she being herself so beautiful!"

"But she loves you now, of course?" suggested I. "And at this very instant you feel her to be your dearest friend?"

"Why do you ask me that question?" exclaimed Priscilla, as if frightened at the scrutiny into her feelings which I compelled her to make. "It somehow puts strange thoughts into my mind. But I do love Zenobia dearly! If she only loves me half as well, I shall be happy!"

"How is it possible to doubt that, Priscilla?" I rejoined. "But observe how pleasantly and happily Zenobia and Hollingsworth are walking together. I call it a delightful spectacle. It truly rejoices me that Hollingsworth had found so fit and affectionate a friend! So many people in the world mistrust him,—so many disbelieve and ridicule, while hardly any do him justice, or acknowledge him for the wonderful man he is,—that it is really a blessed thing for him to have won the sympathy of such a woman as Zenobia. Any man might be proud of that. Any man, even if he be as great as Hollingsworth, might love so magnificent a woman. How very beautiful Zenobia is! And Hollingsworth knows it, too."

There may have been some petty malice in what I said. Generosity is a very fine thing, at a proper time, and within due limits. But it is an insufferable bore to see one man engrossing every thought of all the women, and leaving his friend to shiver in outer seclusion, without even the alternative of solacing himself with what the more fortunate individual has rejected. Yes; it was out of a foolish bitterness of heart that I had spoken.

"Go on before," said Priscilla, abruptly, and with true feminine imperiousness, which heretofore I had never seen her exercise. "It pleases me best to loiter along by myself. I do not walk so fast as you."

With her hand, she made a little gesture of dismissal. It provoked me; yet, on the whole, was the most bewitching thing that Priscilla had ever done. I obeyed her, and strolled moodily homeward, wondering—as I had wondered a thousand times already—how Hollingsworth meant to dispose of these two hearts, which (plainly to my perception, and, as I could not but now suppose, to his) he had engrossed into his own huge egotism.

There was likewise another subject hardly less fruitful of speculation. In what attitude did Zenobia present herself to Hollingsworth? Was it in that of a free woman, with no mortgage on her affections nor claimant to her hand, but fully at liberty to surrender both, in exchange for the heart and hand which she apparently expected to receive? But was it a vision that I had witnessed in the wood? Was Westervelt a goblin? Were those words of passion and agony, which Zenobia had uttered in my hearing, a mere stage declamation? Were they formed of a material lighter than common air? Or, supposing them to bear sterling weight, was it not a perilous and dreadful wrong which she was meditating towards herself and Hollingsworth?

Arriving nearly at the farm-house, I looked back over the long slope of pasture-land, and beheld them standing together, in the light of sunset, just on the spot where, according to the gossip of the Community, they meant to build their cottage. Priscilla, alone and forgotten, was lingering in the shadow of the wood.

XV.

A CRISIS

THUS the summer was passing away;—a summer of toil, of interest, of something that was not pleasure, but which went deep into my heart, and there became a rich experience. I found myself looking forward to years, if not to a lifetime, to be spent on the same system. The Community were now beginning to form their permanent plans. One of our purposes was to erect a Phalanstery (as I think we called it, after Fourier; but the phraseology of those days is not very fresh in my remembrance), where the great and general family should have its abiding-place. Individual members, too, who made it a point of religion to preserve the sanctity of an exclusive home, were selecting sites for their cottages, by the wood-side, or on the breezy swells, or in the sheltered nook of some little valley, according as their taste might lean towards snugness or the picturesque. Altogether, by projecting our minds outward, we had imparted a show of novelty to existence, and contemplated it as hopefully as if the soil beneath our feet had not been fathom-deep with the dust of deluded generations, on every one of which, as on ourselves, the world had imposed itself as a hitherto unwedded bride.

Hollingsworth and myself had often discussed these prospects. It was easy to perceive, however, that he spoke with little or no fervor, but either as questioning the fulfilment of our anticipations, or, at any rate, with a quiet consciousness that it was no personal concern of his. Shortly after the scene at Eliot's pulpit, while he and I were repairing an old stone fence, I amused myself with sallying forward into the future time.

"When we come to be old men," I said, "they will call us uncles, or fathers,—Father Hollingsworth and Uncle Coverdale,—and we will look back cheerfully to these early days, and make a romantic story for the young people (and if a little more romantic than truth may warrant, it will be no harm) out of our severe trials and hardships. In a century or two, we shall, every one of us, be mythical personages, or exceedingly picturesque and poetical ones, at all events. They will have a great public hall, in which your portrait, and mine, and twenty other faces that are living now, shall be hung up; and as for me, I will be painted in my shirt-sleeves, and with the sleeves rolled up, to show my muscular development. What stories will be rife among them about our mighty strength!" continued I, lifting a big stone and putting it into its place; "though our posterity will really be far stronger than ourselves, after several generations of a simple, natural, and active life. What legends of Zenobia's beauty, and Priscilla's slender and shadowy grace, and those mysterious qualities which make her seem diaphanous with spiritual light! In due course of ages, we must all figure heroically in an epic poem; and we will ourselves—at least, I will—bend unseen over the future poet, and lend him inspiration while he writes it."

"You seem," said Hollingsworth, "to be trying how much nonsense you can pour out in a breath."

"I wish you would see fit to comprehend," retorted I, "that the profoundest wisdom must be mingled with nine-tenths of nonsense, else it is not worth the breath that utters it. But I do long for the cottages to be built, that the creeping plants may begin to run over them, and the moss to gather on the walls, and the trees—which we will set out—to cover them with a breadth of shadow. This spick-and-span novelty does not quite suit my taste. It is time, too, for children to be born among us. The first-born child is still to come. And I shall never feel as if this were a real, practical, as well as poetical-system of human life, until somebody has sanctified it by death."

"A pretty occasion for martyrdom, truly!" said Hollingsworth.

"As good as any other," I replied. "I wonder, Hollingsworth, who, of all these strong men, and fair women and maidens, is doomed the first to die. Would it not be well, even before we have absolute need of it, to fix upon a spot for a cemetery? Let us choose the rudest, roughest, most uncultivable spot, for Death's garden ground; and Death shall teach us to beautify it, grave by grave. By our sweet, calm way of dying, and the airy elegance out of which we will shape our funeral rites, and the cheerful allegories which we will model into tomb-stones, the final scene shall lose its terrors; so that hereafter it may be happiness to live, and bliss to die. None of us must die young. Yet, should Providence ordain it so, the event shall not be sorrowful, but affect us with a tender, delicious, only half melancholy and almost smiling pathos!"

"That is to say," muttered Hollingsworth, "you will die like a heathen, as you certainly live like one. But, listen to me, Coverdale. Your fantastic anticipations make me discern all the more forcibly what a wretched, unsubstantial scheme is this, on which we have wasted a precious summer of our lives. Do you seriously imagine that any such realities as you, and many others here, have dreamed of, will ever be brought to pass?"

"Certainly, I do," said I. "Of course, when the reality comes, it will wear the every-day, commonplace, dusty, and rather homely garb, that reality always does put on. But, setting aside the ideal charm, I hold that our highest anticipations have a solid footing on common sense."

"You only half believe what you say," rejoined Hollingsworth; "and as for me, I neither have faith in your dream, nor would care the value of this pebble for its realization, were that possible. And what more do you want of it? It has given you a theme for poetry. Let that content you. But now I ask you to be, at last, a man of sobriety and earnestness, and aid me in an enterprise which is worth all our strength, and the strength of a thousand mightier than we."

There can be no need of giving in detail the conversation that ensued. It is enough to say that Hollingsworth once more brought forward his rigid and unconquerable idea; a scheme for the reformation of the wicked by methods moral, intellectual, and industrial, by the sympathy of pure, humble, and yet exalted minds, and by opening to his pupils the possibility of a worthier life than that which had become their fate. It appeared, unless he over-estimated his own means, that Hollingsworth held it at his choice (and he did so choose) to obtain possession of the very ground on which we had planted our Community, and which had not yet been made irrevocably ours, by purchase. It was just the foundation that he desired. Our beginnings might readily be adapted to his great end. The arrangements already completed would work quietly into his system. So plausible looked his theory, and, more than that, so practical,—such an air of reasonableness had he, by patient thought, thrown over it,—each segment of it was contrived to dove-tail into all the rest with such a complicated applicability, and so ready was he with a response for every objection, that, really, so far as logic and argument went, he had the matter all his own way.

"But," said I, "whence can you, having no means of your own, derive the enormous capital which is essential to this experiment? State-street, I imagine, would not draw its purse-strings very liberally in aid of such a speculation."

"I have the funds—as much, at least, as is needed for a commencement—at command," he answered. "They can be produced within a month, if necessary."

My thoughts reverted to Zenobia. It could only be her wealth which Hollingsworth was appropriating so lavishly. And on what conditions was it to be had? Did she fling it into the scheme with the uncalculating generosity that characterizes a woman when it is her impulse to be generous at all? And did she fling herself along with it? But Hollingsworth did not volunteer an explanation.

"And have you no regrets," I inquired, "in overthrowing this fair system of our new life, which has been planned so deeply, and is now beginning to flourish so hopefully around us? How beautiful it is, and, so far as we can yet see, how practicable! The ages have waited for us, and here we are, the very first that have essayed to carry on our mortal existence in love and mutual help! Hollingsworth, I would be loth to take the ruin of this enterprise upon my conscience."

"Then let it rest wholly upon mine!" he answered, knitting his black brows. "I see through the system. It is full of defects,—irremediable and damning ones!—from first to last, there is nothing else! I grasp it in my hand, and find no substance whatever. There is not human nature in it."

"Why are you so secret in your operations?" I asked. "God forbid that I should accuse you of intentional wrong; but the besetting sin of a philanthropist, it appears to me, is apt to be a moral obliquity. His sense of honor ceases to be the sense of other honorable men. At some point of his course—I know not exactly when or where—he is tempted to palter with the right, and can scarcely forbear persuading himself that the importance of his public ends renders it allowable to throw aside his private conscience. O, my dear friend, beware this error! If you meditate the overthrow of this establishment, call together our companions, state your design, support it with all your eloquence, but allow them an opportunity of defending themselves."

"It does not suit me," said Hollingsworth. "Nor is it my duty to do so."

"I think it is," replied I.

Hollingsworth frowned; not in passion, but, like fate, inexorably.

"I will not argue the point," said he. "What I desire to know of you is,—and you can tell me in one word,—whether I am to look for your coöperation in this great scheme of good? Take it up with me! Be my brother in it! It offers you (what you have told me, over and over again, that you most need) a purpose in life, worthy of the extremest self-devotion,—worthy of martyrdom, should God so order it! In this view, I present it to you. You can greatly benefit mankind. Your peculiar faculties, as I shall direct them, are capable of being so wrought into this enterprise that not one of them need lie idle. Strike hands with me, and from this moment you shall never again feel the languor and vague wretchedness of an indolent or half-occupied man. There may be no more aimless beauty in your life; but, in its stead, there shall be strength, courage, immitigable will—everything that a manly and generous nature should desire! We shall succeed! We shall have done our best for this miserable world; and happiness (which never comes but incidentally) will come to us unawares."

It seemed his intention to say no more. But, after he had quite broken off, his deep eyes filled with tears, and he held out both his hands to me.

"Coverdale," he murmured, "there is not the man in this wide world whom I can love as I could you. Do not forsake me!"

As I look back upon this scene, through the coldness and dimness of so many years, there is still a sensation as if Hollingsworth had caught hold of my heart, and were pulling it towards him with an almost irresistible force. It is a mystery to me how I withstood it. But, in truth, I saw in his scheme of philanthropy nothing but what was odious. A loathsomeness that was to be forever in my daily work! A great, black ugliness of sin, which he proposed to collect out of a thousand human hearts, and that we should spend our lives in an experiment of transmuting it into virtue!

Had I but touched his extended hand, Hollingsworth's magnetism would perhaps have penetrated me with his own conception of all these matters. But I stood aloof. I fortified myself with doubts whether his strength of purpose had not been too gigantic for his integrity, impelling him to trample on considerations that should have been paramount to every other.

"Is Zenobia to take a part in your enterprise?" I asked.

"She is," said Hollingsworth.

"She!—the beautiful!—the gorgeous!" I exclaimed. "And how have you prevailed with such a woman to work in this squalid element?"

"Through no base methods, as you seem to suspect," he answered; "but by addressing whatever is best and noblest in her."

Hollingsworth was looking on the ground. But, as he often did so,—generally, indeed, in his habitual moods of thought,—I could not judge whether it was from any special unwillingness now to meet my eyes. What it was that dictated my next question, I cannot precisely say. Nevertheless, it rose so inevitably into my mouth, and, as it were, asked itself so involuntarily, that there must needs have been an aptness in it.

"What is to become of Priscilla?"

Hollingsworth looked at me fiercely, and with glowing eyes. He could not have shown any other kind of expression than that, had he meant to strike me with a sword.

"Why do you bring in the names of these women?" said he, after a moment of pregnant silence. "What have they to do with the proposal which I make you? I must have your answer! Will you devote yourself, and sacrifice all to this great end, and be my friend of friends forever?"

"In Heaven's name, Hollingsworth," cried I, getting angry, and glad to be angry, because so only was it possible to oppose his tremendous concentrativeness and indomitable will, "cannot you conceive that a man may wish well to the world, and struggle for its good, on some other plan than precisely that which you have laid down? And will you cast off a friend for no unworthiness, but merely because he stands upon his right as an individual being, and looks at matters through his own optics, instead of yours?"

"Be with me," said Hollingsworth, "or be against me! There is no third choice for you."

"Take this, then, as my decision," I answered. "I doubt the wisdom of your scheme. Furthermore, I greatly fear that the methods by which you allow yourself to pursue it are such as cannot stand the scrutiny of an unbiassed conscience."

"And you will not join me?"

"No!"

I never said the word—and certainly can never have it to say hereafter—that cost me a thousandth part so hard an effort as did that one syllable. The heart-pang was not merely figurative, but an absolute torture of the breast. I was gazing steadfastly at Hollingsworth. It seemed to me that it struck him, too, like a bullet. A ghastly paleness—always so terrific on a swarthy face—overspread his features. There was a convulsive movement of his throat, as if he were forcing down some words that struggled and fought for utterance. Whether words of anger, or words of grief, I cannot tell; although, many and many a time, I have vainly tormented myself with conjecturing which of the two they were. One other appeal to my friendship,—such as once, already, Hollingsworth had made,—taking me in the revulsion that followed a strenuous exercise of opposing will, would completely have subdued me. But he left the matter there.

"Well!" said he.

And that was all! I should have been thankful for one word more, even had it shot me through the heart, as mine did him. But he did not speak it; and, after a few moments, with one accord, we set to work again, repairing the stone fence. Hollingsworth, I observed, wrought like a Titan; and, for my own part, I lifted stones which at this day—or, in a calmer mood, at that one—I should no more have thought it possible to stir than to carry off the gates of Gaza on my back.

XVI.

LEAVE-TAKINGS

A FEW days after the tragic passage-at-arms between Hollingsworth and me, I appeared at the dinner-table actually dressed in a coat, instead of my customary blouse; with a satin cravat, too, a white vest, and several other things that made me seem strange and outlandish to myself. As for my companions, this unwonted spectacle caused a great stir upon the wooden benches that bordered either side of our homely board.

"What's in the wind now, Miles?" asked one of them. "Are you deserting us?"

"Yes, for a week or two," said I. "It strikes me that my health demands a little relaxation of labor, and a short visit to the sea-side, during the dog-days."

"You look like it!" grumbled Silas Foster, not greatly pleased with the idea of losing an efficient laborer before the stress of the season was well over. "Now, here's a pretty fellow! His shoulders have broadened a matter of six inches, since he came among us; he can do his day's work, if he likes, with any man or ox on the farm; and yet he talks about going to the sea-shore for his health! Well, well, old woman," added he to his wife, "let me have a plateful of that pork and cabbage! I begin to feel in a very weakly way. When the others have had their turn, you and I will take a jaunt to Newport or Saratoga!"

"Well, but, Mr. Foster," said I, "you must allow me to take a little breath."

"Breath!" retorted the old yeoman. "Your lungs have the play of a pair of blacksmith's bellows already. What on earth do you want more? But go along! I understand the business. We shall never see your face here again. Here ends the reformation of the world, so far as Miles Coverdale has a hand in it!"

"By no means," I replied. "I am resolute to die in the last ditch, for the good of the cause."

"Die in a ditch!" muttered gruff Silas, with genuine Yankee intolerance of any intermission of toil, except on Sunday, the fourth of July, the autumnal cattleshow, Thanksgiving, or the annual Fast. "Die in a ditch! I believe, in my conscience, you would, if there were no steadier means than your own labor to keep you out of it!"

The truth was, that an intolerable discontent and irksomeness had come over me. Blithedale was no longer what it had been. Everything was suddenly faded. The sun-burnt and arid aspect of our woods and pastures, beneath the August sky, did but imperfectly symbolize the lack of dew and moisture that, since yesterday, as it were, had blighted my fields of thought, and penetrated to the innermost and shadiest of my contemplative recesses. The change will be recognized by many, who, after a period of happiness, have endeavored to go on with the same kind of life, in the same scene, in spite of the alteration or withdrawal of some principal circumstance. They discover (what heretofore, perhaps, they had not known) that it was this which gave the bright color and vivid reality to the whole affair.

I stood on other terms than before, not only with Hollingsworth, but with Zenobia and Priscilla. As regarded the two latter, it was that dream-like and miserable sort of change that denies you the privilege to complain, because you can assert no positive injury, nor lay your finger on anything tangible. It is a matter which you do not see, but feel, and which, when you try to analyze it, seems to lose its very existence, and resolve itself into a sickly humor of your own. Your understanding, possibly, may put faith in this denial. But your heart will not so easily rest satisfied. It incessantly remonstrates, though, most of the time, in a bass-note, which you do not separately distinguish; but, now and then, with a sharp cry, importunate to be heard, and resolute to claim belief. "Things are not as they were!" it keeps saying. "You shall not impose on me! I will never be quiet! I will throb painfully! I will be heavy, and desolate, and shiver with cold! For I, your deep heart, know when to be miserable, as once I knew when to be happy! All is changed for us! You are beloved no more!" And, were my life to be spent over again, I would invariably lend my ear to this Cassandra of the inward depths, however clamorous the music and the merriment of a more superficial region.

My outbreak with Hollingsworth, though never definitely known to our associates, had really an effect upon the moral atmosphere of the Community. It was incidental to the closeness of relationship into which we had brought ourselves, that an unfriendly state of feeling could not occur between any two members, without the whole society being more or less commoted and made uncomfortable thereby. This species of nervous sympathy (though a pretty characteristic enough, sentimentally considered, and apparently betokening an actual bond of love among us) was yet found rather inconvenient in its practical operation; mortal tempers being so infirm and variable as they are. If one of us happened to give his neighbor a box on the ear, the tingle was immediately felt on the same side of everybody's head. Thus, even on the supposition that we were far less quarrelsome than the rest of the world, a great deal of time was necessarily wasted in rubbing our ears.

Musing on all these matters, I felt an inexpressible longing for at least a temporary novelty. I thought of going across the Rocky Mountains, or to Europe, or up the Nile; of offering myself a volunteer on the Exploring Expedition; of taking a ramble of years, no matter in what direction, and coming back on the other side of the world. Then, should the colonists of Blithedale have established their enterprise on a permanent basis, I might fling aside my pilgrim staff and dusty shoon, and rest as peacefully here as elsewhere. Or, in case Hollingsworth should occupy the ground with his School of Reform, as he now purposed, I might plead earthly guilt enough, by that time, to give me what I was inclined to think the only trustworthy hold on his affections. Meanwhile, before deciding on any ultimate plan, I determined to remove myself to a little distance, and take an exterior view of what we had all been about.

In truth, it was dizzy work, amid such fermentation of opinions as was going on in the general brain of the Community. It was a kind of Bedlam, for the time being; although out of the very thoughts that were wildest and most destructive might grow a wisdom holy, calm, and pure, and that should incarnate itself with the substance of a noble and happy life. But, as matters now were, I felt myself (and, having a decided tendency towards the actual, I never liked to feel it) getting quite out of my reckoning, with regard to the existing state of the world. I was beginning to lose the sense of what kind of a world it was, among innumerable schemes of what it might or ought to be. It was impossible, situated as we were, not to imbibe the idea that everything in nature and human existence was fluid, or fast becoming so; that the crust of the earth in many places was broken, and its whole surface portentously upheaving; that it was a day of crisis, and that we ourselves were in the critical vortex. Our great globe floated in the atmosphere of infinite space like an unsubstantial bubble. No sagacious man will long retain his sagacity, if he live exclusively among reformers and progressive people, without periodically returning into the settled system of things, to correct himself by a new observation from that old standpoint.

It was now time for me, therefore, to go and hold a little talk with the conservatives, the writers of the North American Review, the merchants, the politicians, the Cambridge men, and all those respectable old blockheads who still, in this intangibility and mistiness of affairs, kept a death-grip on one or two ideas which had not come into vogue since yesterday morning.

The brethren took leave of me with cordial kindness; and as for the sisterhood, I had serious thoughts of kissing them all round, but forbore to do so, because, in all such general salutations, the penance is fully equal to the pleasure. So I kissed none of them; and nobody, to say the truth, seemed to expect it.

"Do you wish me," I said to Zenobia, "to announce in town and at the watering-places, your purpose to deliver a course of lectures on the rights of women?"

"Women possess no rights," said Zenobia, with a half-melancholy smile; "or, at all events, only little girls and grandmothers would have the force to exercise them."

She gave me her hand freely and kindly, and looked at me, I thought, with a pitying expression in her eyes; nor was there any settled light of joy in them on her own behalf, but a troubled and passionate flame, flickering and fitful.

"I regret, on the whole, that you are leaving us," she said; "and all the more, since I feel that this phase of our life is finished, and can never be lived over again. Do you know, Mr. Coverdale, that I have been several times on the point of making you my confidant, for lack of a better and wiser one? But you are too young to be my father confessor; and you would not thank me for treating you like one of those good little handmaidens who share the bosom secrets of a tragedy-queen."

"I would, at least, be loyal and faithful," answered I; "and would counsel you with an honest purpose, if not wisely."

"Yes," said Zenobia, "you would be only too wise, too honest. Honesty and wisdom are such a delightful pastime, at another person's expense!"

"Ah, Zenobia," I exclaimed, "if you would but let me speak!"

"By no means," she replied, "especially when you have just resumed the whole series of social conventionalisms, together with that straight-bodied coat. I would as lief open my heart to a lawyer or a clergyman! No, no, Mr. Coverdale; if I choose a counsellor, in the present aspect of my affairs, it must be either an angel or a madman; and I rather apprehend that the latter would be likeliest of the two to speak the fitting word. It needs a wild steersman when we voyage through chaos! The anchor is up—farewell!"

Priscilla, as soon as dinner was over, had betaken herself into a corner, and set to work on a little purse. As I approached her, she let her eyes rest on me with a calm, serious look; for, with all her delicacy of nerves, there was a singular self-possession in Priscilla, and her sensibilities seemed to lie sheltered from ordinary commotion, like the water in a deep well.

"Will you give me that purse, Priscilla," said I, "as a parting keepsake?"

"Yes," she answered, "if you will wait till it is finished."

"I must not wait, even for that," I replied. "Shall I find you here, on my return?"

"I never wish to go away," said she.

"I have sometimes thought," observed I, smiling, "that you, Priscilla, are a little prophetess; or, at least, that you have spiritual intimations respecting matters which are dark to us grosser people. If that be the case, I should like to ask you what is about to happen; for I am tormented with a strong foreboding that, were I to return even so soon as to-morrow morning, I should find everything changed. Have you any impressions of this nature?"

"Ah, no," said Priscilla, looking at me apprehensively. "If any such misfortune is coming, the shadow has not reached me yet. Heaven forbid! I should be glad if there might never be any change, but one summer follow another, and all just like this."

"No summer ever came back, and no two summers ever were alike," said I, with a degree of Orphic wisdom that astonished myself. "Times change, and people change; and if our hearts do not change as readily, so much the worse for us. Good-by, Priscilla!"

I gave her hand a pressure, which, I think, she neither resisted nor returned. Priscilla's heart was deep, but of small compass; it had room but for a very few dearest ones, among whom she never reckoned me.

On the door-step I met Hollingsworth. I had a momentary impulse to hold out my hand, or at least to give a parting nod, but resisted both. When a real and strong affection has come to an end, it is not well to mock the sacred past with any show of those commonplace civilities that belong to ordinary intercourse. Being dead henceforth to him, and he to me, there could be no propriety in our chilling one another with the touch of two corpse-like hands, or playing at looks of courtesy with eyes that were impenetrable beneath the glaze and the film. We passed, therefore, as if mutually invisible.

I can nowise explain what sort of whim, prank, or perversity it was, that, after all these leave-takings, induced me to go to the pig-sty, and take leave of the swine! There they lay, buried as deeply among the straw as they could burrow, four huge black grunters, the very symbols of slothful ease and sensual comfort. They were asleep, drawing short and heavy breaths, which heaved their big sides up and down. Unclosing their eyes, however, at my approach, they looked dimly forth at the outer world, and simultaneously uttered a gentle grunt; not putting themselves to the trouble of an additional breath for that particular purpose, but grunting with their ordinary inhalation. They were involved, and almost stifled and buried alive, in their own corporeal substance. The very unreadiness and oppression wherewith these greasy citizens gained breath enough to keep their life-machinery in sluggish movement, appeared to make them only the more sensible of the ponderous and fat satisfaction of their existence. Peeping at me, an instant, out of their small, red, hardly perceptible eyes, they dropt asleep again; yet not so far asleep but that their unctuous bliss was still present to them, betwixt dream and reality.

"You must come back in season to eat part of a spare-rib," said Silas Foster, giving my hand a mighty squeeze. "I shall have these fat fellows hanging up by the heels, heads downward, pretty soon, I tell you!"

"O, cruel Silas, what a horrible idea!" cried I. "All the rest of us, men, women, and live-stock, save only these four porkers, are bedevilled with one grief or another; they alone are happy,—and you mean to cut their throats and eat them! It would be more for the general comfort to let them eat us; and bitter and sour morsels we should be!"

XVII.

THE HOTEL

ARRIVING in town (where my bachelor-rooms, long before this time, had received some other occupant), I established myself, for a day or two, in a certain respectable hotel. It was situated somewhat aloof from my former track in life; my present mood inclining me to avoid most of my old companions, from whom I was now sundered by other interests, and who would have been likely enough to amuse themselves at the expense of the amateur working-man. The hotel-keeper put me into a back-room of the third story of his spacious establishment. The day was lowering, with occasional gusts of rain, and an ugly-tempered east wind, which seemed to come right off the chill and melancholy sea, hardly mitigated by sweeping over the roofs, and amalgamating itself with the dusky element of city smoke. All the effeminacy of past days had returned upon me at once. Summer as it still was, I ordered a coal-fire in the rusty grate, and was glad to find myself growing a little too warm with an artificial temperature.

My sensations were those of a traveller, long sojourning in remote regions, and at length sitting down again amid customs once familiar. There was a newness and an oldness oddly combining themselves into one impression. It made me acutely sensible how strange a piece of mosaic-work had lately been wrought into my life. True, if you look at it in one way, it had been only a summer in the country. But, considered in a profounder relation, it was part of another age, a different state of society, a segment of an existence peculiar in its aims and methods, a leaf of some mysterious volume interpolated into the current history which time was writing off. At one moment, the very circumstances now surrounding me — my coal-fire, and the dingy room in the bustling hotel — appeared far off and intangible; the next instant Blithedale looked vague, as if it were at a distance both in time and space, and so shadowy that a question might be raised whether the whole affair had been anything more than the thoughts of a speculative man. I had never before experienced a mood that so robbed the actual world of its solidity. It nevertheless involved a charm, on which — a devoted epicure of my own emotions — I resolved to pause, and enjoy the moral sillabub until quite dissolved away.

Whatever had been my taste for solitude and natural scenery, yet the thick, foggy, stifled element of cities, the entangled life of many men together, sordid as it was, and empty of the beautiful, took quite as strenuous a hold upon my mind. I felt as if there could never be enough of it. Each characteristic sound was too suggestive to be passed over unnoticed. Beneath and around me, I heard the stir of the hotel; the loud voices of guests, landlord, or bar-keeper; steps echoing on the stair-case; the ringing of a bell, announcing arrivals or departures; the porter lumbering past my door with baggage, which he thumped down upon the floors of neighboring chambers; the lighter feet of chambermaids scudding along the passages; — it is ridiculous to think what an interest they had for me! From the street came the tumult of the pavements, pervading the whole house with a continual uproar, so broad and deep that only

an unaccustomed ear would dwell upon it. A company of the city sol-
diery, with a full military band, marched in front of the hotel, invisible to
me, but stirringly audible both by its foot-tramp and the clangor of its
instruments. Once or twice all the city bells jangled together, announcing a fire, which brought out the engine-men and their machines, like
an army with its artillery rushing to battle. Hour by hour the clocks in
many steeples responded one to another. In some public hall, not a great
way off, there seemed to be an exhibition of a mechanical diorama; for,
three times during the day, occurred a repetition of obstreperous music,
winding up with the rattle of imitative cannon and musketry, and a huge
final explosion. Then ensued the applause of the spectators, with clap of
hands, and thump of sticks, and the energetic pounding of their heels.
All this was just as valuable, in its way, as the sighing of the breeze among
the birch-trees that overshadowed Eliot's pulpit.

Yet I felt a hesitation about plunging into this muddy tide of human
activity and pastime. It suited me better, for the present, to linger on the
brink, or hover in the air above it. So I spent the first day and the greater
part of the second in the laziest manner possible, in a rocking-chair, inhal-
ing the fragrance of a series of cigars, with my legs and slippered feet hor-
izontally disposed, and in my hand a novel purchased of a railroad bib-
liopolist. The gradual waste of my cigar accomplished itself with an easy
and gentle expenditure of breath. My book was of the dullest, yet had a
sort of sluggish flow, like that of a stream in which your boat is as often
aground as afloat. Had there been a more impetuous rush, a more absorb-
ing passion of the narrative, I should the sooner have struggled out of its
uneasy current, and have given myself up to the swell and subsidence of
my thoughts. But, as it was, the torpid life of the book served as an unob-
trusive accompaniment to the life within me and about me. At intervals,
however, when its effect grew a little too soporific,—not for my patience,
but for the possibility of keeping my eyes open,—I bestirred myself,
started from the rocking-chair, and looked out of the window.

A gray sky; the weathercock of a steeple, that rose beyond the opposite range of buildings, pointing from the eastward; a sprinkle of small,
spiteful-looking raindrops on the window-pane. In that ebb-tide of my
energies, had I thought of venturing abroad, these tokens would have
checked the abortive purpose.

After several such visits to the window, I found myself getting pretty well
acquainted with that little portion of the backside of the universe which it
presented to my view. Over against the hotel and its adjacent houses, at
the distance of forty or fifty yards, was the rear of a range of buildings,
which appeared to be spacious, modern, and calculated for fashionable
residences. The interval between was apportioned into grass-plots, and
here and there an apology for a garden, pertaining severally to these

dwellings. There were apple-trees, and pear and peach trees, too, the fruit on which looked singularly large, luxuriant and abundant, as well it might, in a situation so warm and sheltered, and where the soil had doubtless been enriched to a more than natural fertility. In two or three places grapevines clambered upon trellises, and bore clusters already purple, and promising the richness of Malta or Madeira in their ripened juice. The blighting winds of our rigid climate could not molest these trees and vines; the sunshine, though descending late into this area, and too early intercepted by the height of the surrounding houses, yet lay tropically there, even when less than temperate in every other region. Dreary as was the day, the scene was illuminated by not a few sparrows and other birds, which spread their wings, and flitted and fluttered, and alighted now here, now there, and busily scratched their food out of the wormy earth. Most of these winged people seemed to have their domicile in a robust and healthy buttonwood-tree. It aspired upward, high above the roof of the houses, and spread a dense head of foliage half across the area.

There was a cat—as there invariably is, in such places—who evidently thought herself entitled to all the privileges of forest-life, in this close heart of city conventionalisms. I watched her creeping along the low, flat roofs of the offices, descending a flight of wooden steps, gliding among the grass, and besieging the buttonwood-tree, with murderous purpose against its feathered citizens. But, after all, they were birds of city breeding, and doubtless knew how to guard themselves against the peculiar perils of their position.

Bewitching to my fancy are all those nooks and crannies, where Nature, like a stray partridge, hides her head among the long-established haunts of men! It is likewise to be remarked, as a general rule, that there is far more of the picturesque, more truth to native and characteristic tendencies, and vastly greater suggestiveness, in the back view of a residence, whether in town or country, than in its front. The latter is always artificial; it is meant for the world's eye, and is therefore a veil and a concealment. Realities keep in the rear, and put forward an advance-guard of show and humbug. The posterior aspect of any old farm-house, behind which a railroad has unexpectedly been opened, is so different from that looking upon the immemorial highway, that the spectator gets new ideas of rural life and individuality in the puff or two of steam-breath which shoots him past the premises. In a city, the distinction between what is offered to the public and what is kept for the family is certainly not less striking.

But, to return to my window, at the back of the hotel. Together with a due contemplation of the fruit-trees, the grape-vines, the buttonwood-tree, the cat, the birds, and many other particulars, I failed not to study the row of fashionable dwellings to which all these appertained. Here, it must be confessed, there was a general sameness. From the upper story to the first floor, they were so much alike, that I could only conceive of the inhabitants as cut out on one identical pattern, like little wooden toy-people of German manufacture. One long, united roof, with its thousands of slates glittering in the rain, extended over the whole. After the distinctness of separate characters to which I had recently been accustomed, it perplexed and annoyed me not to be able to resolve this combination of human interests into well-defined elements. It seemed hardly worth while for more than one of those families to be in existence, since they all had the same glimpse of the sky, all looked into the same area, all received just their equal share of sunshine through the front windows, and all listened to precisely the same noises of the street on which they boarded. Men are so much alike in their nature, that they grow intolerable unless varied by their circumstances.

Just about this time, a waiter entered my room. The truth was, I had rung the bell and ordered a sherry-cobbler.

"Can you tell me," I inquired, "what families reside in any of those houses opposite?"

"The one right opposite is a rather stylish boarding-house," said the waiter. "Two of the gentlemen-boarders keep horses at the stable of our establishment. They do things in very good style, sir, the people that live there."

I might have found out nearly as much for myself, on examining the house a little more closely. In one of the upper chambers I saw a young man in a dressing-gown, standing before the glass and brushing his hair, for a quarter of an hour together. He then spent an equal space of time in the elaborate arrangement of his cravat, and finally made his appearance in a dress-coat, which I suspected to be newly come from the tailor's, and now first put on for a dinner-party. At a window of the next story below, two children, prettily dressed, were looking out. By and by, a middle-aged gentleman came softly behind them, kissed the little girl, and playfully pulled the little boy's ear. It was a papa, no doubt, just come in from his counting-room or office; and anon appeared mamma, stealing as softly behind papa as he had stolen behind the children, and laying her hand on his shoulder, to surprise him. Then followed a kiss between papa and mamma; but a noiseless one, for the children did not turn their heads.

"I bless God for these good folks!" thought I to myself. "I have not seen a prettier bit of nature, in all my summer in the country, than they have shown me here, in a rather stylish boarding-house. I will pay them a little more attention, by and by."

On the first floor, an iron balustrade ran along in front of the tall and spacious windows, evidently belonging to a back drawing-room; and, far into the interior, through the arch of the sliding-doors, I could discern a gleam from the windows of the front apartment. There were no signs of present occupancy in this suite of rooms; the curtains being enveloped in a protective covering, which allowed but a small portion of their crimson material to be seen. But two housemaids were industriously at work; so that there was good prospect that the boarding-house might not long suffer from the absence of its most expensive and profitable guests. Meanwhile, until they should appear, I cast my eyes downward to the lower regions. There, in the dusk that so early settles into such places, I saw the red glow of the kitchen-range. The hot cook, or one of her subordinates, with a ladle in her hand, came to draw a cool breath at the back-door. As soon as she disappeared, an Irish manservant, in a white jacket, crept slyly forth, and threw away the fragments of a china dish, which, unquestionably, he had just broken. Soon afterwards, a lady, showily dressed, with a curling front of what must have been false hair, and reddish-brown, I suppose, in hue,—though my remoteness allowed me only to guess at such particulars,—this respectable mistress of the boarding-house made a momentary transit across the kitchen window, and appeared no more. It was her final, comprehensive glance, in order to make sure that soup, fish, and flesh were in a proper state of readiness, before the serving up of dinner.

There was nothing else worth noticing about the house, unless it be that on the peak of one of the dormer-windows which opened out of the roof sat a dove, looking very dreary and forlorn; insomuch that I wondered why she chose to sit there, in the chilly rain, while her kindred were doubtless nestling in a warm and comfortable dove-cote. All at once, this dove spread her wings, and, launching herself in the air, came flying so straight across the intervening space that I fully expected her to alight directly on my window-sill. In the latter part of her course, however, she swerved aside, flew upward, and vanished, as did, likewise, the slight, fantastic pathos with which I had invested her.

XVIII.

THE BOARDING-HOUSE

THE next day, as soon as I thought of looking again towards the opposite house, there sat the dove again, on the peak of the same dormer-window!

It was by no means an early hour, for, the preceding evening, I had ultimately mustered enterprise enough to visit the theatre, had gone late to bed, and slept beyond all limit, in my remoteness from Silas Foster's awakening horn. Dreams had tormented me, throughout the night. The train of thoughts which, for months past, had worn a track through my mind, and to escape which was one of my chief objects in leaving Blithedale, kept treading remorselessly to and fro in their old footsteps, while slumber left me impotent to regulate them. It was not till I had quitted my three friends that they first began to encroach upon my dreams. In those of the last night, Hollingsworth and Zenobia, standing on either side of my bed, had bent across it to exchange a kiss of passion. Priscilla, beholding this, — for she seemed to be peeping in at the chamber-window, — had melted gradually away, and left only the sadness of her expression in my heart. There it still lingered, after I awoke; one of those unreasonable sadnesses that you know not how to deal with, because it involves nothing for common sense to clutch.

It was a gray and dripping forenoon; gloomy enough in town, and still gloomier in the haunts to which my recollections persisted in transporting me. For, in spite of my efforts to think of something else, I thought how the gusty rain was drifting over the slopes and valleys of our farm; how wet must be the foliage that overshadowed the pulpit-rock; how cheerless, in such a day, my hermitage, — the tree-solitude of my owl-like humors, — in the vine-encircled heart of the tall pine! It was a phase of home-sickness. I had wrenched myself too suddenly out of an accustomed sphere. There was no choice, now, but to bear the pang of whatever heart-strings were snapt asunder, and that illusive torment (like the ache of a limb long ago cut off) by which a past mode of life prolongs itself into the succeeding one. I was full of idle and shapeless regrets. The thought impressed itself upon me that I had left duties unperformed. With the power, perhaps, to act in the place of destiny and avert misfortune from my friends, I had resigned them to their fate. That cold tendency, between instinct and intellect, which made me pry with a speculative interest into people's passions and impulses, appeared to have gone far towards unhumanizing my heart.

But a man cannot always decide for himself whether his own heart is cold or warm. It now impresses me that, if I erred at all in regard to Hollingsworth, Zenobia, and Priscilla, it was through too much sympathy, rather than too little.

To escape the irksomeness of these meditations, I resumed my post at the window. At first sight, there was nothing new to be noticed. The general aspect of affairs was the same as yesterday, except that the more decided inclemency of to-day had driven the sparrows to shelter, and kept the cat within doors; whence, however, she soon emerged, pursued by the cook, and with what looked like the better half of a roast chicken in her mouth. The young man in the dress-coat was invisible; the two children, in the story below, seemed to be romping about the room, under the superintendence of a nursery-maid. The damask curtains of the drawing-room, on the first floor, were now fully displayed, festooned gracefully from top to bottom of the windows, which extended from the ceiling to the carpet. A narrower window, at the left of the drawing-room, gave light to what was probably a small boudoir, within which I caught the faintest imaginable glimpse of a girl's figure, in airy drapery. Her arm was in regular movement, as if she were busy with her German worsted, or some other such pretty and unprofitable handiwork.

While intent upon making out this girlish shape, I became sensible that a figure had appeared at one of the windows of the drawing-room. There was a presentiment in my mind; or perhaps my first glance, imperfect and sidelong as it was, had sufficed to convey subtle information of the truth. At any rate, it was with no positive surprise, but as if I had all along expected the incident, that, directing my eyes thitherward, I beheld—like a full-length picture, in the space between the heavy festoons of the window-curtains—no other than Zenobia! At the same instant, my thoughts made sure of the identity of the figure in the boudoir. It could only be Priscilla.

Zenobia was attired, not in the almost rustic costume which she had heretofore worn, but in a fashionable morning-dress. There was, nevertheless, one familiar point. She had, as usual, a flower in her hair, brilliant and of a rare variety, else it had not been Zenobia. After a brief pause at the window, she turned away, exemplifying, in the few steps that removed her out of sight, that noble and beautiful motion which characterized her as much as any other personal charm. Not one woman in a thousand could move so admirably as Zenobia. Many women can sit gracefully; some can stand gracefully; and a few, perhaps, can assume a series of graceful positions. But natural movement is the result and expression of the whole being, and cannot be well and nobly performed, unless responsive to something in the character. I often used to think that music—light and airy, wild and passionate, or the full harmony of stately marches, in accordance with her varying mood—should have attended Zenobia's footsteps.

I waited for her reappearance. It was one peculiarity, distinguishing Zenobia from most of her sex, that she needed for her moral wellbeing, and never would forego, a large amount of physical exercise. At Blithedale, no inclemency of sky or muddiness of earth had ever impeded her daily walks. Here, in town, she probably preferred to tread the extent of the two drawing-rooms, and measure out the miles by spaces of forty feet, rather than bedraggle her skirts over the sloppy pavements. Accordingly, in about the time requisite to pass through the arch of the sliding-doors to the front window, and to return upon her steps, there she stood again, between the festoons of the crimson curtains. But another personage was now added to the scene. Behind

Zenobia appeared that face which I had first encountered in the wood-path; the man who had passed, side by side with her, in such mysterious familiarity and estrangement, beneath my vine-curtained hermitage in the tall pine-tree. It was Westervelt. And though he was looking closely over her shoulder, it still seemed to me, as on the former occasion, that Zenobia repelled him,—that, perchance, they mutually repelled each other, by some incompatibility of their spheres.

This impression, however, might have been altogether the result of fancy and prejudice in me. The distance was so great as to obliterate any play of feature by which I might otherwise have been made a partaker of their counsels.

There now needed only Hollingsworth and old Moodie to complete the knot of characters, whom a real intricacy of events, greatly assisted by my method of insulating them from other relations, had kept so long upon my mental stage, as actors in a drama. In itself, perhaps, it was no very remarkable event that they should thus come across me, at the moment when I imagined myself free. Zenobia, as I well knew, had retained an establishment in town, and had not unfrequently withdrawn herself from Blithedale during brief intervals, on one of which occasions she had taken Priscilla along with her. Nevertheless, there seemed something fatal in the coincidence that had borne me to this one spot, of all others in a great city, and transfixed me there, and compelled me again to waste my already wearied sympathies on affairs which were none of mine, and persons who cared little for me. It irritated my nerves; it affected me with a kind of heart-sickness. After the effort which it cost me to fling them off,—after consummating my escape, as I thought, from these goblins of flesh and blood, and pausing to revive myself with a breath or two of an atmosphere in which they should have no share,—it was a positive despair, to find the same figures arraying themselves before me, and presenting their old problem in a shape that made it more insoluble than ever.

I began to long for a catastrophe. If the noble temper of Hollingsworth's soul were doomed to be utterly corrupted by the too powerful purpose which had grown out of what was noblest in him; if the rich and generous qualities of Zenobia's womanhood might not save her; if Priscilla must perish by her tenderness and faith, so simple and so devout,—then be it so! Let it all come! As for me, I would look on, as it seemed my part to do, understandingly, if my intellect could fathom the meaning and the moral, and, at all events, reverently and sadly. The curtain fallen, I would pass onward with my poor individual life, which was now attenuated of much of its proper substance, and diffused among many alien interests.

Meanwhile, Zenobia and her companion had retreated from the window. Then followed an interval, during which I directed my eyes towards the figure in the boudoir. Most certainly it was Priscilla, although dressed with a novel and fanciful elegance. The vague perception of it, as viewed so far off, impressed me as if she had suddenly passed out of a chrysalis state and put forth wings. Her hands were not now in motion. She had dropt her work, and sat with her head thrown back, in the same attitude that I had seen several times before, when she seemed to be listening to an imperfectly distinguished sound.

Again the two figures in the drawing-room became visible. They were now a little withdrawn from the window, face to face, and, as I could see by Zenobia's emphatic gestures, were discussing some subject in which she, at least, felt a passionate concern. By and by she broke away, and vanished beyond my ken. Westervelt approached the window, and leaned his forehead against a pane of glass, displaying the sort of smile on his handsome features which, when I before met him, had let me into the secret of his gold-bordered teeth. Every human being, when given over to the devil, is sure to have the wizard mark upon him, in one form or another. I fancied that this smile, with its peculiar revelation, was the devil's signet on the Professor.

This man, as I had soon reason to know, was endowed with a cat-like circumspection; and though precisely the most unspiritual quality in the world, it was almost as effective as spiritual insight in making him acquainted with whatever it suited him to discover. He now proved it, considerably to my discomfiture, by detecting and recognizing me, at my post of observation. Perhaps I ought to have blushed at being caught in such an evident scrutiny of Professor Westervelt and his affairs. Perhaps I did blush. Be that as it might, I retained presence of mind enough not to make my position yet more irksome, by the poltroonery of drawing back.

Westervelt looked into the depths of the drawing-room, and beckoned. Immediately afterwards, Zenobia appeared at the window, with color much heightened, and eyes which, as my conscience whispered me, were shooting bright arrows, barbed with scorn, across the intervening space, directed full at my sensibilities as a gentleman. If the truth must be told, far as her flight-shot was, those arrows hit the mark. She signified her recognition of me by a gesture with her head and hand, comprising at once a salutation and dismissal. The next moment, she administered one of those pitiless rebukes which a woman always has at hand, ready for an offence (and which she so seldom spares, on due occasion), by letting down a white linen curtain between the festoons of the damask ones. It fell like the drop-curtain of a theatre, in the interval between the acts.

Priscilla had disappeared from the boudoir. But the dove still kept her desolate perch on the peak of the attic-window.

XIX.

ZENOBIA'S DRAWING-ROOM

THE remainder of the day, so far as I was concerned, was spent in meditating on these recent incidents. I contrived, and alternately rejected, innumerable methods of accounting for the presence of Zenobia and Priscilla, and the connection of Westervelt with both. It must be owned, too, that I had a keen, revengeful sense of the insult inflicted by Zenobia's scornful recognition, and more particularly by her letting down the curtain; as if such were the proper barrier to be interposed between a character like hers and a perceptive faculty like mine. For, was mine a mere vulgar curiosity? Zenobia should have known me better than to suppose it. She should have been able to appreciate that quality of the intellect and the heart which impelled me (often against my own will, and to the detriment of my own comfort) to live in other lives, and to endeavor—by generous sympathies, by delicate intuitions, by taking note of things too slight for record, and by bringing my human spirit into manifold accordance with the companions whom God assigned me—to learn the secret which was hidden even from themselves.

Of all possible observers, methought a woman like Zenobia and a man like Hollingsworth should have selected me. And, now, when the event has long been past, I retain the same opinion of my fitness for the office. True, I might have condemned them. Had I been judge, as well as witness, my sentence might have been stern as that of destiny itself. But, still, no trait of original nobility of character, no struggle against temptation,—no iron necessity of will, on the one hand, nor extenuating circumstance to be derived from passion and despair, on the other,—no remorse that might coëxist with error, even if powerless to prevent it,—no proud repentance that should claim retribution as a meed,—would go unappreciated. True, again, I might give my full assent to the punishment which was sure to follow. But it would be given mournfully, and with undiminished love. And, after all was finished, I would come, as if to gather up the white ashes of those who had perished at the stake, and to tell the world—the wrong being now atoned for—how much had perished there which it had never yet known how to praise.

I sat in my rocking-chair, too far withdrawn from the window to expose myself to another rebuke like that already inflicted. My eyes still wandered towards the opposite house, but without effecting any new discoveries. Late in the afternoon, the weathercock on the church-spire indicated a change of wind; the sun shone dimly out, as if the golden wine of its beams were mingled half-and-half with water. Nevertheless, they kindled up the whole range of edifices, threw a glow over the windows, glistened on the wet roofs, and, slowly withdrawing upward, perched upon the chimney-tops; thence they took a higher flight, and lingered an instant on the tip of the spire, making it the final point of more cheerful light in the whole sombre scene. The next moment, it was all gone. The twilight fell into the area like a shower of dusky snow; and before it was quite dark, the gong of the hotel summoned me to tea.

When I returned to my chamber, the glow of an astral-lamp was penetrating mistily through the white curtain of Zenobia's drawing-room. The shadow of a passing figure was now and then cast upon this medium, but with too vague an outline for even my adventurous conjectures to read the hieroglyphic that it presented.

All at once, it occurred to me how very absurd was my behavior, in thus tormenting myself with crazy hypotheses as to what was going on within that drawing-room, when it was at my option to be personally present there. My relations with Zenobia, as yet unchanged,—as a familiar friend, and associated in the same life-long enterprise,—gave me the right, and made it no more than kindly courtesy demanded, to call on her. Nothing, except our habitual independence of conventional rules at Blithedale, could have kept me from sooner recognizing this duty. At all events, it should now be performed.

In compliance with this sudden impulse, I soon found myself actually within the house, the rear of which, for two days past, I had been so sedulously watching. A servant took my card, and immediately returning, ushered me up stairs. On the way, I heard a rich, and, as it were, triumphant burst of music from a piano, in which I felt Zenobia's character, although heretofore I had known nothing of her skill upon the instrument. Two or three canary-birds, excited by this gush of sound, sang piercingly, and did their utmost to produce a kindred melody. A bright illumination streamed through the door of the front drawing-room; and I had barely stept across the threshold before Zenobia came forward to meet me, laughing, and with an extended hand.

"Ah, Mr. Coverdale," said·she, still smiling, but, as I thought, with a good deal of scornful anger underneath, "it has gratified me to see the interest which you continue to take in my affairs! I have long recognized you as a sort of transcendental Yankee, with all the native propensity of your countrymen to investigate matters that come within their range, but rendered almost poetical, in your case, by the refined methods which you adopt for its gratification. After all, it was an unjustifiable stroke, on my part,—was it not?—to let down the window-curtain!"

"I cannot call it a very wise one," returned I, with a secret bitterness, which, no doubt, Zenobia appreciated. "It is really impossible to hide anything, in this world, to say nothing of the next. All that we ought to ask, therefore, is, that the witnesses of our conduct, and the speculators on our motives, should be capable of taking the highest view which the circumstances of the case may admit. So much being secured, I, for one, would be most happy in feeling myself followed everywhere by an indefatigable human sympathy."

"We must trust for intelligent sympathy to our guardian angels, if any there be," said Zenobia. "As long as the only spectator of my poor tragedy is a young man at the window of his hotel, I must still claim the liberty to drop the curtain."

While this passed, as Zenobia's hand was extended, I had applied the very slightest touch of my fingers to her own. In spite of an external freedom, her manner made me sensible that we stood upon no real terms of confidence. The thought came sadly across me, how great was the contrast betwixt this interview and our first meeting. Then, in the warm light of the country fireside, Zenobia had greeted me cheerily and hopefully, with a full, sisterly grasp of the hand, conveying as much kindness in it as other women could have evinced by the pressure of both arms around my neck, or by yielding a cheek to the brotherly salute. The difference was as complete as between her appearance at that time,—so simply attired, and with only the one superb flower in her hair,—and now, when her beauty was set off by all that dress and ornament could do for it. And they did much. Not, indeed, that they created or added anything to what Nature had lavishly done for Zenobia. But, those costly robes which she had on, those flaming jewels on her neck, served as lamps to display the personal advantages which required nothing less than such an illumination to be fully seen. Even her characteristic flower, though it seemed to be still there, had undergone a cold and bright transfiguration; it was a flower exquisitely imitated in jeweller's work, and imparting the last touch that transformed Zenobia into a work of art.

"I scarcely feel," I could not forbear saying, "as if we had ever met before. How many years ago it seems since we last sat beneath Eliot's pulpit, with Hollingsworth extended on the fallen leaves, and Priscilla at his feet! Can it be, Zenobia, that you ever really numbered yourself with our little band of earnest, thoughtful, philanthropic laborers?"

"Those ideas have their time and place," she answered, coldly. "But I fancy it must be a very circumscribed mind that can find room for no others."

Her manner bewildered me. Literally, moreover, I was dazzled by the brilliancy of the room. A chandelier hung down in the centre, glowing with I know not how many lights; there were separate lamps, also, on two or three tables, and on marble brackets, adding their white radiance to that of the chandelier. The furniture was exceedingly rich. Fresh from our old farm-house, with its homely board and benches in the dining-room, and a few wicker chairs in the best parlor, it struck me that here was the fulfilment of every fantasy of an imagination revelling in various methods of costly self-indulgence and splendid ease. Pictures, marbles, vases,—in brief, more shapes of luxury than there could be any object in enumerating, except for an auctioneer's advertisement,— and the whole repeated and doubled by the reflection of a great mirror, which showed me Zenobia's proud figure, likewise, and my own. It cost me, I acknowledge, a bitter sense of shame, to perceive in myself a positive effort to bear up against the effect which Zenobia sought to impose on me. I reasoned against her, in my secret mind, and strove so to keep my footing. In the gorgeousness with which she had surrounded herself,—in the redundance of personal ornament, which the largeness of her physical nature and the rich type of her beauty caused to seem so suitable,—I malevolently beheld the true character of the woman, passionate, luxurious, lacking simplicity, not deeply refined, incapable of pure and perfect taste.

But, the next instant, she was too powerful for all my opposing struggles. I saw how fit it was that she should make herself as gorgeous as she pleased, and should do a thousand things that would have been ridiculous in the poor, thin, weakly characters of other women. To this day, however, I hardly know whether I then beheld Zenobia in her truest attitude, or whether that were the truer one in which she had presented herself at Blithedale. In both, there was something like the illusion which a great actress flings around her.

"Have you given up Blithedale forever?" I inquired.

"Why should you think so?" asked she.

"I cannot tell," answered I; "except that it appears all like a dream that we were ever there together."

"It is not so to me," said Zenobia. "I should think it a poor and meagre nature, that is capable of but one set of forms, and must convert all the past into a dream merely because the present happens to be unlike it. Why should we be content with our homely life of a few months past, to the exclusion of all other modes? It was good; but there are other lives as good, or better. Not, you will understand, that I condemn those who give themselves up to it more entirely than I, for myself, should deem it wise to do."

It irritated me, this self-complacent, condescending, qualified approval and criticism of a system to which many individuals—perhaps as highly endowed as our gorgeous Zenobia—had contributed their all of earthly endeavor, and their loftiest aspirations. I determined to make proof if there were any spell that would exorcise her out of the part which she

seemed to be acting. She should be compelled to give me a glimpse of something true; some nature, some passion, no matter whether right or wrong, provided it were real.

"Your allusion to that class of circumscribed characters, who can live only in one mode of life," remarked I, coolly, "reminds me of our poor friend Hollingsworth. Possibly he was in your thoughts when you spoke thus. Poor fellow! It is a pity that, by the fault of a narrow education, he should have so completely immolated himself to that one idea of his; especially as the slightest modicum of common sense would teach him its utter impracticability. Now that I have returned into the world, and can look at his project from a distance, it requires quite all my real regard for this respectable and well-intentioned man, to prevent me laughing at him, — as I find society at large does."

Zenobia's eyes darted lightning; her cheeks flushed; the vividness of her expression was like the effect of a powerful light flaming up suddenly within her. My experiment had fully succeeded. She had shown me the true flesh and blood of her heart, by thus involuntarily resenting my slight, pitying, half-kind, half-scornful mention of the man who was all in all with her. She herself probably felt this; for it was hardly a moment before she tranquillized her uneven breath, and seemed as proud and self-possessed as ever.

"I rather imagine," said she, quietly, "that your appreciation falls short of Mr. Hollingsworth's just claims. Blind enthusiasm, absorption in one idea, I grant, is generally ridiculous, and must be fatal to the respectability of an ordinary man; it requires a very high and powerful character to make it otherwise. But a great man — as, perhaps, you do not know — attains his normal condition only through the inspiration of one great idea. As a friend of Mr. Hollingsworth, and, at the same time, a calm observer, I must tell you that he seems to me such a man. But you are very pardonable for fancying him ridiculous. Doubtless, he is so — to you! There can be no truer test of the noble and heroic, in any individual, than the degree in which he possesses the faculty of distinguishing heroism from absurdity."

I dared make no retort to Zenobia's concluding apothegm. In truth, I admired her fidelity. It gave me a new sense of Hollingsworth's native power, to discover that his influence was no less potent with this beautiful woman, here, in the midst of artificial life, than it had been at the foot of the gray rock, and among the wild birch-trees of the wood-path, when she so passionately pressed his hand against her heart. The great, rude, shaggy, swarthy man! And Zenobia loved him!

"Did you bring Priscilla with you?" I resumed. "Do you know I have sometimes fancied it not quite safe, considering the susceptibility of her temperament, that she should be so constantly within the sphere of a

man like Hollingsworth. Such tender and delicate natures, among your sex, have often, I believe, a very adequate appreciation of the heroic element in men. But then, again, I should suppose them as likely as any other women to make a reciprocal impression. Hollingsworth could hardly give his affections to a person capable of taking an independent stand, but only to one whom he might absorb into himself. He has certainly shown great tenderness for Priscilla."

Zenobia had turned aside. But I caught the reflection of her face in the mirror, and saw that it was very pale, — as pale, in her rich attire, as if a shroud were round her.

"Priscilla is here," said she, her voice a little lower than usual. "Have not you learnt as much from your chamber window? Would you like to see her?"

She made a step or two into the back drawing-room, and called, "Priscilla! Dear Priscilla!"

XX.

THEY VANISH

PRISCILLA immediately answered the summons, and made her appearance through the door of the boudoir.

I had conceived the idea, which I now recognized as a very foolish one, that Zenobia would have taken measures to debar me from an interview with this girl, between whom and herself there was so utter an opposition of their dearest interests, that, on one part or the other, a great grief, if not likewise a great wrong, seemed a matter of necessity. But, as Priscilla was only a leaf floating on the dark current of events, without influencing them by her own choice or plan, — as she probably guessed not whither the stream was bearing her, nor perhaps even felt its inevitable movement, — there could be no peril of her communicating to me any intelligence with regard to Zenobia's purposes.

On perceiving me, she came forward with great quietude of manner; and when I held out my hand, her own moved slightly towards it, as if attracted by a feeble degree of magnetism.

"I am glad to see you, my dear Priscilla," said I, still holding her hand; "but everything that I meet with, now-a-days, makes me wonder whether I am awake. You, especially, have always seemed like a figure in a dream, and now more than ever."

"O there is substance in these fingers of mine," she answered, giving

my hand the faintest possible pressure, and then taking away her own. "Why do you call me a dream? Zenobia is much more like one than I; she is so very, very beautiful! And, I suppose," added Priscilla, as if thinking aloud, "everybody sees it, as I do."

But, for my part, it was Priscilla's beauty, not Zenobia's, of which I was thinking at that moment. She was a person who could be quite obliterated, so far as beauty went, by anything unsuitable in her attire; her charm was not positive and material enough to bear up against a mistaken choice of color, for instance, or fashion. It was safest, in her case, to attempt no art of dress; for it demanded the most perfect taste, or else the happiest accident in the world, to give her precisely the adornment which she needed. She was now dressed in pure white, set off with some kind of a gauzy fabric, which—as I bring up her figure in my memory, with a faint gleam on her shadowy hair, and her dark eyes bent shyly on mine, through all the vanished years—seems to be floating about her like a mist. I wondered what Zenobia meant by evolving so much loveliness out of this poor girl. It was what few women could afford to do; for, as I looked from one to the other, the sheen and splendor of Zenobia's presence took nothing from Priscilla's softer spell, if it might not rather be thought to add to it.

"What do you think of her?" asked Zenobia.

I could not understand the look of melancholy kindness with which Zenobia regarded her. She advanced a step, and beckoning Priscilla near her, kissed her cheek; then, with a slight gesture of repulse, she moved to the other side of the room. I followed.

"She is a wonderful creature," I said. "Ever since she came among us, I have been dimly sensible of just this charm which you have brought out. But it was never absolutely visible till now. She is as lovely as a flower!"

"Well, say so, if you like," answered Zenobia. "You are a poet,—at least, as poets go, now-a-days,—and must be allowed to make an opera-glass of your imagination, when you look at women. I wonder, in such Arcadian freedom of falling in love as we have lately enjoyed, it never occurred to you to fall in love with Priscilla. In society, indeed, a genuine American never dreams of stepping across the inappreciable air-line which separates one class from another. But what was rank to the colonists of Blithedale?"

"There were other reasons," I replied, "why I should have demonstrated myself an ass, had I fallen in love with Priscilla. By the by, has Hollingsworth ever seen her in this dress?"

"Why do you bring up his name at every turn?" asked Zenobia, in an under tone, and with a malign look which wandered from my face to Priscilla's. "You know not what you do! It is dangerous, sir, believe me, to tamper thus with earnest human passions, out of your own mere idleness, and for your sport. I will endure it no longer! Take care that it does not happen again! I warn you!"

"You partly wrong me, if not wholly," I responded. "It is an uncertain sense of some duty to perform, that brings my thoughts, and therefore my words, continually to that one point."

"O, this stale excuse of duty!" said Zenobia, in a whisper so full of scorn that it penetrated me like the hiss of a serpent. "I have often heard it before, from those who sought to interfere with me, and I know precisely what it signifies. Bigotry; self-conceit; an insolent curiosity; a meddlesome temper; a cold-blooded criticism, founded on a shallow interpretation of half-perceptions; a monstrous scepticism in regard to any conscience or any wisdom, except one's own; a most irreverent propensity to thrust Providence aside, and substitute one's self in its awful place;—out of these, and other motives as miserable as these, comes your idea of duty! But, beware, sir! With all your fancied acuteness, you step blindfold into these affairs. For any mischief that may follow your interference, I hold you responsible!"

It was evident that, with but a little further provocation, the lioness would turn to bay; if, indeed, such were not her attitude already. I bowed, and, not very well knowing what else to do, was about to withdraw. But, glancing again towards Priscilla, who had retreated into a corner, there fell upon my heart an intolerable burthen of despondency, the purport of which I could not tell, but only felt it to bear reference to her. I approached her, and held out my hand; a gesture, however, to which she made no response. It was always one of her peculiarities that she seemed to shrink from even the most friendly touch, unless it were Zenobia's or Hollingsworth's. Zenobia, all this while, stood watching us, but with a careless expression, as if it mattered very little what might pass.

"Priscilla," I inquired, lowering my voice, "when do you go back to Blithedale?"

"Whenever they please to take me," said she.

"Did you come away of your own free will?" I asked.

"I am blown about like a leaf," she replied. "I never have any free will."

"Does Hollingsworth know that you are here?" said I.

"He bade me come," answered Priscilla.

She looked at me, I thought, with an air of surprise, as if the idea were incomprehensible that she should have taken this step without his agency.

"What a gripe this man has laid upon her whole being!" muttered I, between my teeth. "Well, as Zenobia so kindly intimates, I have no more business here. I wash my hands of it all. On Hollingsworth's head be the consequences! Priscilla," I added, aloud, "I know not that ever we may meet again. Farewell!"

As I spoke the word, a carriage had rumbled along the street, and stopt before the house. The door-bell rang, and steps were immediately afterwards heard on the staircase. Zenobia had thrown a shawl over her dress.

"Mr. Coverdale," said she, with cool courtesy, "you will perhaps excuse us. We have an engagement, and are going out."

"Whither?" I demanded.

"Is not that a little more than you are entitled to inquire?" said she, with a smile. "At all events, it does not suit me to tell you."

The door of the drawing-room opened, and Westervelt appeared. I observed that he was elaborately dressed, as if for some grand entertainment. My dislike for this man was infinite. At that moment it amounted to nothing less than a creeping of the flesh, as when, feeling about in a dark place, one touches something cold and slimy, and questions what the secret hatefulness may be. And still I could not but acknowledge that, for personal beauty, for polish of manner, for all that externally befits a gentleman, there was hardly another like him. After bowing to Zenobia, and graciously saluting Priscilla in her corner, he recognized me by a slight but courteous inclination.

"Come, Priscilla," said Zenobia; "it is time. Mr. Coverdale, good-evening."

As Priscilla moved slowly forward, I met her in the middle of the drawing-room.

"Priscilla," said I, in the hearing of them all, "do you know whither you are going?"

"I do not know," she answered.

"Is it wise to go, and is it your choice to go?" I asked. "If not, I am your friend, and Hollingsworth's friend. Tell me so, at once."

"Possibly," observed Westervelt, smiling, "Priscilla sees in me an older friend than either Mr. Coverdale or Mr. Hollingsworth. I shall willingly leave the matter at her option."

While thus speaking, he made a gesture of kindly invitation, and Priscilla passed me, with the gliding movement of a sprite, and took his offered arm. He offered the other to Zenobia; but she turned her proud and beautiful face upon him, with a look which—judging from what I caught of it in profile—would undoubtedly have smitten the man dead, had he possessed any heart, or had this glance attained to it. It seemed to rebound, however, from his courteous visage, like an arrow from polished steel. They all three descended the stairs; and when I likewise reached the street-door, the carriage was already rolling away.

XXI.

AN OLD ACQUAINTANCE

THUS excluded from everybody's confidence, and attaining no further, by my most earnest study, than to an uncertain sense of something hidden from me, it would appear reasonable that I should have flung off all these alien perplexities. Obviously, my best course was to betake myself to new scenes. Here I was only an intruder. Elsewhere there might be circumstances in which I could establish a personal interest, and people who would respond, with a portion of their sympathies, for so much as I should bestow of mine.

Nevertheless, there occurred to me one other thing to be done. Remembering old Moodie, and his relationship with Priscilla, I determined to seek an interview, for the purpose of ascertaining whether the knot of affairs was as inextricable on that side as I found it on all others. Being tolerably well acquainted with the old man's haunts, I went, the next day, to the saloon of a certain establishment about which he often lurked. It was a reputable place enough, affording good entertainment in the way of meat, drink, and fumigation; and there, in my young and idle days and nights, when I was neither nice nor wise, I had often amused myself with watching the staid humors and sober jollities of the thirsty souls around me.

At my first entrance, old Moodie was not there. The more patiently to await him, I lighted a cigar, and establishing myself in a corner, took a quiet, and, by sympathy, a boozy kind of pleasure in the customary life that was going forward. The saloon was fitted up with a good deal of taste. There were pictures on the walls, and among them an oil-painting of a beef-steak, with such an admirable show of juicy tenderness, that the beholder sighed to think it merely visionary, and incapable of ever being put upon a gridiron. Another work of high art was the lifelike representation of a noble sirloin; another, the hindquarters of a deer, retaining the hoofs and tawny fur; another, the head and shoulders of a salmon; and, still more exquisitely finished, a brace of canvas-back ducks, in which the mottled feathers were depicted with the accuracy of a daguerreotype. Some very hungry painter, I suppose, had wrought these subjects of still life, heightening his imagination with his appetite, and earning, it is to be hoped, the privilege of a daily dinner off whichever of his pictorial viands he liked best. Then, there was a fine old cheese, in which you could almost discern the mites; and some sardines, on a small plate, very richly done, and looking as if oozy with the oil in which they had been smothered. All these things were so perfectly imitated, that you seemed to have the genuine article before you, and yet with an indescribable ideal charm; it took away the grossness from what was fleshiest and fattest, and thus helped the life of man, even in its earthliest relations, to appear rich and noble, as well as warm, cheerful, and substantial. There were pictures, too, of gallant revellers,—those of the old time,—Flemish, apparently,—with doublets and slashed sleeves,—drinking their wine out of fantastic long-stemmed glasses; quaffing joyously, quaffing forever, with inaudible laughter and song, while the Champagne bubbled immortally against their mustaches, or the purple tide of Burgundy ran inexhaustibly down their throats.

But, in an obscure corner of the saloon, there was a little picture— excellently done, moreover, of a ragged, bloated, New England toper, stretched out on a bench, in the heavy, apoplectic sleep of drunkenness. The death-in-life was too well portrayed. You smelt the fumy liquor that had brought on this syncope. Your only comfort lay in the forced reflection, that, real as he looked, the poor caitiff was but imaginary,—a bit of painted canvas, whom no delirium tremens, nor so much as a retributive headache, awaited, on the morrow.

By this time, it being past eleven o'clock, the two barkeepers of the saloon were in pretty constant activity. One of these young men had a rare faculty in the concoction of gin-cocktails. It was a spectacle to behold, how, with a tumbler in each hand, he tossed the contents from one to the other. Never conveying it awry, nor spilling the least drop, he compelled the frothy liquor, as it seemed to me, to spout forth from one glass and descend into the other, in a great parabolic curve, as well defined and calculable as a planet's orbit. He had a good forehead, with a particularly large development just above the eyebrows; fine intellectual gifts, no doubt, which he had educated to this profitable end; being famous for nothing but gin-cocktails, and commanding a fair salary by his one accomplishment. These cocktails, and other artificial combinations of liquor (of which there were at least a score, though mostly, I suspect, fantastic in their differences), were much in favor with the younger class of customers, who, at furthest, had only reached the second stage of potatory life. The stanch, old soakers, on the other hand,—men who, if put on tap, would have yielded a red alcoholic liquor by way of blood,— usually confined themselves to plain brandy-and-water, gin, or West India rum; and, oftentimes, they prefaced their dram with some medicinal remark as to the wholesomeness and stomachic qualities of that particular drink. Two or three appeared to have bottles of their own behind the counter; and, winking one red eye to the barkeeper, he forthwith produced these choicest and peculiar cordials, which it was a matter of great interest and favor, among their acquaintances, to obtain a sip of.

Agreeably to the Yankee habit, under whatever circumstances, the deportment of all these good fellows, old or young, was decorous and thoroughly correct. They grew only the more sober in their cups; there was no confused babble nor boisterous laughter. They sucked in the joyous fire of the decanters, and kept it smouldering in their inmost recesses, with a bliss known only to the heart which it warmed and comforted. Their eyes twinkled a little, to be sure; they hemmed vigorously after each glass, and laid a hand upon the pit of the stomach, as if the pleasant titillation there was what constituted the tangible part of their enjoyment. In that spot, unquestionably, and not in the brain, was the acme of the whole affair. But the true purpose of their drinking—and one that will induce men to drink, or do something equivalent, as long as this weary world shall endure—was the renewed youth and vigor, the brisk, cheerful sense of things present and to come, with which, for about a quarter of an hour, the dram permeated their systems. And when such quarters of an hour can be obtained in some mode less baneful to the great sum of a man's life,—but, nevertheless, with a little spice of impropriety, to give it a wild flavor,—we temperance people may ring out our bells for victory!

The prettiest object in the saloon was a tiny fountain, which threw up its feathery jet through the counter, and sparkled down again into an oval basin, or lakelet, containing several gold-fishes. There was a bed of bright sand at the bottom, strewn with coral and rock-work; and the fishes went gleaming about, now turning up the sheen of a golden side, and now vanishing into the shadows of the water, like the fanciful thoughts that coquet with a poet in his dream. Never before, I imagine, did a company of water-drinkers remain so entirely uncontaminated by the bad example around them; nor could I help wondering that it had not occurred to any freakish inebriate to empty a glass of liquor into their lakelet. What a delightful idea! Who would not be a fish, if he could inhale jollity with the essential element of his existence!

I had begun to despair of meeting old Moodie, when, all at once, I recognized his hand and arm protruding from behind a screen that was set up for the accommodation of bashful topers. As a matter of course, he had one of Priscilla's little purses, and was quietly insinuating it under the notice of a person who stood near. This was always old Moodie's way. You hardly ever saw him advancing towards you, but became aware of his proximity without being able to guess how he had come thither. He glided about like a spirit, assuming visibility close to your elbow, offering his petty trifles of merchandise, remaining long enough for you to purchase, if so disposed, and then taking himself off, between two breaths, while you happened to be thinking of something else.

By a sort of sympathetic impulse that often controlled me in those more impressible days of my life, I was induced to approach this old man in a mode as undemonstrative as his own. Thus, when, according to his custom, he was probably just about to vanish, he found me at his elbow.

"Ah!" said he, with more emphasis than was usual with him. "It is Mr. Coverdale!"

"Yes, Mr. Moodie, your old acquaintance," answered I. "It is some time now since we ate our luncheon together at Blithedale, and a good deal longer since our little talk together at the street corner."

"That was a good while ago," said the old man.

And he seemed inclined to say not a word more. His existence looked so colorless and torpid,—so very faintly shadowed on the canvas of reality,—that I was half afraid lest he should altogether disappear, even while my eyes were fixed full upon his figure. He was certainly the wretchedest old ghost in the world, with his crazy hat, the dingy handkerchief about his throat, his suit of threadbare gray, and especially that patch over his right eye, behind which he always seemed to be hiding himself. There was one method, however, of bringing him out into somewhat stronger relief. A glass of brandy would effect it. Perhaps the gentler influence of a bottle of claret might do the same. Nor could I think it a matter for the recording angel to write down against me, if—with my painful consciousness of the frost in this old man's blood, and the positive ice that had congealed about his heart— I should thaw him out, were it only for an hour, with the summer warmth of a little wine. What else could possibly be done for him? How else could he be imbued with energy enough to hope for a happier state hereafter? How else be inspired to say his prayers? For there are states of our spiritual system when the throb of the soul's life is too faint and weak to render us capable of religious aspiration.

"Mr. Moodie," said I, "shall we lunch together? And would you like to drink a glass of wine?"

His one eye gleamed. He bowed; and it impressed me that he grew to be more of a man at once, either in anticipation of the wine, or as a grateful response to my good fellowship in offering it.

"With pleasure," he replied.

The barkeeper, at my request, showed us into a private room, and soon afterwards set some fried oysters and a bottle of claret on the table; and I saw the old man glance curiously at the label of the bottle, as if to learn the brand.

"It should be good wine," I remarked, "if it have any right to its label."

"You cannot suppose, sir," said Moodie, with a sigh, "that a poor old fellow like me knows any difference in wines."

And yet, in his way of handling the glass, in his preliminary snuff at the aroma, in his first cautious sip of the wine, and the gustatory skill with which he gave his palate the full advantage of it, it was impossible not to recognize the connoisseur.

"I fancy, Mr. Moodie," said I, "you are a much better judge of wines than I have yet learned to be. Tell me fairly,—did you never drink it where the grape grows?"

"How should that have been, Mr. Coverdale?" answered old Moodie, shyly; but then he took courage, as it were, and uttered a feeble little laugh. "The flavor of this wine," added he, "and its perfume, still more than its taste, makes me remember that I was once a young man."

"I wish, Mr. Moodie," suggested I, — not that I greatly cared about it, however, but was only anxious to draw him into some talk about Priscilla and Zenobia, — "I wish, while we sit over our wine, you would favor me with a few of those youthful reminiscences."

"Ah," said he, shaking his head, "they might interest you more than you suppose. But I had better be silent, Mr. Coverdale. If this good wine, — though claret, I suppose, is not apt to play such a trick, — but if it should make my tongue run too freely, I could never look you in the face again."

"You never did look me in the face, Mr. Moodie," I replied, "until this very moment."

"Ah!" sighed old Moodie.

It was wonderful, however, what an effect the mild grape-juice wrought upon him. It was not in the wine, but in the associations which it seemed to bring up. Instead of the mean, slouching, furtive, painfully depressed air of an old city vagabond, more like a gray kennel-rat than any other living thing, he began to take the aspect of a decayed gentleman. Even his garments — especially after I had myself quaffed a glass or two — looked less shabby than when we first sat down. There was, by and by, a certain exuberance and elaborateness of gesture and manner, oddly in contrast with all that I had hitherto seen of him. Anon, with hardly any impulse from me, old Moodie began to talk. His communications referred exclusively to a long past and more fortunate period of his life, with only a few unavoidable allusions to the circumstances that had reduced him to his present state. But, having once got the clue, my subsequent researches acquainted me with the main facts of the following narrative; although, in writing it out, my pen has perhaps allowed itself a trifle of romantic and legendary license, worthier of a small poet than of a grave biographer.

XXII.

FAUNTLEROY

FIVE-AND-TWENTY years ago, at the epoch of this story, there dwelt in one of the Middle States a man whom we shall call Fauntleroy; a man of wealth, and magnificent tastes, and prodigal expenditure. His home might almost be styled a palace; his habits, in the ordinary sense, princely. His whole being seemed to have crystallized itself into an external splendor, wherewith he glittered in the eyes of the world, and had no other life than upon this gaudy surface. He had married a lovely woman, whose nature was deeper than his own. But his affection for her, though it showed largely, was superficial, like all his other manifestations and developments; he did not so truly keep this noble creature in his heart, as wear her beauty for the most brilliant ornament of his outward state. And there was born to him a child, a beautiful daughter, whom he took from the beneficent hand of God with no just sense of her immortal value, but as a man already rich in gems would receive another jewel. If he loved her, it was because she shone.

After Fauntleroy had thus spent a few empty years, coruscating continually an unnatural light, the source of it—which was merely his gold—began to grow more shallow, and finally became exhausted. He saw himself in imminent peril of losing all that had heretofore distinguished him; and, conscious of no innate worth to fall back upon, he recoiled from this calamity, with the instinct of a soul shrinking from annihilation. To avoid it—wretched man!—or, rather to defer it, if but for a month, a day, or only to procure himself the life of a few breaths more amid the false glitter which was now less his own than ever,—he made himself guilty of a crime. It was just the sort of crime, growing out of its artificial state, which society (unless it should change its entire constitution for this man's unworthy sake) neither could nor ought to pardon. More safely might it pardon murder. Fauntleroy's guilt was discovered. He fled; his wife perished, by the necessity of her innate nobleness, in its alliance with a being so ignoble; and betwixt her mother's death and her father's ignominy, his daughter was left worse than orphaned.

There was no pursuit after Fauntleroy. His family connections, who had great wealth, made such arrangements with those whom he had attempted to wrong as secured him from the retribution that would have overtaken an unfriended criminal. The wreck of his estate was divided among his creditors. His name, in a very brief space, was forgotten by the multitude who had passed it so diligently from mouth to mouth. Seldom, indeed, was it recalled, even by his closest former intimates. Nor could it have been otherwise. The man had laid no real touch on any mortal's heart. Being a mere image, an optical delusion, created by the sunshine of prosperity, it was his law to vanish into the shadow of the first intervening cloud. He seemed to leave no vacancy; a phenomenon which, like many others that attended his brief career, went far to prove the illusiveness of his existence.

Not, however, that the physical substance of Fauntleroy had literally melted into vapor. He had fled northward to the New England metropolis, and had taken up his abode, under another name, in a squalid street or court of the older portion of the city. There he dwelt among poverty-stricken wretches, sinners, and forlorn good people, Irish, and whomsoever else were neediest. Many families were clustered in each house together, above stairs and below, in the little peaked garrets, and even in the dusky cellars. The house where Fauntleroy paid weekly rent for a chamber and a closet had been a stately habitation in its day. An old colonial governor had built it, and lived there, long ago, and held his levees in a great room where now slept twenty Irish bedfellows; and died in Fauntleroy's chamber, which his embroidered and white-wigged ghost still haunted. Tattered hangings, a marble hearth, traversed with many cracks and fissures, a richly-carved oaken mantel-piece, partly hacked away for kindling-stuff, a stuccoed ceiling, defaced with great, unsightly patches of the naked laths,—such was the chamber's aspect, as if, with its splinters and rags of dirty splendor, it were a kind of practical gibe at this poor, ruined man of show.

At first, and at irregular intervals, his relatives allowed Fauntleroy a little pittance to sustain life; not from any love, perhaps, but lest poverty should compel him, by new offences, to add more shame to that with which he had already stained them. But he showed no tendency to further guilt. His character appeared to have been radically changed (as, indeed, from its shallowness, it well might) by his miserable fate; or, it may be, the traits now seen in him were portions of the same character, presenting itself in another phase. Instead of any longer seeking to live in the sight of the world, his impulse was to shrink into the nearest obscurity, and to be unseen of men, were it possible, even while standing before their eyes. He had no pride; it was all trodden in the dust. No ostentation; for how could it survive, when there was nothing left of Fauntleroy, save penury and shame! His very gait demonstrated that he would gladly have faded out of view, and have crept about invisibly, for the sake of sheltering himself from the irksomeness of a human glance. Hardly, it was averred, within the memory of those who knew him now, had he the hardihood to show his full front to the world. He skulked in corners, and crept about in a sort of noon-day twilight, making himself gray and misty, at all hours, with his morbid intolerance of sunshine.

In his torpid despair, however, he had done an act which that condition of the spirit seems to prompt almost as often as prosperity and hope. Fauntleroy was again married. He had taken to wife a forlorn, meek-spirited, feeble young woman, a seamstress, whom he found dwelling with her mother in a contiguous chamber of the old gubernatorial residence. This poor phantom—as the beautiful and noble companion of his former life had done—brought him a daughter. And sometimes, as from one dream into another, Fauntleroy looked forth out of his present grimy environment into that past magnificence, and wondered whether the grandee of yesterday or the pauper of to-day were real. But, in my mind, the one and the other were alike impalpable. In truth, it was Fauntleroy's fatality to behold whatever he touched dissolve. After a few years, his second wife (dim shadow that she had always been) faded finally out of the world, and left Fauntleroy to deal as he might with their pale and nervous child. And, by this time, among his distant relatives—with whom he had grown a weary thought, linked with contagious infamy, and which they were only too willing to get rid of—he was himself supposed to be no more.

The younger child, like his elder one, might be considered as the true offspring of both parents, and as the reflection of their state. She was a tremulous little creature, shrinking involuntarily from all mankind, but in timidity, and no sour repugnance. There was a lack of human substance in her; it seemed as if, were she to stand up in a sunbeam, it would pass right through her figure, and trace out the cracked and dusty window-panes upon the naked floor. But, nevertheless, the poor child had a heart; and from her mother's gentle character she had inherited a profound and still capacity of affection. And so her life was one of love. She bestowed it partly on her father, but in greater part on an idea.

For Fauntleroy, as they sat by their cheerless fireside,—which was no fireside, in truth, but only a rusty stove,—had often talked to the little girl about his former wealth, the noble loveliness of his first wife, and the beautiful child whom she had given him. Instead of the fairy tales which other parents tell, he told Priscilla this. And, out of the loneliness of her sad little existence, Priscilla's love grew, and tended upward, and twined itself perseveringly around this unseen sister; as a grapevine might strive to clamber out of a gloomy hollow among the rocks, and embrace a young tree standing in the sunny warmth above. It was almost like worship, both in its earnestness and its humility; nor was it the less humble,—though the more earnest,—because Priscilla could claim human kindred with the being whom she so devoutly loved. As with worship, too, it gave her soul the refreshment of a purer atmosphere. Save for this singular, this melancholy, and yet beautiful affection, the child could hardly have lived; or, had she lived, with a heart shrunken for lack of any sentiment to fill it, she must have yielded to the barren miseries of her position, and have grown to womanhood characterless and worthless. But now, amid all the sombre coarseness of her father's outward life, and of her own, Priscilla had a higher and imaginative life within. Some faint gleam thereof was often visible upon her face. It was as if, in her spiritual visits to her brilliant sister, a portion of the latter's brightness had permeated our dim Priscilla, and still lingered, shedding a faint illumination through the cheerless chamber, after she came back.

As the child grew up, so pallid and so slender, and with much unaccountable nervousness, and all the weaknesses of neglected infancy still haunting her, the gross and simple neighbors whispered strange things about Priscilla. The big, red, Irish matrons, whose innumerable progeny swarmed out of the adjacent doors, used to mock at the pale, western child. They fancied—or, at least, affirmed it, between jest and earnest—that she was not so solid flesh and blood as other children, but mixed largely with a thinner element. They called her ghost-child, and said that she could indeed vanish when she pleased, but could never, in her densest moments, make herself quite visible. The sun, at mid-day, would shine through her; in the first gray of the twilight, she lost all the distinctness of her outline; and, if you followed the dim thing into a dark corner, behold! she was not there. And it was true that Priscilla had strange ways; strange ways, and stranger words, when she uttered any words at all. Never stirring out of the old governor's dusky house, she sometimes talked of distant places and splendid rooms, as if she had just left them. Hidden things were visible to her (at least, so the people inferred from obscure hints escaping unawares out of her mouth), and silence was audible. And in all the world there was nothing so difficult to be endured, by those who had any dark secret to conceal, as the glance of Priscilla's timid and melancholy eyes.

Her peculiarities were the theme of continual gossip among the other inhabitants of the gubernatorial mansion. The rumor spread thence into a wider circle. Those who knew old Moodie, as he was now called, used often to jeer him, at the very street corners, about his daughter's gift of second sight and prophecy. It was a period when science (though mostly through its empirical professors) was bringing forward, anew, a hoard of facts and imperfect theories, that had partially won credence in elder times, but which modern scepticism had swept away as rubbish. These things were now tossed up again, out of the surging ocean of human thought and experience. The story of Priscilla's preternatural manifestations, therefore, attracted a kind of notice of which it would have been deemed wholly unworthy a few years earlier. One day, a gentleman ascended the creaking staircase, and inquired which was old Moodie's chamber-door. And, several times, he came again. He was a marvellously handsome man,—still youthful, too, and fashionably dressed. Except that Priscilla, in those days, had no beauty, and, in the languor of her existence, had not yet blossomed into womanhood, there would have been rich food for scandal in these visits; for the girl was unquestionably their sole object, although her father was supposed always to be present. But, it must likewise be added, there was something about Priscilla that calumny could not meddle with; and thus far was she privileged, either by the preponderance of what was spiritual, or the thin and watery blood that left her cheek so pallid.

Yet, if the busy tongues of the neighborhood spared Priscilla in one way, they made themselves amends by renewed and wilder babble on another score. They averred that the strange gentleman was a wizard, and that he had taken advantage of Priscilla's lack of earthly substance to subject her to himself, as his familiar spirit, through whose medium he gained cognizance of whatever happened, in regions near or remote. The boundaries of his power were defined by the verge of the pit of Tartarus on the one hand, and the third sphere of the celestial world on the other. Again, they declared their suspicion that the wizard, with all his show of manly beauty, was really an aged and wizened figure, or else that his semblance of a human body was only a necromantic, or perhaps a mechanical contrivance, in which a demon walked about. In proof of it, however, they could merely instance a gold band around his upper teeth, which had once been visible to several old women, when he smiled at them from the top of the governor's staircase. Of course, this was all absurdity, or mostly so. But, after every possible deduction, there remained certain very mysterious points about the stranger's character, as well as the connection that he established with Priscilla. Its nature at that period was even less understood than now, when miracles of this kind have grown so absolutely stale, that I would gladly, if the truth allowed, dismiss the whole matter from my narrative.

We must now glance backward, in quest of the beautiful daughter of Fauntleroy's prosperity. What had become of her? Fauntleroy's only brother, a bachelor, and with no other relative so near, had adopted the forsaken child. She grew up in affluence, with native graces clustering luxuriantly about her. In her triumphant progress towards womanhood, she was adorned with every variety of feminine accomplishment. But she lacked a mother's care. With no adequate control, on any hand (for a man, however stern, however wise, can never sway and guide a female child), her character was left to shape itself. There was good in it, and evil. Passionate, self-willed and imperious, she had a warm and generous nature; showing the richness of the soil, however, chiefly by the weeds that flourished in it, and choked up the herbs of grace. In her girlhood her uncle died. As Fauntleroy was supposed to be likewise dead, and no other heir was known to exist, his wealth devolved on her, although, dying suddenly, the uncle left no will. After his death, there were obscure passages in Zenobia's history. There were whispers of an attachment, and even a secret marriage, with a fascinating and accomplished but unprincipled young man. The incidents and appearances, however, which led to this surmise, soon passed away, and were forgotten.

Nor was her reputation seriously affected by the report. In fact, so great was her native power and influence, and such seemed the careless purity of her nature, that whatever Zenobia did was generally acknowledged as right for her to do. The world never criticized her so harshly as it does most women who transcend its rules. It almost yielded its assent, when it beheld her stepping out of the common path, and asserting the more extensive privileges of her sex, both theoretically and by her practice. The sphere of ordinary womanhood was felt to be narrower than her development required.

A portion of Zenobia's more recent life is told in the foregoing pages. Partly in earnest—and, I imagine, as was her disposition, half in a proud jest, or in a kind of recklessness that had grown upon her, out of some hidden grief,—she had given her countenance, and promised liberal pecuniary aid, to our experiment of a better social state. And Priscilla followed her to Blithedale. The sole bliss of her life had been a dream of this beautiful sister, who had never so much as known of her existence. By this time, too, the poor girl was enthralled in an intolerable bondage, from which she must either free herself or perish. She deemed herself safest near Zenobia, into whose large heart she hoped to nestle.

One evening, months after Priscilla's departure, when Moodie (or shall we call him Fauntleroy?) was sitting alone in the state-chamber of the old governor, there came footsteps up the staircase. There was a pause on the landing-place. A lady's musical yet haughty accents were heard making an inquiry from some denizen of the house, who had thrust a head out of a contiguous chamber. There was then a knock at Moodie's door.

"Come in!" said he.

And Zenobia entered. The details of the interview that followed being unknown to me,—while, notwithstanding, it would be a pity quite to lose the picturesqueness of the situation,—I shall attempt to sketch it, mainly from fancy, although with some general grounds of surmise in regard to the old man's feelings.

She gazed wonderingly at the dismal chamber. Dismal to her, who beheld it only for an instant; and how much more so to him, into whose brain each bare spot on the ceiling, every tatter of the paper-hangings, and all the splintered carvings of the mantel-piece, seen wearily through long years, had worn their several prints! Inexpressibly miserable is this familiarity with objects that have been from the first disgustful.

"I have received a strange message," said Zenobia, after a moment's silence, "requesting, or rather enjoining it upon me, to come hither. Rather from curiosity than any other motive,—and because, though a woman, I have not all the timidity of one,—I have complied. Can it be you, sir, who thus summoned me?"

"It was," answered Moodie.

"And what was your purpose?" she continued. "You require charity, perhaps? In that case, the message might have been more fitly worded.

But you are old and poor, and age and poverty should be allowed their privileges. Tell me, therefore, to what extent you need my aid."

"Put up your purse," said the supposed mendicant, with an inexplicable smile. "Keep it, — keep all your wealth, — until I demand it all, or none! My message had no such end in view. You are beautiful, they tell me; and I desired to look at you."

He took the one lamp that showed the discomfort and sordidness of his abode, and approaching Zenobia, held it up, so as to gain the more perfect view of her, from top to toe. So obscure was the chamber, that you could see the reflection of her diamonds thrown upon the dingy wall, and flickering with the rise and fall of Zenobia's breath. It was the splendor of those jewels on her neck, like lamps that burn before some fair temple, and the jewelled flower in her hair, more than the murky, yellow light, that helped him to see her beauty. But he beheld it, and grew proud at heart; his own figure, in spite of his mean habiliments, assumed an air of state and grandeur.

"It is well," cried old Moodie. "Keep your wealth. You are right worthy of it. Keep it, therefore; but with one condition only."

Zenobia thought the old man beside himself, and was moved with pity.

"Have you none to care for you?" asked she. "No daughter? — no kind-hearted neighbor? — no means of procuring the attendance which you need? Tell me, once again, can I do nothing for you?"

"Nothing," he replied. "I have beheld what I wished. Now leave me. Linger not a moment longer, or I may be tempted to say what would bring a cloud over that queenly brow. Keep all your wealth, but with only this one condition: Be kind — be no less kind than sisters are — to my poor Priscilla!"

And, it may be, after Zenobia withdrew, Fauntleroy paced his gloomy chamber, and communed with himself as follows; — or, at all events, it is the only solution which I can offer of the enigma presented in his character:

"I am unchanged, — the same man as of yore!" said he. "True, my brother's wealth — he dying intestate — is legally my own. I know it; yet, of my own choice, I live a beggar, and go meanly clad, and hide myself behind a forgotten ignominy. Looks this like ostentation? Ah! But in Zenobia I live again! Beholding her, so beautiful, — so fit to be adorned with all imaginable splendor of outward state, — the cursed vanity, which, half a lifetime since, dropt off like tatters of once gaudy apparel from my debased and ruined person, is all renewed for her sake. Were I to reappear, my shame would go with me from darkness into daylight. Zenobia has the splendor, and not the shame. Let the world admire her, and be dazzled by her, the brilliant child of my prosperity! It is Fauntleroy that still shines through her!"

But then, perhaps, another thought occurred to him.

"My poor Priscilla! And am I just to her, in surrendering all to this beautiful Zenobia? Priscilla! I love her best,—I love her only!—but with shame, not pride. So dim, so pallid, so shrinking,—the daughter of my long calamity! Wealth were but a mockery in Priscilla's hands. What is its use, except to fling a golden radiance around those who grasp it? Yet let Zenobia take heed! Priscilla shall have no wrong!"

But, while the man of show thus meditated,—that very evening, so far as I can adjust the dates of these strange incidents,—Priscilla—poor, pallid flower!—was either snatched from Zenobia's hand, or flung wilfully away!

XXIII.

A VILLAGE-HALL

WELL, I betook myself away, and wandered up and down, like an exorcised spirit that had been driven from its old haunts after a mighty struggle. It takes down the solitary pride of man, beyond most other things, to find the impracticability of flinging aside affections that have grown irksome. The bands that were silken once are apt to become iron fetters when we desire to shake them off. Our souls, after all, are not our own. We convey a property in them to those with whom we associate; but to what extent can never be known, until we feel the tug, the agony, of our abortive effort to resume an exclusive sway over ourselves. Thus, in all the weeks of my absence, my thoughts continually revert back, brooding over the by-gone months, and bringing up incidents that seemed hardly to have left a trace of themselves in their passage. I spent painful hours in recalling these trifles, and rendering them more misty and unsubstantial than at first by the quantity of speculative musing thus kneaded in with them. Hollingsworth, Zenobia, Priscilla! These three had absorbed my life into themselves. Together with an inexpressible longing to know their fortunes, there was likewise a morbid resentment of my own pain, and a stubborn reluctance to come again within their sphere.

All that I learned of them, therefore, was comprised in a few brief and pungent squibs, such as the newspapers were then in the habit of bestowing on our socialist enterprise. There was one paragraph, which, if I rightly guessed its purport, bore reference to Zenobia, but was too darkly hinted to convey even thus much of certainty. Hollingsworth, too, with his philanthropic project, afforded the penny-a-liners a theme for some savage and bloody-minded jokes; and, considerably to my surprise, they affected me with as much indignation as if we had still been friends.

Thus passed several weeks; time long enough for my brown and toil-hardened hands to reäccustom themselves to gloves. Old habits, such as were merely external, returned upon me with wonderful promptitude. My superficial talk, too, assumed altogether a worldly tone. Meeting former acquaintances, who showed themselves inclined to ridicule my heroic devotion to the cause of human welfare, I spoke of the recent phase of my life as indeed fair matter for a jest. But I also gave them to understand that it was, at most, only an experiment, on which I had staked no valuable amount of hope or fear. It had enabled me to pass the summer in a novel and agreeable way, had afforded me some grotesque specimens of artificial simplicity, and could not, therefore, so far as I was concerned, be reckoned a failure. In no one instance, however, did I voluntarily speak of my three friends. They dwelt in a profounder region. The more I consider myself as I then was, the more do I recognize how deeply my connection with those three had affected all my being.

As it was already the epoch of annihilated space, I might, in the time I was away from Blithedale, have snatched a glimpse at England, and been back again. But my wanderings were confined within a very limited sphere. I hopped and fluttered, like a bird with a string about its leg, gyrating round a small circumference, and keeping up a restless activity to no purpose. Thus it was still in our familiar Massachusetts,—in one of its white country-villages,—that I must next particularize an incident.

The scene was one of those lyceum-halls, of which almost every village has now its own, dedicated to that sober and pallid, or rather drab-colored, mode of winter-evening entertainment, the lecture. Of late years, this has come strangely into vogue, when the natural tendency of things would seem to be to substitute lettered for oral methods of addressing the public. But, in halls like this, besides the winter course of lectures, there is a rich and varied series of other exhibitions. Hither comes the ventriloquist, with all his mysterious tongues; the thaumaturgist, too, with his miraculous transformations of plates, doves, and rings, his pancakes smoking in your hat, and his cellar of choice liquors represented in one small bottle. Here, also, the itinerant professor instructs separate classes of ladies and gentlemen in physiology, and demonstrates his lessons by the aid of real skeletons, and mannikins in wax, from Paris. Here is to be heard the choir of Ethiopian melodists, and to be seen the diorama of Moscow or Bunker Hill, or the moving panorama of the Chinese wall. Here is displayed the museum of wax figures, illustrating the wide catholicism of earthly renown, by mixing up heroes and statesmen, the pope and the Mormon prophet, kings, queens, murderers, and beautiful ladies; every sort of person, in short, except authors, of whom I never beheld even the most famous done in wax. And here, in this many-purposed hall (unless the selectmen of the village chance to have more than their share of the Puritanism which, however diversified with later patchwork, still gives its prevailing tint to New England character), here the company of strolling players sets up its little stage, and claims patronage for the legitimate drama.

But, on the autumnal evening which I speak of, a number of printed handbills—stuck up in the bar-room, and on the sign-post of the hotel, and on the meeting-house porch, and distributed largely through the village—had promised the inhabitants an interview with that celebrated and hitherto inexplicable phenomenon, the Veiled Lady!

The hall was fitted up with an amphitheatrical descent of seats towards a platform, on which stood a desk, two lights, a stool, and a capacious antique chair. The audience was of a generally decent and respectable character: old farmers, in their Sunday black coats, with shrewd, hard, sun-dried faces, and a cynical humor, oftener than any other expression, in their eyes; pretty girls, in many-colored attire; pretty young men,—the schoolmaster, the lawyer or student at law, the shopkeeper,—all looking rather suburban than rural. In these days, there is absolutely no rusticity, except when the actual labor of the soil leaves its earth-mould on the person. There was likewise a considerable proportion of young and middle-aged women, many of them stern in feature, with marked foreheads, and a very definite line of eyebrow; a type of womanhood in which a bold intellectual development seems to be keeping pace with the progressive delicacy of the physical constitution. Of all these people I took note, at first, according to my custom. But I ceased to do so the moment that my eyes fell on an individual who sat two or three seats below me, immovable, apparently deep in thought, with his back, of course, towards me, and his face turned steadfastly upon the platform.

After sitting a while in contemplation of this person's familiar contour, I was irresistibly moved to step over the intervening benches, lay my hand on his shoulder, put my mouth close to his ear, and address him in a sepulchral, melo-dramatic whisper:

"Hollingsworth! where have you left Zenobia?"

His nerves, however, were proof against my attack. He turned half around, and looked me in the face with great, sad eyes, in which there was neither kindness nor resentment, nor any perceptible surprise.

"Zenobia, when I last saw her," he answered, "was at Blithedale."

He said no more. But there was a great deal of talk going on near me, among a knot of people who might be considered as representing the mysticism, or rather the mystic sensuality, of this singular age. The nature of the exhibition that was about to take place had probably given the turn to their conversation.

I heard, from a pale man in blue spectacles, some stranger stories than ever were written in a romance; told, too, with a simple, unimaginative steadfastness, which was terribly efficacious in compelling the auditor to receive them into the category of established facts. He cited instances of the miraculous power of one human being over the will and passions of another; insomuch that settled grief was but a shadow beneath the influence of a man possessing this potency, and the strong love of years melted away like a vapor. At the bidding of one of these wizards, the maiden, with her lover's kiss still burning on her lips, would turn from him with icy indifference; the newly-made widow would dig up her buried heart out of her young husband's grave before the sods had taken root upon it; a mother, with her babe's milk in her bosom, would thrust away her child. Human character was but soft wax in his hands; and guilt, or virtue, only the forms into which he should see fit to mould it. The religious sentiment was a flame which he could blow up with his breath, or a spark that he could utterly extinguish. It is unutterable, the horror and disgust with which I listened, and saw that, if these things were to be believed, the individual soul was virtually annihilated, and all that is sweet and pure in our present life debased, and that the idea of man's eternal responsibility was made ridiculous, and immortality rendered at once impossible, and not worth acceptance. But I would have perished on the spot, sooner than believe it.

The epoch of rapping spirits, and all the wonders that have followed in their train,—such as tables upset by invisible agencies, bells self-tolled at funerals, and ghostly music performed on jews-harps,—had not yet arrived. Alas, my countrymen, methinks we have fallen on an evil age! If these phenomena have not humbug at the bottom, so much the worse for us. What can they indicate, in a spiritual way, except that the soul of man is descending to a lower point than it has ever before reached while incarnate? We are pursuing a downward course in the eternal march, and thus bring ourselves into the same range with beings whom death, in requital of their gross and evil lives, has degraded below humanity! To hold intercourse with spirits of this order, we must stoop and grovel in some element more vile than earthly dust. These goblins, if they exist at all, are but the shadows of past mortality, outcasts, mere refuse-stuff, adjudged unworthy of the eternal world, and, on the most favorable supposition, dwindling gradually into nothingness. The less we have to say to them the better, lest we share their fate!

The audience now began to be impatient; they signified their desire for the entertainment to commence by thump of sticks and stamp of boot-heels. Nor was it a great while longer before, in response to their call, there appeared a bearded personage in oriental robes, looking like one of the enchanters of the Arabian Nights. He came upon the platform from a side-door, saluted the spectators, not with a salaam, but a bow, took his station at the desk, and first blowing his nose with a white handkerchief, prepared to speak. The environment of the homely vil-lage-hall, and the absence of many ingenious contrivances of stage-effect with which the exhibition had heretofore been set off, seemed to bring the artifice of this character more openly upon the surface. No sooner did I behold the bearded enchanter, than, laying my hand again on Hollingsworth's shoulder, I whispered in his ear,

"Do you know him?"

"I never saw the man before," he muttered, without turning his head.

But I had seen him three times already. Once, on occasion of my first visit to the Veiled Lady; a second time, in the wood-path at Blithedale; and lastly, in Zenobia's drawing-room. It was Westervelt. A quick association of ideas made me shudder from head to foot; and again, like an evil spirit, bringing up reminiscences of a man's sins, I whispered a question in Hollingsworth's ear, —

"What have you done with Priscilla?"

He gave a convulsive start, as if I had thrust a knife into him, writhed himself round on his seat, glared fiercely into my eyes, but answered not a word.

The Professor began his discourse, explanatory of the psychological phenomena, as he termed them, which it was his purpose to exhibit to the spectators. There remains no very distinct impression of it on my memory. It was eloquent, ingenious, plausible, with a delusive show of spirituality, yet really imbued throughout with a cold and dead materi-alism. I shivered, as at a current of chill air issuing out of a sepulchral vault, and bringing the smell of corruption along with it. He spoke of a new era that was dawning upon the world; an era that would link soul to soul, and the present life to what we call futurity, with a closeness that should finally convert both worlds into one great, mutually con-scious brotherhood. He described (in a strange, philosophical guise, with terms of art, as if it were a matter of chemical discovery) the agency by which this mighty result was to be effected; nor would it have surprised me, had he pretended to hold up a portion of his universally pervasive fluid, as he affirmed it to be, in a glass phial.

At the close of his exordium, the Professor beckoned with his hand, — once, twice, thrice, — and a figure came gliding upon the platform, enveloped in a long veil of silvery whiteness. It fell about her like the texture of a summer cloud, with a kind of vagueness, so that the outline of the form beneath it could not be accurately discerned. But the movement of the Veiled Lady was graceful, free and unembarrassed, like that of a person accustomed to be the spectacle of thousands; or, possibly, a blindfold prisoner within the sphere with which this dark earthly magician had surrounded her, she was wholly unconscious of being the central object to all those straining eyes.

Pliant to his gesture (which had even an obsequious courtesy, but at the same time a remarkable decisiveness), the figure placed itself in the great chair. Sitting there, in such visible obscurity, it was perhaps as much like the actual presence of a disembodied spirit as anything that stage trickery could devise. The hushed breathing of the spectators proved how high-wrought were their anticipations of the wonders to be performed through the medium of this incomprehensible creature. I, too, was in breathless suspense, but with a far different presentiment of some strange event at hand.

"You see before you the Veiled Lady," said the bearded Professor, advancing to the verge of the platform. "By the agency of which I have just spoken, she is at this moment in communion with the spiritual world. That silvery veil is, in one sense, an enchantment, having been dipped, as it were, and essentially imbued, through the potency of my art, with the fluid medium of spirits. Slight and ethereal as it seems, the limitations of time and space have no existence within its folds. This hall—these hundreds of faces, encompassing her within so narrow an amphitheatre—are of thinner substance, in her view, than the airiest vapor that the clouds are made of. She beholds the Absolute!"

As preliminary to other and far more wonderful psychological experiments, the exhibitor suggested that some of his auditors should endeavor to make the Veiled Lady sensible of their presence by such methods—provided only no touch were laid upon her person—as they might deem best adapted to that end. Accordingly, several deep-lunged country-fellows, who looked as if they might have blown the apparition away with a breath, ascended the platform. Mutually encouraging one another, they shouted so close to her ear that the veil stirred like a wreath of vanishing mist; they smote upon the floor with bludgeons; they perpetrated so hideous a clamor, that methought it might have reached, at least, a little way into the eternal sphere. Finally, with the assent of the Professor, they laid hold of the great chair, and were startled, apparently, to find it soar upward, as if lighter than the air through which it rose. But the Veiled Lady remained seated and motionless, with a composure that was hardly less than awful, because implying so immeasurable a distance betwixt her and these rude persecutors.

"These efforts are wholly without avail," observed the Professor, who had been looking on with an aspect of serene indifference. "The roar of a battery of cannon would be inaudible to the Veiled Lady. And yet, were I to will it, sitting in this very hall, she could hear the desert wind sweeping over the sands as far off as Arabia; the icebergs grinding one against the other in the polar seas; the rustle of a leaf in an East Indian forest; the lowest whispered breath of the bashfulest maiden in the world, uttering the first confession of her love. Nor does there exist the moral inducement, apart from my own behest, that could persuade her to lift the silvery veil, or arise out of that chair."

Greatly to the Professor's discomposure, however, just as he spoke these words, the Veiled Lady arose. There was a mysterious tremor that shook the magic veil. The spectators, it may be, imagined that she was about to take flight into that invisible sphere, and to the society of those purely spiritual beings with whom they reckoned her so near akin. Hollingsworth, a moment ago, had mounted the platform, and now stood gazing at the figure, with a sad intentness that brought the whole power of his great, stern, yet tender soul into his glance.

"Come," said he, waving his hand towards her. "You are safe!"

She threw off the veil, and stood before that multitude of people pale, tremulous, shrinking, as if only then had she discovered that a thousand eyes were gazing at her. Poor maiden! How strangely had she been betrayed! Blazoned abroad as a wonder of the world, and performing what were adjudged as miracles,—in the faith of many, a seeress and a prophetess; in the harsher judgment of others, a mountebank,—she had kept, as I religiously believe, her virgin reserve and sanctity of soul throughout it all. Within that encircling veil, though an evil hand had flung it over her, there was as deep a seclusion as if this forsaken girl had, all the while, been sitting under the shadow of Eliot's pulpit, in the Blithedale woods, at the feet of him who now summoned her to the shelter of his arms. And the true heart-throb of a woman's affection was too powerful for the jugglery that had hitherto environed her. She uttered a shriek, and fled to Hollingsworth, like one escaping from her deadliest enemy, and was safe forever!

XXIV.

THE MASQUERADERS

TWO nights had passed since the foregoing occurrences, when, in a breezy September forenoon, I set forth from town, on foot, towards Blithedale.

It was the most delightful of all days for a walk, with a dash of invigorating ice-temper in the air, but a coolness that soon gave place to the brisk glow of exercise, while the vigor remained as elastic as before. The atmosphere had a spirit and sparkle in it. Each breath was like a sip of ethereal wine, tempered, as I said, with a crystal lump of ice. I had started on this expedition in an exceedingly sombre mood, as well befitted one who found himself tending towards home, but was conscious that nobody would be quite overjoyed to greet him there. My feet were hardly off the pavement, however, when this morbid sensation began to yield to the lively influences of air and motion. Nor had I gone far, with fields yet green on either side, before my step became as swift and light as if Hollingsworth were waiting to exchange a friendly hand-grip, and Zenobia's and Priscilla's open arms would welcome the wanderer's reappearance. It has happened to me, on other occasions, as well as this, to prove how a state of physical well-being can create a kind of joy, in spite of the profoundest anxiety of mind.

The pathway of that walk still runs along, with sunny freshness, through my memory. I know not why it should be so. But my mental eye can even now discern the September grass, bordering the pleasant roadside with a brighter verdure than while the summer heats were scorching it; the trees, too, mostly green, although here and there a branch or shrub has donned its vesture of crimson and gold a week or two before its fellows. I see the tufted barberry-bushes, with their small clusters of scarlet fruit; the toadstools, likewise, — some spotlessly white, others yellow or red, — mysterious growths, springing suddenly from no root or seed, and growing nobody can tell how or wherefore. In this respect they resembled many of the emotions in my breast. And I still see the little rivulets, chill, clear and bright, that murmured beneath the road, through subterranean rocks, and deepened into mossy pools, where tiny fish were darting to and fro, and within which lurked the hermit-frog. But no, — I never can account for it, that, with a yearning interest to learn the upshot of all my story, and returning to Blithedale for that sole purpose, I should examine these things so like a peaceful-bosomed naturalist. Nor why, amid all my sympathies and fears, there shot, at times, a wild exhilaration through my frame.

Thus I pursued my way along the line of the ancient stone wall that Paul Dudley built, and through white villages, and past orchards of ruddy apples, and fields of ripening maize, and patches of woodland, and all such sweet rural scenery as looks the fairest, a little beyond the suburbs of a town. Hollingsworth, Zenobia, Priscilla! They glided mistily before me, as I walked. Sometimes, in my solitude, I laughed with the bitterness of self-scorn, remembering how unreservedly I had given up my heart and soul to interests that were not mine. What had I ever had to do with them? And why, being now free, should I take this thraldom on me once again? It was both sad and dangerous, I whispered to myself, to be in too close affinity with the passions, the errors, and the misfortunes, of individuals who stood within a circle of their own, into which, if I stept at all, it must be as an intruder, and at a peril that I could not estimate.

Drawing nearer to Blithedale, a sickness of the spirits kept alternating with my flights of causeless buoyancy. I indulged in a hundred odd and extravagant conjectures. Either there was no such place as Blithedale, nor ever had been, nor any brotherhood of thoughtful laborers like what I seemed to recollect there, or else it was all changed during my absence. It had been nothing but dream-work and enchantment. I should seek in vain for the old farm-house, and for the greensward, the potato-fields, the root-crops, and acres of Indian corn, and for all that configuration of the land which I had imagined. It would be another spot, and an utter strangeness.

These vagaries were of the spectral throng so apt to steal out of an unquiet heart. They partly ceased to haunt me, on my arriving at a point whence, through the trees, I began to catch glimpses of the Blithedale farm. That surely was something real. There was hardly a square foot of all those acres on which I had not trodden heavily, on one or another kind of toil. The curse of Adam's posterity—and, curse or blessing be it, it gives substance to the life around us—had first come upon me there. In the sweat of my brow I had there earned bread and eaten it, and so established my claim to be on earth, and my fellowship with all the sons of labor. I could have knelt down, and have laid my breast against that soil. The red clay of which my frame was moulded seemed nearer akin to those crumbling furrows than to any other portion of the world's dust. There was my home, and there might be my grave.

I felt an invincible reluctance, nevertheless, at the idea of presenting myself before my old associates, without first ascertaining the state in which they were. A nameless foreboding weighed upon me. Perhaps, should I know all the circumstances that had occurred, I might find it my wisest course to turn back, unrecognized, unseen, and never look at Blithedale more. Had it been evening, I would have stolen softly to some lighted window of the old farm-house, and peeped darkling in, to see all their well-known faces round the supper-board. Then, were there a vacant seat, I might noiselessly unclose the door, glide in, and take my place among them, without a word. My entrance might be so quiet, my aspect so familiar, that they would forget how long I had been away, and suffer me to melt into the scene, as a wreath of vapor melts into a larger cloud. I dreaded a boisterous greeting. Beholding me at table, Zenobia, as a matter of course, would send me a cup of tea, and Hollingsworth fill my plate from the great dish of pan-dowdy, and Priscilla, in her quiet way, would hand the cream, and others help me to the bread and butter. Being one of them again, the knowledge of what had happened would come to me without a shock. For still, at every turn of my shifting fantasies, the thought stared me in the face that some evil thing had befallen us, or was ready to befall.

Yielding to this ominous impression, I now turned aside into the woods, resolving to spy out the posture of the Community, as craftily as the wild Indian before he makes his onset. I would go wandering about the outskirts of the farm, and, perhaps, catching sight of a solitary acquaintance, would approach him amid the brown shadows of the trees (a kind of medium fit for spirits departed and revisitant, like myself), and entreat him to tell me how all things were.

The first living creature that I met was a partridge which sprung up beneath my feet, and whirred away; the next was a squirrel, who chattered angrily at me from an overhanging bough. I trod along by the dark, sluggish river, and remember pausing on the bank, above one of its blackest and most placid pools—(the very spot, with the barkless stump of a tree aslantwise over the water, is depicting itself to my fancy at this instant),—and wondering how deep it was, and if any over-laden soul had ever flung its weight of mortality in thither, and if it thus escaped the burthen, or only made it heavier. And perhaps the skeleton of the drowned wretch still lay beneath the inscrutable depth, clinging to some sunken log at the bottom with the gripe of its old despair. So slight, however, was the track of these gloomy ideas, that I soon forgot them in the contemplation of a brood of wild ducks, which were floating on the river, and anon took flight, leaving each a bright streak over the black surface. By and by, I came to my hermitage, in the heart of the white-pine tree, and clambering up into it, sat down to rest. The grapes, which I had watched throughout the summer, now dangled around me in abundant clusters of the deepest purple, deliciously sweet to the taste, and, though wild, yet free from that ungentle flavor which distinguishes nearly all our native and uncultivated grapes. Methought a wine might be pressed out of them possessing a passionate zest, and endowed with a new kind of intoxicating quality, attended with such bacchanalian ecstasies as the tamer grapes of Madeira, France, and the Rhine, are inadequate to produce. And I longed to quaff a great goblet of it at that moment!

While devouring the grapes, I looked on all sides out of the peep-holes of my hermitage, and saw the farm-house, the fields, and almost every part of our domain, but not a single human figure in the landscape. Some of the windows of the house were open, but with no more signs of life than in a dead man's unshut eyes. The barn-door was ajar, and swinging in the breeze. The big old dog,—he was a relic of the former dynasty of the farm,—that hardly ever stirred out of the yard, was nowhere to be seen. What, then, had become of all the fraternity and sisterhood? Curious to ascertain this point, I let myself down out of the tree, and going to the edge of the wood, was glad to perceive our herd of cows chewing the cud or grazing not far off. I fancied, by their manner, that two or three of them recognized me (as, indeed, they ought, for I had milked them and been their chamberlain times without number); but, after staring me in the face a little while, they phlegmatically began grazing and chewing their cuds again. Then I grew foolishly angry at so cold a reception, and flung some rotten fragments of an old stump at these unsentimental cows.

Skirting further round the pasture, I heard voices and much laughter proceeding from the interior of the wood. Voices, male and feminine; laughter, not only of fresh young throats, but the bass of grown people, as if solemn organ-pipes should pour out airs of merriment. Not a voice spoke, but I knew it better than my own; not a laugh, but its cadences were familiar. The wood, in this portion of it, seemed as full of jollity as if Comus and his crew were holding their revels in one of its usually lonesome glades. Stealing onward as far as I durst, without hazard of discovery, I saw a concourse of strange figures beneath the overshadowing branches. They appeared, and vanished, and came again, confusedly, with the streaks of sunlight glimmering down upon them.

Among them was an Indian chief, with blanket, feathers and war-paint, and uplifted tomahawk; and near him, looking fit to be his woodland-bride, the goddess Diana, with the crescent on her head, and attended by our big lazy dog, in lack of any fleeter hound. Drawing an arrow from her quiver, she let it fly at a venture, and hit the very tree behind which I happened to be lurking. Another group consisted of a Bavarian broom-girl, a negro of the Jim Crow order, one or two foresters of the middle ages, a Kentucky woodsman in his trimmed hunting-shirt and deerskin leggings, and a Shaker elder, quaint, demure, broad-brimmed, and square-skirted. Shepherds of Arcadia, and allegoric figures from the Faerie Queen, were oddly mixed up with these. Arm in arm, or otherwise huddled together in strange discrepancy, stood grim Puritans, gay Cavaliers, and Revolutionary officers with three-cornered cocked hats, and queues longer than their swords. A bright-complexioned, dark-haired, vivacious little gypsy, with a red shawl over her head, went from one group to another, telling fortunes by palmistry; and Moll Pitcher, the renowned old witch of Lynn, broomstick in hand, showed herself prominently in the midst, as if announcing all these apparitions to be the offspring of her necromantic art. But Silas Foster, who leaned against a tree near by, in his customary blue frock, and smoking a short pipe, did more to disenchant the scene, with his look of shrewd, acrid, Yankee observation, than twenty witches and necromancers could have done in the way of rendering it weird and fantastic.

A little further off, some old-fashioned skinkers and drawers, all with portentously red noses, were spreading a banquet on the leaf-strewn earth; while a horned and long-tailed gentleman (in whom I recognized the fiendish musician erst seen by Tam O'Shanter) tuned his fiddle, and summoned the whole motley rout to a dance, before partaking of the festal cheer. So they joined hands in a circle, whirling round so swiftly, so madly, and so merrily, in time and tune with the Satanic music, that their separate incongruities were blended all together, and they became a kind of entanglement that went nigh to turn one's brain with merely looking at it. Anon they stopt all of a sudden, and staring at one another's figures, set up a roar of laughter; whereat a shower of the September leaves (which, all day long, had been hesitating whether to fall or no) were shaken off by the movement of the air, and came eddying down upon the revellers.

Then, for lack of breath, ensued a silence; at the deepest point of which, tickled by the oddity of surprising my grave associates in this masquerading trim, I could not possibly refrain from a burst of laughter on my own separate account.

"Hush!" I heard the pretty gypsy fortune-teller say. "Who is that laughing?"

"Some profane intruder!" said the goddess Diana. "I shall send an arrow through his heart, or change him into a stag, as I did Actaeon, if he peeps from behind the trees!"

"Me take his scalp!" cried the Indian chief, brandishing his tomahawk, and cutting a great caper in the air.

"I'll root him in the earth with a spell that I have at my tongue's end!" squeaked Moll Pitcher. "And the green moss shall grow all over him, before he gets free again!"

"The voice was Miles Coverdale's," said the fiendish fiddler, with a whisk of his tail and a toss of his horns. "My music has brought him hither. He is always ready to dance to the devil's tune!"

Thus put on the right track, they all recognized the voice at once, and set up a simultaneous shout.

"Miles! Miles! Miles Coverdale, where are you?" they cried. "Zenobia! Queen Zenobia! here is one of your vassals lurking in the wood. Command him to approach, and pay his duty!"

The whole fantastic rabble forthwith streamed off in pursuit of me, so that I was like a mad poet hunted by chimeras. Having fairly the start of them, however, I succeeded in making my escape, and soon left their merriment and riot at a good distance in the rear. Its fainter tones assumed a kind of mournfulness, and were finally lost in the hush and solemnity of the wood. In my haste, I stumbled over a heap of logs and sticks that had been cut for fire-wood, a great while ago, by some former possessor of the soil, and piled up square, in order to be carted or sledded away to the farm-house. But, being forgotten, they had lain there perhaps fifty years, and possibly much longer, until, by the accumulation of moss, and the leaves falling over them and decaying there, from autumn to autumn, a green mound was formed, in which the softened outline of the woodpile was still perceptible. In the fitful mood that then swayed my mind, I found something strangely affecting in this simple circumstance. I imagined the long-dead woodman, and his long-dead wife and children, coming out of their chill graves, and essaying to make a fire with this heap of mossy fuel!

From this spot I strayed onward, quite lost in reverie, and neither knew nor cared whither I was going, until a low, soft, well-remembered voice spoke, at a little distance.

"There is Mr. Coverdale!"

"Miles Coverdale!" said another voice,—and its tones were very stern. "Let him come forward, then!"

"Yes, Mr. Coverdale," cried a woman's voice,—clear and melodious, but, just then, with something unnatural in its chord,—"you are welcome! But you come half an hour too late, and have missed a scene which you would have enjoyed!"

I looked up, and found myself nigh Eliot's pulpit, at the base of which sat Hollingsworth, with Priscilla at his feet, and Zenobia standing before them.

XXV.

THE THREE TOGETHER

HOLLINGSWORTH was in his ordinary working-dress. Priscilla wore a pretty and simple gown, with a kerchief about her neck, and a calash, which she had flung back from her head, leaving it suspended by the strings. But Zenobia (whose part among the maskers, as may be supposed, was no inferior one) appeared in a costume of fanciful magnificence, with her jewelled flower as the central ornament of what resembled a leafy crown, or coronet. She represented the oriental princess by whose name we were accustomed to know her. Her attitude was free and noble; yet, if a queen's, it was not that of a queen triumphant, but dethroned, on trial for her life, or, perchance, condemned, already. The spirit of the conflict seemed, nevertheless, to be alive in her. Her eyes were on fire; her cheeks had each a crimson spot, so exceedingly vivid, and marked with so definite an outline, that I at first doubted whether it were not artificial. In a very brief space, however, this idea was shamed by the paleness that ensued, as the blood sunk suddenly away. Zenobia now looked like marble.

One always feels the fact, in an instant, when he has intruded on those who love, or those who hate, at some acme of their passion that puts them into a sphere of their own, where no other spirit can pretend to stand on equal ground with them. I was confused,—affected even with a species of terror,—and wished myself away. The intentness of their feelings gave them the exclusive property of the soil and atmosphere, and left me no right to be or breathe there.

"Hollingsworth,—Zenobia,—I have just returned to Blithedale," said I, "and had no thought of finding you here. We shall meet again at the house, I will retire."

"This place is free to you," answered Hollingsworth.

"As free as to ourselves," added Zenobia. "This long while past, you have been following up your game, groping for human emotions in the dark corners of the heart. Had you been here a little sooner, you might have seen them dragged into the daylight. I could even wish to have my trial over again, with you standing by to see fair play! Do you know, Mr. Coverdale, I have been on trial for my life?"

She laughed, while speaking thus. But, in truth, as my eyes wandered from one of the group to another, I saw in Hollingsworth all that an artist could desire for the grim portrait of a Puritan magistrate holding inquest of life and death in a case of witchcraft;—in Zenobia, the sorceress herself, not aged, wrinkled and decrepit, but fair enough to tempt Satan with a force reciprocal to his own;—and, in Priscilla, the pale victim, whose soul and body had been wasted by her spells. Had a pile of fagots been heaped against the rock, this hint of impending doom would have completed the suggestive picture.

"It was too hard upon me," continued Zenobia, addressing Hollingsworth, "that judge, jury and accuser, should all be comprehended in one man! I demur, as I think the lawyers say, to the jurisdiction. But let the learned Judge Coverdale seat himself on the top of the rock, and you and me stand at its base, side by side, pleading our cause before him! There might, at least, be two criminals, instead of one."

"You forced this on me," replied Hollingsworth, looking her sternly in the face. "Did I call you hither from among the masqueraders yonder? Do I assume to be your judge? No; except so far as I have an unquestionable right of judgment, in order to settle my own line of behavior towards those with whom the events of life bring me in contact. True, I have already judged you, but not on the world's part,—neither do I pretend to pass a sentence!"

"Ah, this is very good!" said Zenobia, with a smile. "What strange beings you men are, Mr. Coverdale!—is it not so? It is the simplest thing in the world with you to bring a woman before your secret tribunals, and judge and condemn her unheard, and then tell her to go free without a sentence. The misfortune is, that this same secret tribunal chances to be the only judgment-seat that a true woman stands in awe of, and that any verdict short of acquittal is equivalent to a death-sentence!"

The more I looked at them, and the more I heard, the stronger grew my impression that a crisis had just come and gone. On Hollingsworth's brow it had left a stamp like that of irrevocable doom, of which his own will was the instrument. In Zenobia's whole person, beholding her more closely, I saw a riotous agitation; the almost delirious disquietude of a great struggle, at the close of which the vanquished one felt her strength and courage still mighty within her, and longed to renew the contest. My sensations were as if I had come upon a battle-field before the smoke was as yet cleared away.

And what subjects had been discussed here? All, no doubt, that for so many months past had kept my heart and my imagination idly feverish. Zenobia's whole character and history; the true nature of her mysterious connection with Westervelt; her later purposes towards Hollingsworth, and, reciprocally, his in reference to her; and, finally, the degree in which Zenobia had been cognizant of the plot against Priscilla, and what, at last, had been the real object of that scheme. On these points, as before, I was left to my own conjectures. One thing, only, was certain. Zenobia and Hollingsworth were friends no longer. If their heart-strings were ever intertwined, the knot had been adjudged an entanglement, and was now violently broken.

But Zenobia seemed unable to rest content with the matter in the posture which it had assumed.

"Ah! do we part so?" exclaimed she, seeing Hollingsworth about to retire.

"And why not?" said he, with almost rude abruptness. "What is there further to be said between us?"

"Well, perhaps nothing," answered Zenobia, looking him in the face, and smiling. "But we have come, many times before, to this gray rock, and we have talked very softly among the whisperings of the birch-trees. They were pleasant hours! I love to make the latest of them, though not altogether so delightful, loiter away as slowly as may be. And, besides, you have put many queries to me at this, which you design to be our last, interview; and being driven, as I must acknowledge, into a corner, I have responded with reasonable frankness. But, now, with your free consent, I desire the privilege of asking a few questions, in my turn."

"I have no concealments," said Hollingsworth.

"We shall see," answered Zenobia. "I would first inquire whether you have supposed me to be wealthy?"

"On that point," observed Hollingsworth, "I have had the opinion which the world holds."

"And I held it, likewise," said Zenobia. "Had I not, Heaven is my witness, the knowledge should have been as free to you as me. It is only three days since I knew the strange fact that threatens to make me poor; and your own acquaintance with it, I suspect, is of at least as old a date. I fancied myself affluent. You are aware, too, of the disposition which I purposed making of the larger portion of my imaginary opulence; — nay, were it all, I had not hesitated. Let me ask you, further, did I ever propose or intimate any terms of compact, on which depended this — as the world would consider it — so important sacrifice?"

"You certainly spoke of none," said Hollingsworth.

"Nor meant any," she responded. "I was willing to realize your dream, freely, — generously, as some might think, — but, at all events, fully, and heedless though it should prove the ruin of my fortune. If, in your own thoughts, you have imposed any conditions of this expenditure, it is you that must be held responsible for whatever is sordid and unworthy in them. And now, one other question. Do you love this girl?"

"O, Zenobia!" exclaimed Priscilla, shrinking back, as if longing for the rock to topple over and hide her.

"Do you love her?" repeated Zenobia.

"Had you asked me that question a short time since," replied Hollingsworth, after a pause, during which, it seemed to me, even the birch-trees held their whispering breath, "I should have told you — 'No!' My feelings for Priscilla differed little from those of an elder brother, watching tenderly over the gentle sister whom God has given him to protect."

"And what is your answer now?" persisted Zenobia.

"I do love her!" said Hollingsworth, uttering the words with a deep inward breath, instead of speaking them outright. "As well declare it thus as in any other way. I do love her!"

"Now, God be judge between us," cried Zenobia, breaking into sudden passion, "which of us two has most mortally offended him! At least, I am a woman, with every fault, it may be, that a woman ever had, — weak, vain, unprincipled (like most of my sex; for our virtues, when we have any, are merely impulsive and intuitive), passionate, too, and pursuing my foolish and unattainable ends by indirect and cunning, though absurdly chosen means, as an hereditary bond-slave must; false, moreover, to the whole circle of good, in my reckless truth to the little good I saw before me,—but still a woman! A creature whom only a little change of earthly fortune, a little kinder smile of Him who sent me hither, and one true heart to encourage and direct me, might have made all that a woman can be! But how is it with you? Are you a man? No; but a monster! A cold, heartless, self-beginning and self-ending piece of mechanism!"

"With what, then, do you charge me!" asked Hollingsworth, aghast and greatly disturbed by this attack. "Show me one selfish end, in all I ever aimed at, and you may cut it out of my bosom with a knife!"

"It is all self!" answered Zenobia, with still intenser bitterness. "Nothing else; nothing but self, self, self! The fiend, I doubt not, has made his choicest mirth of you, these seven years past, and especially in the mad summer which we have spent together. I see it now! I am awake, disenchanted, disenthralled! Self, self, self! You have embodied yourself in a project. You are a better masquerader than the witches and gypsies yonder; for your disguise is a self-deception. See whither it has brought you! First, you aimed a death-blow, and a treacherous one, at this scheme of a purer and higher life, which so many noble spirits had wrought out. Then, because Coverdale could not be quite your slave, you threw him ruthlessly away. And you took me, too, into your plan, as long as there was hope of my being available, and now fling me aside again, a broken tool! But, foremost and blackest of your sins, you stifled down your inmost consciousness!—you did a deadly wrong to your own heart!—you were ready to sacrifice this girl, whom, if God ever visibly showed a purpose, he put into your charge, and through whom he was striving to redeem you!"

"This is a woman's view," said Hollingsworth, growing deadly pale,—"a woman's, whose whole sphere of action is in the heart, and who can conceive of no higher nor wider one!"

"Be silent!" cried Zenobia, imperiously. "You know neither man nor woman! The utmost that can be said in your behalf,—and because I would not be wholly despicable in my own eyes, but would fain excuse my wasted feelings, nor own it wholly a delusion, therefore I say it,—is, that a great and rich heart has been ruined in your breast. Leave me, now. You have done with me, and I with you. Farewell!"

"Priscilla," said Hollingsworth, "come."

Zenobia smiled; possibly I did so too. Not often, in human life, has a gnawing sense of injury found a sweeter morsel of revenge than was conveyed in the tone with which Hollingsworth spoke those two words. It was the abased and tremulous tone of a man whose faith in himself was shaken, and who sought, at last, to lean on an affection. Yes; the strong man bowed himself, and rested on this poor Priscilla! O! could she have failed him, what a triumph for the lookers-on!

And, at first, I half imagined that she was about to fail him. She rose up, stood shivering like the birch-leaves that trembled over her head, and then slowly tottered, rather than walked, towards Zenobia. Arriving at her feet, she sank down there, in the very same attitude which she had assumed on their first meeting, in the kitchen of the old farm-house. Zenobia remembered it.

"Ah, Priscilla!" said she, shaking her head, "how much is changed since then! You kneel to a dethroned princess. You, the victorious one! But he is waiting for you. Say what you wish, and leave me."

"We are sisters!" gasped Priscilla.

I fancied that I understood the word and action. It meant the offering of herself, and all she had, to be at Zenobia's disposal. But the latter would not take it thus.

"True, we are sisters!" she replied; and, moved by the sweet word, she stooped down and kissed Priscilla; but not lovingly, for a sense of fatal harm received through her seemed to be lurking in Zenobia's heart. "We had one father! You knew it from the first; I, but a little while—else some things that have chanced might have been spared you. But I never wished you harm. You stood between me and an end which I desired. I wanted a clear path. No matter what I meant. It is over now. Do you forgive me?"

"O, Zenobia," sobbed Priscilla, "it is I that feel like the guilty one!"

"No, no, poor little thing!" said Zenobia, with a sort of contempt. "You have been my evil fate; but there never was a babe with less strength or will to do an injury. Poor child! Methinks you have but a melancholy lot before you, sitting all alone in that wide, cheerless heart, where, for aught you know,—and as I, alas! believe,—the fire which you have kindled may soon go out. Ah, the thought makes me shiver for you! What will you do, Priscilla, when you find no spark among the ashes?"

"Die!" she answered.

"That was well said!" responded Zenobia, with an approving smile. "There is all a woman in your little compass, my poor sister. Meanwhile, go with him, and live!"

She waved her away, with a queenly gesture, and turned her own face to the rock. I watched Priscilla, wondering what judgment she would pass between Zenobia and Hollingsworth; how interpret his behavior, so as to reconcile it with true faith both towards her sister and herself; how compel her love for him to keep any terms whatever with her sisterly affection. But, in truth, there was no such difficulty as I imagined. Her engrossing love made it all clear. Hollingsworth could have no fault. That was the one principle at the centre of the universe. And the doubtful guilt or possible integrity of other people, appearances, self-evident facts, the testimony of her own senses,—even Hollingsworth's self-accusation, had he volunteered it,—would have weighed not the value of a mote of thistledown on the other side. So secure was she of his right, that she never thought of comparing it with another's wrong, but left the latter to itself.

Hollingsworth drew her arm within his, and soon disappeared with her among the trees. I cannot imagine how Zenobia knew when they were out of sight; she never glanced again towards them. But, retaining a proud attitude so long as they might have thrown back a retiring look, they were no sooner departed,—utterly departed,—than she began slowly to sink down. It was as if a great, invisible, irresistible weight were pressing her to the earth. Settling upon her knees, she leaned her forehead against the rock, and sobbed convulsively; dry sobs they seemed to be, such as have nothing to do with tears.

XXVI.

ZENOBIA AND COVERDALE

ZENOBIA had entirely forgotten me. She fancied herself alone with her great grief. And had it been only a common pity that I felt for her,—the pity that her proud nature would have repelled, as the one worst wrong which the world yet held in reserve—the sacredness and awfulness of the crisis might have impelled me to steal away silently, so that not a dry leaf should rustle under my feet. I would have left her to struggle, in that solitude with only the eye of God upon her. But, so it happened, I never once dreamed of questioning my right to be there now, as I had questioned it just before, when I came so suddenly upon Hollingsworth and herself, in the passion of their recent debate. It suits me not to explain what was the analogy that I saw, or imagined, between Zenobia's situation and mine; nor, I believe, will the reader detect this one secret, hidden beneath many a revelation which perhaps concerned me less. In simple truth, however, as Zenobia leaned her forehead against the rock, shaken with that tearless agony, it seemed to me that the self-same pang, with hardly mitigated torment, leaped thrilling from her heart-strings to my own. Was it wrong, therefore, if I felt myself consecrated to the priesthood by sympathy like this, and called upon to minister to this woman's affliction, so far as mortal could?

But, indeed, what could mortal do for her? Nothing! The attempt would be a mockery and an anguish. Time, it is true, would steal away her grief, and bury it and the best of her heart in the same grave. But destiny itself, methought, in its kindliest mood, could do no better for Zenobia, in the way of quick relief, than to cause the impending rock to impend a little further, and fall upon her head. So I leaned against a tree, and listened to her sobs, in unbroken silence. She was half prostrate, half kneeling, with her forehead still pressed against the rock. Her sobs were the only sound; she did not groan, nor give any other utterance to her distress. It was all involuntary.

At length, she sat up, put back her hair, and stared about her with a bewildered aspect, as if not distinctly recollecting the scene through which she had passed, nor cognizant of the situation in which it left her. Her face and brow were almost purple with the rush of blood. They whitened, however, by and by, and for some time retained this death-like hue. She put her hand to her forehead, with a gesture that made me forcibly conscious of an intense and living pain there.

Her glance, wandering wildly to and fro, passed over me several times, without appearing to inform her of my presence. But, finally, a look of recognition gleamed from her eyes into mine.

"Is it you, Miles Coverdale?" said she, smiling. "Ah, I perceive what you are about! You are turning this whole affair into a ballad. Pray let me hear as many stanzas as you happen to have ready!"

"O, hush, Zenobia!" I answered. "Heaven knows what an ache is in my soul!"

"It is genuine tragedy, is it not?" rejoined Zenobia, with a sharp, light laugh. "And you are willing to allow, perhaps, that I have had hard measure. But it is a woman's doom, and I have deserved it like a woman; so let there be no pity, as, on my part, there shall be no complaint. It is all right, now, or will shortly be so. But, Mr. Coverdale, by all means write this ballad, and put your soul's ache into it, and turn your sympathy to good account, as other poets do, and as poets must, unless they choose to give us glittering icicles instead of lines of fire. As for the moral, it shall be distilled into the final stanza, in a drop of bitter honey."

"What shall it be, Zenobia?" I inquired, endeavoring to fall in with her mood.

"O, a very old one will serve the purpose," she replied. "There are no new truths, much as we have prided ourselves on finding some. A moral? Why, this:—that, in the battle-field of life, the downright stroke, that would fall only on a man's steel head-piece, is sure to light on a woman's heart, over which she wears no breastplate, and whose wisdom it is, therefore, to keep out of the conflict. Or, this:—that the whole universe, her own sex and yours, and Providence, or Destiny, to boot, make common cause against the woman who swerves one hair's breadth out of the beaten track. Yes; and add (for I may as well own it, now) that, with that one hair's breadth, she goes all astray, and never sees the world in its true aspect afterwards!"

"This last is too stern a moral," I observed. "Cannot we soften it a little?"

"Do it if you like, at your own peril, not on my responsibility," she answered. Then, with a sudden change of subject, she went on: "After all, he has flung away what would have served him better than the poor, pale flower he kept. What can Priscilla do for him? Put passionate warmth into his heart, when it shall be chilled with frozen hopes? Strengthen his hands, when they are weary with much doing and no performance? No! but only tend towards him with a blind, instinctive love, and hang her little, puny weakness for a clog upon his arm! She cannot even give him such sympathy as is worth the name. For will he never, in many an hour of darkness, need that proud intellectual sympathy which he might have had from me?—the sympathy that would flash light along his course, and guide as well as cheer him? Poor Hollingsworth! Where will he find it now?"

"Hollingsworth has a heart of ice!" said I, bitterly. "He is a wretch!"

"Do him no wrong," interrupted Zenobia, turning haughtily upon me. "Presume not to estimate a man like Hollingsworth. It was my fault, all along, and none of his. I see it now! He never sought me. Why should he seek me? What had I to offer him? A miserable, bruised and battered heart, spoilt long before he met me. A life, too, hopelessly entangled with a villain's! He did well to cast me off. God be praised, he did it! And yet, had he trusted me, and borne with me a little longer, I would have saved him all this trouble."

She was silent for a time, and stood with her eyes fixed on the ground. Again raising them, her look was more mild and calm.

"Miles Coverdale!" said she.

"Well, Zenobia," I responded. "Can I do you any service?"

"Very little," she replied. "But it is my purpose, as you may well imagine, to remove from Blithedale; and, most likely, I may not see Hollingsworth again. A woman in my position, you understand, feels scarcely at her ease among former friends. New faces—unaccustomed looks—those only can she tolerate. She would pine among familiar scenes; she would be apt to blush, too, under the eyes that knew her secret; her heart might throb uncomfortably; she would mortify herself, I suppose, with foolish notions of having sacrificed the honor of her sex at the foot of proud, contumacious man. Poor womanhood, with its rights and wrongs. Here will be new matter for my course of lectures, at the idea of which you smiled, Mr. Coverdale, a month or two ago.

But, as you have really a heart and sympathies, as far as they go, and as I shall depart without seeing Hollingsworth, I must entreat you to be a messenger between him and me."

"Willingly," said I, wondering at the strange way in which her mind seemed to vibrate from the deepest earnest to mere levity. "What is the message?"

"True,—what is it?" exclaimed Zenobia. "After all, I hardly know. On better consideration, I have no message. Tell him,—tell him something pretty and pathetic, that will come nicely and sweetly into your ballad,—anything you please, so it be tender and submissive enough. Tell him he has murdered me! Tell him that I'll haunt him!"—she spoke these words with the wildest energy.—"And give him—no, give Priscilla—this!"

Thus saying, she took the jewelled flower out of her hair; and it struck me as the act of a queen, when worsted in a combat, discrowning herself, as if she found a sort of relief in abasing all her pride.

"Bid her wear this for Zenobia's sake," she continued. "She is a pretty little creature, and will make as soft and gentle a wife as the veriest Bluebeard could desire. Pity that she must fade so soon! These delicate and puny maidens always do. Ten years hence, let Hollingsworth look at my face and Priscilla's, and then choose betwixt them. Or, if he pleases, let him do it now."

How magnificently Zenobia looked, as she said this! The effect of her beauty was even heightened by the over-consciousness and self-recognition of it, into which, I suppose, Hollingsworth's scorn had driven her. She understood the look of admiration in my face; and—Zenobia to the last—it gave her pleasure.

"It is an endless pity," said she, "that I had not bethought myself of winning your heart, Mr. Coverdale, instead of Hollingsworth's. I think I should have succeeded; and many women would have deemed you the worthier conquest of the two. You are certainly much the handsomest man. But there is a fate in these things. And beauty, in a man, has been of little account with me, since my earliest girlhood, when, for once, it turned my head. Now, farewell!"

"Zenobia, whither are you going?" I asked.

"No matter where," said she. "But I am weary of this place, and sick to death of playing at philanthropy and progress. Of all varieties of mock-life, we have surely blundered into the very emptiest mockery, in our effort to establish the one true system. I have done with it; and Blithedale must find another woman to superintend the laundry, and you, Mr. Coverdale, another nurse to make your gruel, the next time you fall ill. It was, indeed, a foolish dream! Yet it gave us some pleasant summer days, and bright hopes, while they lasted. It can do no more;

nor will it avail us to shed tears over a broken bubble. Here is my hand! Adieu!"

She gave me her hand, with the same free, whole-souled gesture as on the first afternoon of our acquaintance; and, being greatly moved, I bethought me of no better method of expressing my deep sympathy than to carry it to my lips. In so doing, I perceived that this white hand — so hospitably warm when I first touched it, five months since — was now cold as a veritable piece of snow.

"How very cold!" I exclaimed, holding it between both my own, with the vain idea of warming it. "What can be the reason? It is really death-like!"

"The extremities die first, they say," answered Zenobia, laughing. "And so you kiss this poor, despised, rejected hand! Well, my dear friend, I thank you. You have reserved your homage for the fallen. Lip of man will never touch my hand again. I intend to become a Catholic, for the sake of going into a nunnery. When you next hear of Zenobia, her face will be behind the black veil; so look you last at it now — for all is over! Once more, farewell!"

She withdrew her hand, yet left a lingering pressure, which I felt long afterwards. So intimately connected as I had been with perhaps the only man in whom she was ever truly interested, Zenobia looked on me as the representative of all the past, and was conscious that, in bidding me adieu, she likewise took final leave of Hollingsworth, and of this whole epoch of her life. Never did her beauty shine out more lustrously than in the last glimpse that I had of her. She departed, and was soon hidden among the trees.

But, whether it was the strong impression of the foregoing scene, or whatever else the cause, I was affected with a fantasy that Zenobia had not actually gone, but was still hovering about the spot and haunting it. I seemed to feel her eyes upon me. It was as if the vivid coloring of her character had left a brilliant stain upon the air. By degrees, however, the impression grew less distinct. I flung myself upon the fallen leaves at the base of Eliot's pulpit. The sunshine withdrew up the tree-trunks, and flickered on the top most boughs; gray twilight made the wood obscure; the stars brightened out; the pendent boughs became wet with chill autumnal dews. But I was listless, worn out with emotion on my own behalf and sympathy for others, and had no heart to leave my comfortless lair beneath the rock.

I must have fallen asleep, and had a dream, all the circumstances of which utterly vanished at the moment when they converged to some tragical catastrophe, and thus grew too powerful for the thin sphere of slumber that enveloped them. Starting from the ground, I found the risen moon shining upon the rugged face of the rock, and myself all in a tremble.

XXVII.

MIDNIGHT

IT could not have been far from midnight when I came beneath Hollingsworth's window, and, finding it open, flung in a tuft of grass with earth at the roots, and heard it fall upon the floor. He was either awake or sleeping very lightly; for scarcely a moment had gone by, before he looked out, and discerned me standing in the moonlight.

"Is it you, Coverdale?" he asked. "What is the matter?"

"Come down to me, Hollingsworth!" I answered. "I am anxious to speak with you."

The strange tone of my own voice startled me, and him, probably, no less. He lost no time, and soon issued from the house-door, with his dress half arranged.

"Again, what is the matter?" he asked, impatiently.

"Have you seen Zenobia," said I, "since you parted from her at Eliot's pulpit?"

"No," answered Hollingsworth; "nor did I expect it."

His voice was deep, but had a tremor in it. Hardly had he spoken, when Silas Foster thrust his head, done up in a cotton handkerchief, out of another window, and took what he called—as it literally was—a squint at us.

"Well, folks, what are ye about here?" he demanded. "Aha! are you there, Miles Coverdale? You have been turning night into day, since you left us, I reckon; and so you find it quite natural to come prowling about the house at this time o' night, frightening my old woman out of her wits, and making her disturb a tired man out of his best nap. In with you, you vagabond, and to bed!"

"Dress yourself quietly, Foster," said I. "We want your assistance."

I could not, for the life of me, keep that strange tone out of my voice. Silas Foster, obtuse as were his sensibilities, seemed to feel the ghastly earnestness that was conveyed in it as well as Hollingsworth did. He immediately withdrew his head, and I heard him yawning, muttering to his wife, and again yawning heavily, while he hurried on his clothes. Meanwhile, I showed Hollingsworth a delicate handkerchief, marked with a well-known cipher, and told where I had found it, and other circumstances, which had filled me with a suspicion so terrible that I left him, if he dared, to shape it out for himself. By the time my brief explanation was finished, we were joined by Silas Foster, in his blue woollen frock.

"Well, boys," cried he, peevishly, "what is to pay now?"

"Tell him, Hollingsworth," said I.

Hollingsworth shivered, perceptibly, and drew in a hard breath betwixt his teeth. He steadied himself, however, and, looking the matter more firmly in the face than I had done, explained to Foster my suspicions, and the grounds of them, with a distinctness from which, in spite of my utmost efforts, my words had swerved aside. The tough-nerved yeoman, in his comment, put a finish on the business, and brought out the hideous idea in its full terror, as if he were removing the napkin from the face of a corpse.

"And so you think she's drowned herself?" he cried.

I turned away my face.

"What on earth should the young woman do that for?" exclaimed Silas, his eyes half out of his head with mere surprise. "Why, she has more means than she can use or waste, and lacks nothing to make her comfortable, but a husband, and that's an article she could have, any day. There's some mistake about this, I tell you!"

"Come," said I, shuddering; "let us go and ascertain the truth."

"Well, well," answered Silas Foster; "just as you say. We'll take the long pole, with the hook at the end, that serves to get the bucket out of the draw-well, when the rope is broken. With that, and a couple of long-handled hay-rakes, I'll answer for finding her, if she's anywhere to be found. Strange enough! Zenobia drown herself! No, no; I don't believe it. She had too much sense, and too much means, and enjoyed life a great deal too well."

When our few preparations were completed, we hastened, by a shorter than the customary route, through fields and pastures, and across a portion of the meadow, to the particular spot on the river-bank which I had paused to contemplate in the course of my afternoon's ramble. A nameless presentiment had again drawn me thither, after leaving Eliot's pulpit. I showed my companions where I had found the handkerchief, and pointed to two or three footsteps, impressed into the clayey margin, and tending towards the water. Beneath its shallow verge, among the water-weeds, there were further traces, as yet unobliterated by the sluggish current, which was there almost at a stand-still. Silas Foster thrust his face down close to these footsteps, and picked up a shoe that had escaped my observation, being half imbedded in the mud.

"There's a kid shoe that never was made on a Yankee last," observed he. "I know enough of shoemaker's craft to tell that. French manufacture; and, see what a high instep! And how evenly she trod in it! There never was a woman that stept handsomer in her shoes than Zenobia did. Here," he added, addressing Hollingsworth; "would you like to keep the shoe?"

Hollingsworth started back.

"Give it to me, Foster," said I.

I dabbled it in the water, to rinse off the mud, and have kept it ever since. Not far from this spot lay an old, leaky punt, drawn up on the oozy river-side, and generally half full of water. It served the angler to go in quest of pickerel, or the sportsman to pick up his wild ducks. Setting this crazy bark afloat, I seated myself in the stern with the paddle, while Hollingsworth sat in the bows with the hooked pole, and Silas Foster amidships with a hay-rake.

"It puts me in mind of my young days," remarked Silas, "when I used to steal out of bed to go bobbing for horn-pouts and eels. Heigh-ho!— well, life and death together make sad work for us all! Then I was a boy, bobbing for fish; and now I am getting to be an old fellow, and here I be, groping for a dead body! I tell you what, lads. If I thought anything had really happened to Zenobia, I should feel kind o' sorrowful."

"I wish, at least, you would hold your tongue," muttered I.

The moon, that night, though past the full, was still large and oval, and having risen between eight and nine o'clock, now shone aslantwise over the river, throwing the high, opposite bank, with its woods, into deep shadow, but lighting up the hither shore pretty effectually. Not a ray appeared to fall on the river itself. It lapsed imperceptibly away, a broad, black, inscrutable depth, keeping its own secrets from the eye of man, as impenetrably as mid-ocean could.

"Well, Miles Coverdale," said Foster, "you are the helmsman. How do you mean to manage this business?"

"I shall let the boat drift, broadside foremost, past that stump," I replied. "I know the bottom, having sounded it in fishing. The shore, on this side, after the first step or two, goes off very abruptly; and there is a pool, just by the stump, twelve or fifteen feet deep. The current could not have force enough to sweep any sunken object, even if partially buoyant, out of that hollow."

"Come, then," said Silas; "but I doubt whether I can touch bottom with this hay-rake, if it's as deep as you say. Mr. Hollingsworth, I think you'll be the lucky man tonight, such luck as it is."

We floated past the stump. Silas Foster plied his rake manfully, poking it as far as he could into the water, and immersing the whole length of his arm besides. Hollingsworth at first sat motionless, with the hooked pole elevated in the air. But, by and by, with a nervous and jerky movement, he began to plunge it into the blackness that upbore us, setting his teeth, and making precisely such thrusts, methought, as if he were stabbing at a deadly enemy. I bent over the side of the boat. So obscure, however, so awfully mysterious, was that dark stream, that—and the thought made me shiver like a leaf—I might as well have tried to look into the enigma of the eternal world, to discover what had become of Zenobia's soul, as into the river's depths, to find her body. And there, perhaps, she lay, with her face upward, while the shadow of the boat, and my own pale face peering downward, passed slowly betwixt her and the sky!

Once, twice, thrice, I paddled the boat up stream, and again suffered it to glide, with the river's slow, funereal motion, downward. Silas Foster had raked up a large mass of stuff, which, as it came towards the surface, looked somewhat like a flowing garment, but proved to be a monstrous tuft of water-weeds. Hollingsworth, with a gigantic effort, upheaved a sunken log. When once free of the bottom, it rose partly out of water,— all weedy and slimy, a devilish-looking object, which the moon had not shone upon for half a hundred years,—then plunged again, and sullenly returned to its old resting-place, for the remnant of the century.

"That looked ugly!" quoth Silas. "I half thought it was the evil one, on the same errand as ourselves,—searching for Zenobia."

"He shall never get her," said I, giving the boat a strong impulse.

"That's not for you to say, my boy," retorted the yeoman. "Pray God he never has, and never may. Slow work this, however! I should really be glad to find something! Pshaw! What a notion that is, when the only good luck would be to paddle, and drift, and poke, and grope, hereabouts, till morning, and have our labor for our pains! For my part, I shouldn't wonder if the creature had only lost her shoe in the mud, and saved her soul alive, after all. My stars! how she will laugh at us, to-morrow morning!"

It is indescribable what an image of Zenobia—at the breakfast-table, full of warm and mirthful life—this surmise of Silas Foster's brought before my mind. The terrible phantasm of her death was thrown by it into the remotest and dimmest back-ground, where it seemed to grow as improbable as a myth.

"Yes, Silas, it may be as you say," cried I.

The drift of the stream had again borne us a little below the stump, when I felt,—yes, felt, for it was as if the iron hook had smote my breast,—felt Hollingsworth's pole strike some object at the bottom of the river! He started up, and almost overset the boat.

"Hold on!" cried Foster; "you have her!"

Putting a fury of strength into the effort, Hollingsworth heaved amain, and up came a white swash to the surface of the river. It was the flow of a woman's garments. A little higher, and we saw her dark hair streaming down the current. Black River of Death, thou hadst yielded up thy victim! Zenobia was found!

Silas Foster laid hold of the body; Hollingsworth, likewise, grappled with it; and I steered towards the bank, gazing all the while at Zenobia, whose limbs were swaying in the current close at the boat's side. Arriving near the shore, we all three stept into the water, bore her out, and laid her on the ground beneath a tree.

"Poor child!" said Foster,—and his dry old heart, I verily believe, vouchsafed a tear,—"I'm sorry for her!"

Were I to describe the perfect horror of the spectacle, the reader might justly reckon it to me for a sin and shame. For more than twelve long years I have borne it in my memory, and could now reproduce it as freshly as if it were still before my eyes. Of all modes of death, methinks it is the ugliest. Her wet garments swathed limbs of terrible inflexibility. She was the marble image of a death-agony. Her arms had grown rigid in the act of struggling, and were bent before her with clenched hands; her knees, too, were bent, and—thank God for it—in the attitude of prayer. Ah, that rigidity! It is impossible to bear the terror of it. It seemed,—I must needs impart so much of my own miserable idea,—it seemed as if her body must keep the same position in the coffin, and that her skeleton would keep it in the grave; and that when Zenobia rose at the day of judgment, it would be in just the same attitude as now!

One hope I had; and that, too, was mingled half with fear. She knelt, as if in prayer. With the last, choking consciousness, her soul, bubbling out through her lips, it may be, had given itself up to the Father, reconciled and penitent. But her arms! They were bent before her, as if she struggled against Providence in never-ending hostility. Her hands! They were clenched in immitigable defiance. Away with the hideous thought! The flitting moment after Zenobia sank into the dark pool— when her breath was gone, and her soul at her lips—was as long, in its capacity of God's infinite forgiveness, as the lifetime of the world!

Foster bent over the body, and carefully examined it.

"You have wounded the poor thing's breast," said he to Hollingsworth; "close by her heart, too!"

"Ha!" cried Hollingsworth, with a start.

And so he had, indeed, both before and after death!

"See!" said Foster. "That's the place where the iron struck her. It looks cruelly, but she never felt it!"

He endeavored to arrange the arms of the corpse decently by its side. His utmost strength, however, scarcely sufficed to bring them down; and rising again, the next instant, they bade him defiance, exactly as before. He made another effort, with the same result.

"In God's name, Silas Foster," cried I, with bitter indignation, "let that dead woman alone!"

"Why, man, it's not decent!" answered he, staring at me in amazement. "I can't bear to see her looking so! Well, well," added he, after a third effort, "'t is of no use, sure enough; and we must leave the women to do their best with her, after we get to the house. The sooner that's done, the better."

We took two rails from a neighboring fence, and formed a bier by laying across some boards from the bottom of the boat. And thus we bore Zenobia homeward. Six hours before, how beautiful! At midnight, what a horror! A reflection occurs to me that will show ludicrously, I doubt not, on my page, but must come in, for its sterling truth. Being the woman that she was, could Zenobia have foreseen all these ugly circumstances of death,—how ill it would become her, the altogether unseemly aspect which she must put on, and especially old Silas Foster's efforts to improve the matter,—she would no more have committed the dreadful act than have exhibited herself to a public assembly in a badly-fitting garment! Zenobia, I have often thought, was not quite simple in her death. She had seen pictures, I suppose, of drowned persons in lithe and graceful attitudes. And she deemed it well and decorous to die as so many village maidens have, wronged in their first love, and seeking peace in the bosom of the old, familiar stream,—so familiar that they could not dread it,—where, in childhood, they used to bathe their little feet, wading mid-leg deep, unmindful of wet skirts. But in Zenobia's case there was some tint of the Arcadian affectation that had been visible enough in all our lives, for a few months past.

This, however, to my conception, takes nothing from the tragedy. For, has not the world come to an awfully sophisticated pass, when, after a certain degree of acquaintance with it, we cannot even put ourselves to death, in whole-hearted simplicity?

Slowly, slowly, with many a dreary pause,—resting the bier often on some rock, or balancing it across a mossy log, to take fresh hold,—we bore our burthen onward through the moonlight, and at last laid Zenobia on the floor of the old farm-house. By and by came three or four withered women, and stood whispering around the corpse, peering at it through their spectacles, holding up their skinny hands, shaking their night-capt heads, and taking counsel of one another's experience what was to be done.

With those tire-women we left Zenobia!

XXVIII.

BLITHEDALE PASTURE

BLITHEDALE, thus far in its progress, had never found the necessity of a burial-ground. There was some consultation among us in what spot Zenobia might most fitly be laid. It was my own wish that she should sleep at the base of Eliot's pulpit, and that on the rugged front of the rock the name by which we familiarly knew her,—Zenobia,—and not another word, should be deeply cut, and left for the moss and lichens to fill up at their long leisure. But Hollingsworth (to whose ideas on this point great deference was due) made it his request that her grave might be dug on the gently sloping hillside, in the wide pasture, where, as we once supposed, Zenobia and he had planned to build their cottage. And thus it was done, accordingly.

She was buried very much as other people have been for hundreds of years gone by. In anticipation of a death, we Blithedale colonists had sometimes set our fancies at work to arrange a funereal ceremony, which should be the proper symbolic expression of our spiritual faith and eternal hopes; and this we meant to substitute for those customary rites which were moulded originally out of the Gothic gloom, and by long use, like an old velvet pall, have so much more than their first death-smell in them. But when the occasion came, we found it the simplest and truest thing, after all, to content ourselves with the old fashion, taking away what we could, but interpolating no novelties, and particularly avoiding all frippery of flowers and cheerful emblems. The procession moved from the farm-house. Nearest the dead walked an old man in deep mourning, his face mostly concealed in a white handkerchief, and with Priscilla leaning on his arm. Hollingsworth and myself came next. We all stood around the narrow niche in the cold earth; all saw the coffin lowered in; all heard the rattle of the crumbly soil upon its lid,—that final sound, which mortality awakens on the utmost verge of sense, as if in the vain hope of bringing an echo from the spiritual world.

I noticed a stranger,—a stranger to most of those present, though known to me,—who, after the coffin had descended, took up a handful of earth, and flung it first into the grave. I had given up Hollingsworth's arm, and now found myself near this man.

"It was an idle thing—a foolish thing—for Zenobia to do," said he. "She was the last woman in the world to whom death could have been necessary. It was too absurd! I have no patience with her."

"Why so?" I inquired, smothering my horror at his cold comment in my eager curiosity to discover some tangible truth as to his relation with Zenobia. "If any crisis could justify the sad wrong she offered to herself, it was surely that in which she stood. Everything had failed her;—prosperity in the world's sense, for her opulence was gone,—the heart's prosperity, in love. And there was a secret burthen on her, the nature of which is best known to you. Young as she was, she had tried life fully, had no more to hope, and something, perhaps, to fear. Had Providence taken her away in its own holy hand, I should have thought it the kindest dispensation that could be awarded to one so wrecked."

"You mistake the matter completely," rejoined Westervelt.

"What, then, is your own view of it?" I asked.

"Her mind was active, and various in its powers," said he. "Her heart had a manifold adaptation; her constitution an infinite buoyancy, which (had she possessed only a little patience to await the reflux of her troubles) would have borne her upward, triumphantly, for twenty years to come. Her beauty would not have waned—or scarcely so, and surely not beyond the reach of art to restore it—in all that time. She had life's summer all before her, and a hundred varieties of brilliant success. What an actress Zenobia might have been! It was one of her least valuable capabilities. How forcibly she might have wrought upon the world, either directly in her own person, or by her influence upon some man, or a series of men, of controlling genius! Every prize that could be worth a woman's having—and many prizes which other women are too timid to desire—lay within Zenobia's reach."

"In all this," I observed, "there would have been nothing to satisfy her heart."

"Her heart!" answered Westervelt, contemptuously. "That troublesome organ (as she had hitherto found it) would have been kept in its due place and degree, and have had all the gratification it could fairly claim. She would soon have established a control over it. Love had failed her, you say! Had it never failed her before? Yet she survived it, and loved again,—possibly not once alone, nor twice either. And now to drown herself for yonder dreamy philanthropist!"

"Who are you," I exclaimed, indignantly, "that dare to speak thus of the dead? You seem to intend a eulogy, yet leave out whatever was noblest in her, and blacken while you mean to praise. I have long considered you as Zenobia's evil fate. Your sentiments confirm me in the idea, but leave me still ignorant as to the mode in which you have influenced her life. The connection may have been indissoluble, except by death. Then, indeed,—always in the hope of God's infinite mercy,—I cannot deem it a misfortune that she sleeps in yonder grave!"

"No matter what I was to her," he answered, gloomily, yet without actual emotion. "She is now beyond my reach. Had she lived, and hearkened to my counsels, we might have served each other well. But there Zenobia lies in yonder pit, with the dull earth over her. Twenty years of a brilliant lifetime thrown away for a mere woman's whim!"

Heaven deal with Westervelt according to his nature and deserts!—that is to say, annihilate him. He was altogether earthy, worldly, made for time and its gross objects, and incapable—except by a sort of dim reflection caught from other-minds—of so much as one spiritual idea. Whatever stain Zenobia had was caught from him; nor does it seldom happen that a character of admirable qualities loses its better life because the atmosphere that should sustain it is rendered poisonous by such breath as this man mingled with Zenobia's. Yet his reflections possessed their share of truth. It was a woful thought, that a woman of Zenobia's diversified capacity should have fancied herself irretrievably defeated on the broad battlefield of life, and with no refuge, save to fall on her own sword, merely because Love had gone against her. It is nonsense, and a miserable wrong,—the result, like so many others, of masculine egotism,—that the success or failure of woman's existence should be made to depend wholly on the affections, and on one species of affection, while man has such a multitude of other chances, that this seems but an incident. For its own sake, if it will do no more, the world should throw open all its avenues to the passport of a woman's bleeding heart.

As we stood around the grave, I looked often towards Priscilla, dreading to see her wholly overcome with grief. And deeply grieved, in truth, she was. But a character so simply constituted as hers has room only for a single predominant affection. No other feeling can touch the heart's inmost core, nor do it any deadly mischief. Thus, while we see that such a being responds to every breeze with tremulous vibration, and imagine that she must be shattered by the first rude blast, we find her retaining her equilibrium amid shocks that might have overthrown many a sturdier frame. So with Priscilla;—her one possible misfortune was Hollingsworth's unkindness; and that was destined never to befall her,—never yet, at least,—for Priscilla has not died.

But Hollingsworth! After all the evil that he did, are we to leave him thus, blest with the entire devotion of this one true heart, and with wealth at his disposal, to execute the long-contemplated project that had led him so far astray? What retribution is there here? My mind being vexed with precisely this query, I made a journey, some years since, for the sole purpose of catching a last glimpse of Hollingsworth, and judging for myself whether he were a happy man or no. I learned that he inhabited a small cottage, that his way of life was exceedingly retired, and that my only chance of encountering him or Priscilla was to meet them in a secluded lane, where, in the latter part of the afternoon, they were accustomed to walk. I did meet them, accordingly. As they approached me, I observed in Hollingsworth's face a depressed and melancholy look, that seemed habitual;—the powerfully-built man showed a self-distrustful weakness, and a childlike or childish tendency to press close, and closer still, to the side of the slender woman whose arm was within his. In Priscilla's manner there was a protective and watchful quality, as if she felt herself the guardian of her companion; but, likewise, a deep, submissive, unquestioning reverence, and also a veiled happiness in her fair and quiet countenance.

Drawing nearer, Priscilla recognized me, and gave me a kind of friendly smile, but with a slight gesture, which I could not help interpreting as an entreaty not to make myself known to Hollingsworth.

Nevertheless, an impulse took possession of me, and compelled me to address him.

"I have come, Hollingsworth," said I, "to view your grand edifice for the reformation of criminals. Is it finished yet?"

"No, nor begun," answered he, without raising his eyes. "A very small one answers all my purposes."

Priscilla threw me an upbraiding glance. But I spoke again, with a bitter and revengeful emotion, as if flinging a poisoned arrow at Hollingsworth's heart.

"Up to this moment," I inquired, "how many criminals have you reformed?"

"Not one," said Hollingsworth, with his eyes still fixed on the ground. "Ever since we parted, I have been busy with a single murderer."

Then the tears gushed into my eyes, and I forgave him; for I remembered the wild energy, the passionate shriek, with which Zenobia had spoken those words,—"Tell him he has murdered me! Tell him that I'll haunt him!"—and I knew what murderer he meant, and whose vindictive shadow dogged the side where Priscilla was not.

The moral which presents itself to my reflections, as drawn from Hollingsworth's character and errors, is simply this,—that, admitting what is called philanthropy, when adopted as a profession, to be often useful by its energetic impulse to society at large, it is perilous to the individual whose ruling passion, in one exclusive channel, it thus becomes. It ruins, or is fearfully apt to ruin, the heart, the rich juices of which God never meant should be pressed violently out, and distilled into alcoholic liquor, by an unnatural process, but should render life sweet, bland, and gently beneficent, and insensibly influence other hearts and other lives to the same blessed end. I see in Hollingsworth an exemplification of the most awful truth in Bunyan's book of such;—from the very gate of heaven there is a by-way to the pit!

But, all this while, we have been standing by Zenobia's grave. I have never since beheld it, but make no question that the grass grew all the better on that little parallelogram of pasture-land, for the decay of the beautiful woman who slept beneath. How much Nature seems to love us! And how readily, nevertheless, without a sigh or a complaint, she converts us to a meaner purpose, when her highest one—that of conscious intellectual life and sensibility—has been untimely balked! While Zenobia lived, Nature was proud of her, and directed all eyes upon that radiant presence, as her fairest handiwork. Zenobia perished. Will not Nature shed a tear? Ah, no!—she adopts the calamity at once into her system, and is just as well pleased, for aught we can see, with the tuft of ranker vegetation that grew out of Zenobia's heart, as with all the beauty which has bequeathed us no earthly representative except in this crop of weeds. It is because the spirit is inestimable that the lifeless body is so little valued.

XXIX.

MILES COVERDALE'S CONFESSION

I⊤ remains only to say a few words about myself. Not improbably, the reader might be willing to spare me the trouble; for I have made but a poor and dim figure in my own narrative, establishing no separate interest, and suffering my colorless life to take its hue from other lives. But one still retains some little consideration for one's self; so I keep these last two or three pages for my individual and sole behoof.

But what, after all, have I to tell? Nothing, nothing, nothing! I left Blithedale within the week after Zenobia's death, and went back thither no more. The whole soil of our farm, for a long time afterwards, seemed but the sodded earth over her grave. I could not toil there, nor live upon its products. Often, however, in these years that are darkening around me, I remember our beautiful scheme of a noble and unselfish life; and how fair, in that first summer, appeared the prospect that it might endure for generations, and be perfected, as the ages rolled away, into the system of a people and a world! Were my former associates now there, — were there only three or four of those true-hearted men still laboring in the sun, — I sometimes fancy that I should direct my world-weary footsteps thitherward, and entreat them to receive me, for old friendship's sake. More and more I feel that we had struck upon what ought to be a truth. Posterity may dig it up, and profit by it. The experiment, so far as its original projectors were concerned, proved, long ago, a failure; first lapsing into Fourierism, and dying, as it well deserved, for this infidelity to its own higher spirit. Where once we toiled with our whole hopeful hearts, the town-paupers, aged, nerveless, and disconsolate, creep sluggishly a-field. Alas, what faith is requisite to bear up against such results of generous efforts!

My subsequent life has passed, — I was going to say happily — but, at all events, tolerably enough. I am now at middle age, — well, well, a step or two beyond the mid-most point, and I care not a fig who knows it! — a bachelor, with no very decided purpose of ever being otherwise. I have been twice to Europe, and spent a year or two rather agreeably at each visit. Being well to do in the world, and having nobody but myself to care for, I live very much at my ease, and fare sumptuously every day. As for poetry, I have given it up, notwithstanding that Doctor Griswold — as the reader, of course, knows — has placed me at a fair elevation among our minor minstrelsy, on the strength of my pretty little volume, published ten years ago. As regards human progress (in spite of my irrepressible yearnings over the Blithedale reminiscences), let them believe in it who can, and aid in it who choose. If I could earnestly do either, it might be all the better for my comfort. As Hollingsworth once told me,

I lack a purpose. How strange! He was ruined, morally, by an overplus of the very same ingredient, the want of which, I occasionally suspect, has rendered my own life all an emptiness. I by no means wish to die. Yet, were there any cause, in this whole chaos of human struggle, worth a sane man's dying for, and which my death would benefit, then—provided, however, the effort did not involve an unreasonable amount of trouble—methinks I might be bold to offer up my life. If Kossuth, for example, would pitch the battle-field of Hungarian rights within an easy ride of my abode, and choose a mild, sunny morning, after breakfast, for the conflict, Miles Coverdale would gladly be his man, for one brave rush upon the levelled bayonets. Further than that, I should be loth to pledge myself.

I exaggerate my own defects. The reader must not take my own word for it, nor believe me altogether changed from the young man who once hoped strenuously, and struggled not so much amiss. Frostier heads than mine have gained honor in the world; frostier hearts have imbibed new warmth, and been newly happy. Life, however, it must be owned, has come to rather an idle pass with me. Would my friends like to know what brought it thither? There is one secret,—I have concealed it all along, and never meant to let the least whisper of it escape,—one foolish little secret, which possibly may have had something to do with these inactive years of meridian manhood, with my bachelorship, with the unsatisfied retrospect that I fling back on life, and my listless glance towards the future. Shall I reveal it? It is an absurd thing for a man in his afternoon,—a man of the world, moreover, with these three white hairs in his brown mustache, and that deepening track of a crow's-foot on each temple,—an absurd thing ever to have happened, and quite the absurdest for an old bachelor, like me, to talk about. But it rises in my throat; so let it come.

I perceive, moreover, that the confession, brief as it shall be, will throw a gleam of light over my behavior throughout the foregoing incidents, and is, indeed, essential to the full understanding of my story. The reader, therefore, since I have disclosed so much, is entitled to this one word more. As I write it, he will charitably suppose me to blush, and turn away my face:—

I—I myself—was in love—with—PRISCILLA!

FICTION

FLATLAND: A ROMANCE OF MANY DIMENSIONS, Edwin A. Abbott. (0-486-27263-X)

PRIDE AND PREJUDICE, Jane Austen. (0-486-28473-5)

CIVIL WAR SHORT STORIES AND POEMS, Edited by Bob Blaisdell. (0-486-48226-X)

THE DECAMERON: Selected Tales, Giovanni Boccaccio. Edited by Bob Blaisdell. (0-486-41113-3)

JANE EYRE, Charlotte Brontë. (0-486-42449-9)

WUTHERING HEIGHTS, Emily Brontë. (0-486-29256-8)

THE THIRTY-NINE STEPS, John Buchan. (0-486-28201-5)

ALICE'S ADVENTURES IN WONDERLAND, Lewis Carroll. (0-486-27543-4)

MY ÁNTONIA, Willa Cather. (0-486-28240-6)

THE AWAKENING, Kate Chopin. (0-486-27786-0)

HEART OF DARKNESS, Joseph Conrad. (0-486-26464-5)

LORD JIM, Joseph Conrad. (0-486-40650-4)

THE RED BADGE OF COURAGE, Stephen Crane. (0-486-26465-3)

THE WORLD'S GREATEST SHORT STORIES, Edited by James Daley. (0-486-44716-2)

A CHRISTMAS CAROL, Charles Dickens. (0-486-26865-9)

GREAT EXPECTATIONS, Charles Dickens. (0-486-41586-4)

A TALE OF TWO CITIES, Charles Dickens. (0-486-40651-2)

CRIME AND PUNISHMENT, Fyodor Dostoyevsky. Translated by Constance Garnett. (0-486-41587-2)

THE ADVENTURES OF SHERLOCK HOLMES, Sir Arthur Conan Doyle. (0-486-47491-7)

THE HOUND OF THE BASKERVILLES, Sir Arthur Conan Doyle. (0-486-28214-7)

BLAKE: PROPHET AGAINST EMPIRE, David V. Erdman. (0-486-26719-9)

WHERE ANGELS FEAR TO TREAD, E. M. Forster. (0-486-27791-7)

BEOWULF, Translated by R. K. Gordon. (0-486-27264-8)

THE RETURN OF THE NATIVE, Thomas Hardy. (0-486-43165-7)

THE SCARLET LETTER, Nathaniel Hawthorne. (0-486-28048-9)

SIDDHARTHA, Hermann Hesse. (0-486-40653-9)

THE ODYSSEY, Homer. (0-486-40654-7)

THE TURN OF THE SCREW, Henry James. (0-486-26684-2)

DUBLINERS, James Joyce. (0-486-26870-5)

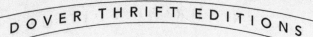

FICTION

THE METAMORPHOSIS AND OTHER STORIES, Franz Kafka. (0-486-29030-1)

SONS AND LOVERS, D. H. Lawrence. (0-486-42121-X)

THE CALL OF THE WILD, Jack London. (0-486-26472-6)

GREAT AMERICAN SHORT STORIES, Edited by Paul Negri. (0-486-42119-8)

THE GOLD-BUG AND OTHER TALES, Edgar Allan Poe. (0-486-26875-6)

ANTHEM, Ayn Rand. (0-486-49277-X)

FRANKENSTEIN, Mary Shelley. (0-486-28211-2)

THE JUNGLE, Upton Sinclair. (0-486-41923-1)

THREE LIVES, Gertrude Stein. (0-486-28059-4)

THE STRANGE CASE OF DR. JEKYLL AND MR. HYDE, Robert Louis Stevenson. (0-486-26688-5)

DRACULA, Bram Stoker. (0-486-41109-5)

UNCLE TOM'S CABIN, Harriet Beecher Stowe. (0-486-44028-1)

ADVENTURES OF HUCKLEBERRY FINN, Mark Twain. (0-486-28061-6)

THE ADVENTURES OF TOM SAWYER, Mark Twain. (0-486-40077-8)

CANDIDE, Voltaire. Edited by Francois-Marie Arouet. (0-486-26689-3)

THE COUNTRY OF THE BLIND: and Other Science-Fiction Stories, H. G. Wells. Edited by Martin Gardner. (0-486-48289-8)

THE WAR OF THE WORLDS, H. G. Wells. (0-486-29506-0)

ETHAN FROME, Edith Wharton. (0-486-26690-7)

THE PICTURE OF DORIAN GRAY, Oscar Wilde. (0-486-27807-7)

MONDAY OR TUESDAY: Eight Stories, Virginia Woolf. (0-486-29453-6)

NONFICTION

POETICS, Aristotle. (0-486-29577-X)

MEDITATIONS, Marcus Aurelius. (0-486-29823-X)

THE WAY OF PERFECTION, St. Teresa of Avila. Edited and Translated by E. Allison Peers. (0-486-48451-3)

THE DEVIL'S DICTIONARY, Ambrose Bierce. (0-486-27542-6)

GREAT SPEECHES OF THE 20TH CENTURY, Edited by Bob Blaisdell. (0-486-47467-4)

THE COMMUNIST MANIFESTO AND OTHER REVOLUTIONARY WRITINGS: Marx, Marat, Paine, Mao Tse-Tung, Gandhi and Others, Edited by Bob Blaisdell. (0-486-42465-0)

INFAMOUS SPEECHES: From Robespierre to Osama bin Laden, Edited by Bob Blaisdell. (0-486-47849-1)

GREAT ENGLISH ESSAYS: From Bacon to Chesterton, Edited by Bob Blaisdell. (0-486-44082-6)

GREEK AND ROMAN ORATORY, Edited by Bob Blaisdell. (0-486-49622-8)

THE UNITED STATES CONSTITUTION: The Full Text with Supplementary Materials, Edited and with supplementary materials by Bob Blaisdell. (0-486-47166-7)

GREAT SPEECHES BY NATIVE AMERICANS, Edited by Bob Blaisdell. (0-486-41122-2)

GREAT SPEECHES BY AFRICAN AMERICANS: Frederick Douglass, Sojourner Truth, Dr. Martin Luther King, Jr., Barack Obama, and Others, Edited by James Daley. (0-486-44761-8)

GREAT SPEECHES BY AMERICAN WOMEN, Edited by James Daley. (0-486-46141-6)

HISTORY'S GREATEST SPEECHES, Edited by James Daley. (0-486-49739-9)

GREAT INAUGURAL ADDRESSES, Edited by James Daley. (0-486-44577-1)

GREAT SPEECHES ON GAY RIGHTS, Edited by James Daley. (0-486-47512-3)

ON THE ORIGIN OF SPECIES: By Means of Natural Selection, Charles Darwin. (0-486-45006-6)

NARRATIVE OF THE LIFE OF FREDERICK DOUGLASS, Frederick Douglass. (0-486-28499-9)

THE SOULS OF BLACK FOLK, W. E. B. Du Bois. (0-486-28041-1)

NATURE AND OTHER ESSAYS, Ralph Waldo Emerson. (0-486-46947-6)

SELF-RELIANCE AND OTHER ESSAYS, Ralph Waldo Emerson. (0-486-27790-9)

THE LIFE OF OLAUDAH EQUIANO, Olaudah Equiano. (0-486-40661-X)

WIT AND WISDOM FROM POOR RICHARD'S ALMANACK, Benjamin Franklin. (0-486-40891-4)

THE AUTOBIOGRAPHY OF BENJAMIN FRANKLIN, Benjamin Franklin. (0-486-29073-5)

DOVER THRIFT EDITIONS

NONFICTION

THE DECLARATION OF INDEPENDENCE AND OTHER GREAT DOCUMENTS OF AMERICAN HISTORY: 1775-1865, Edited by John Grafton. (0-486-41124-9)

INCIDENTS IN THE LIFE OF A SLAVE GIRL, Harriet Jacobs. (0-486-41931-2)

GREAT SPEECHES, Abraham Lincoln. (0-486-26872-1)

THE WIT AND WISDOM OF ABRAHAM LINCOLN: A Book of Quotations, Abraham Lincoln. Edited by Bob Blaisdell. (0-486-44097-4)

THE SECOND TREATISE OF GOVERNMENT AND A LETTER CONCERNING TOLERATION, John Locke. (0-486-42464-2)

THE PRINCE, Niccolò Machiavelli. (0-486-27274-5)

MICHEL DE MONTAIGNE: Selected Essays, Michel de Montaigne. Translated by Charles Cotton. Edited by William Carew Hazlitt. (0-486-48603-6)

UTOPIA, Sir Thomas More. (0-486-29583-4)

BEYOND GOOD AND EVIL: Prelude to a Philosophy of the Future, Friedrich Nietzsche. (0-486-29868-X)

TWELVE YEARS A SLAVE, Solomon Northup. (0-486-78962-4)

COMMON SENSE, Thomas Paine. (0-486-29602-4)

BOOK OF AFRICAN-AMERICAN QUOTATIONS, Edited by Joslyn Pine. (0-486-47589-1)

THE TRIAL AND DEATH OF SOCRATES: Four Dialogues, Plato. (0-486-27066-1)

THE REPUBLIC, Plato. (0-486-41121-4)

SIX GREAT DIALOGUES: Apology, Crito, Phaedo, Phaedrus, Symposium, The Republic, Plato. Translated by Benjamin Jowett. (0-486-45465-7)

WOMEN'S WIT AND WISDOM: A Book of Quotations, Edited by Susan L. Rattiner. (0-486-41123-0)

GREAT SPEECHES, Franklin Delano Roosevelt. (0-486-40894-9)

THE CONFESSIONS OF ST. AUGUSTINE, St. Augustine. (0-486-42466-9)

A MODEST PROPOSAL AND OTHER SATIRICAL WORKS, Jonathan Swift. (0-486-28759-9)

THE IMITATION OF CHRIST, Thomas à Kempis. Translated by Aloysius Croft and Harold Bolton. (0-486-43185-1)

CIVIL DISOBEDIENCE AND OTHER ESSAYS, Henry David Thoreau. (0-486-27563-9)

WALDEN; OR, LIFE IN THE WOODS, Henry David Thoreau. (0-486-28495-6)

NARRATIVE OF SOJOURNER TRUTH, Sojourner Truth. (0-486-29899-X)

THE WIT AND WISDOM OF MARK TWAIN: A Book of Quotations, Mark Twain. (0-486-40664-4)

UP FROM SLAVERY, Booker T. Washington. (0-486-28738-6)

A VINDICATION OF THE RIGHTS OF WOMAN, Mary Wollstonecraft. (0-486-29036-0)

PLAYS